W9-CCM-965

"PREPARE YOUR WEAPONS!"

"Warriors of Ra!" Hathor spoke suddenly, a hidden mechanism augmenting her voice to fill the chamber. "Our forces now hold only a few strong points, protecting the civilian survivors of the initial rebel attacks. Mighty Ra dispatched me with the necessary amulet to open the StarGate to this destination." She gestured to the golden Eye of Ra hanging between her breasts.

She faced the silenced throng. "Contact has been broken with the StarGate of Earth. But already we hasten back to that planet at the best speed this vessel's engines can deliver. Our dread Lord and your own people await rescue. Prepare your weapons, brave Setim. . . . Our enemies will be numerous and powerful!"

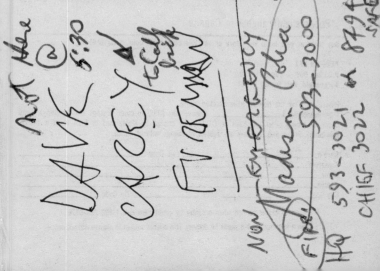

▣ ROC   ⦻ SIGNET

ENTER THE *STARGATE* UNIVERSE!

☐ **STARGATE™: RETALIATION by Bill McCay.** The action-packed adventure
continues in this explosive story of war over a planet's fate. Major O'Neal
and Daniel Jackson must now face the terrible revenge of Hathor, Ra's
treacherous successor. Having bided her time, Hathor plots the re-
conquest of a world and brings a weapon more awesome than any the
rebels can imagine.   (455169—$5.99)

☐ **STARGATE: REBELLION by Bill McCay.** When the crack team of scientists
and soldiers entered the Stargate,™ armed rebellion on a planet a
million light-years away was the last thing on their minds. Now that
it's started, commando Jack O'Neil and renegade Egyptologist Daniel
Jackson can't ignore it. But both the U.S. Army and Ra's vicious successor, Hathor, have other ideas for the Stargate.™   (455029—$4.99)

☐ **STARGATE by Dean Devlin & Roland Emmerich. Based on the Major
Motion Picture from MGM.** Something long forgotten. Something un-
earthed only in the 20th century. And now a crack team of scientists
and soldiers has the power to go beyond the last frontier of space on
an ultrasecret mission to probe the greatest mystery in the universe.
                                                    (184106—$4.99)

*Prices slightly higher in Canada

Buy them at your local bookstore or use this convenient coupon for ordering.

PENGUIN USA
P.O. Box 999 — Dept. #17109
Bergenfield, New Jersey 07621

Please send me the books I have checked above.
I am enclosing $_____ (please add $2.00 to cover postage and handling). Send
check or money order (no cash or C.O.D.'s) or charge by Mastercard or VISA (with a $15.00
minimum). Prices and numbers are subject to change without notice.

Card #_____ Exp. Date _____
Signature_____
Name_____
Address_____
City _____ State _____ Zip Code _____

For faster service when ordering by credit card call 1-800-253-6476

Allow a minimum of 4-6 weeks for delivery. This offer is subject to change without notice.

STARGATE™

RETRIBUTION

BILL McCAY

BASED ON STORY AND
CHARACTERS CREATED BY
DEAN DEVLIN & ROLAND EMMERICH

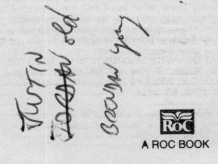

A ROC BOOK

ROC
Published by the Penguin Group
Penguin Putnam Inc., 375 Hudson Street,
New York, New York 10014, U.S.A.
Penguin Books Ltd, 27 Wrights Lane,
London W8 5TZ, England
Penguin Books Australia Ltd,
Ringwood, Victoria, Australia
Penguin Books Canada Ltd, 10 Alcorn Avenue,
Toronto, Ontario, Canada M4V 3B2
Penguin Books (N.Z.) Ltd, 182–190 Wairau Road,
Auckland 10, New Zealand

Penguin Books Ltd, Registered Offices:
Harmondsworth, Middlesex, England

First published by Roc, an imprint of Dutton Signet,
a member of Penguin Putnam Inc.

First Printing, October, 1997
10 9 8 7 6 5 4 3 2 1

STARGATE™ TM & Copyright © 1997 Canal + (U.S.). All Rights Reserved.
TM designates a trademark of Canal + (U.S.). Based on story and characters
created by Dean Devlin & Roland Emmerich.

 REGISTERED TRADEMARK—MARCA REGISTRADA

Printed in the United States of America

Without limiting the rights under copyright reserved above, no part of this
publication may be reproduced, stored in or introduced into a retrieval
system, or transmitted, in any form, or by any means (electronic, mechanical,
photocopying, recording, or otherwise), without the prior written permission
of both the copyright owner and the above publisher of this book.

BOOKS ARE AVAILABLE AT QUANTITY DISCOUNTS WHEN USED TO
PROMOTE PRODUCTS OR SERVICES. FOR INFORMATION PLEASE
WRITE TO PREMIUM MARKETING DIVISION, PENGUIN PUTNAM INC.,
375 HUDSON STREET, NEW YORK, NY 10014.

If you purchased this book without a cover you should be aware that this
book is stolen property. It was reported as "unsold and destroyed" to the
publisher and neither the author nor the publisher has received any payment
for this "stripped book."

CHAPTER 1
CAREER CHOICES

Holding his breath, Skaara endured the interminable elevator ride up from the Creek Mountain missile silo. To pass the time, he considered the ceaseless round of the fates.

Mere months ago, he'd been a mastadge herder on the world of Abydos—the son of a council member, it's true, but no more distinguished than any other animal handler. Then the strangers had arrived through the StarGate, the enigmatic doorway to other worlds. Skaara had been befriended by the visitors, until the god-king Ra had come to take them prisoner . . . and Skaara had found himself leading a rebellion.

He'd risen higher, forming the strongest native military force his recently freed planet had ever seen and leading it in a desperate sortie against a new attack from Ra's empire. The militia had seized the starship *Ra's Eye* from the would-be goddess Hathor and gained powerful new weapons. But factionalism raised its ugly head. The militia, like the government of Abydos, quickly developed fractures—and then had shattered at Hathor's counterstroke, attacked from without and within.

Skaara had become ruler and peacekeeper of the city of Nagada—at least as much of it as he could control. When Hathor produced a monstrous new space vessel, Skaara led off the remnants of his troops to protect a stream of refugees fleeing from the doomed city to the StarGate. Skaara himself had passed through the portal, arriving on the planet Earth.

From mastadge keeper to rebel leader, military commander, lawgiver, refugee ... and finally, mastadge herder.

Skaara's lungs gave out, as they inevitably did on the long ride. He breathed in—and just as inevitably, wished he hadn't.

The elevator was too small and stuffy—especially now, with the available air redolent from the trio of fifty-gallon garbage cans full of mastadge dung.

Skaara was used to the smell, but he'd always encountered it out in the open, in the fresh air. The handful of mastadges who had transited the StarGate to Earth were kept in the artificial caverns that housed the StarGate here. Machines piped air as artificial as these underground warrens. In the stagnant atmosphere the smell of the animal droppings seemed to flavor the whole complex.

It clung to Skaara's clothing and lingered in his nose.

But that was not the worst of it. The mastadges weren't used to being pent up so far underground. The beasts, large as an earthly elephant, always lived in the open on Abydos. They could survive even the killer sandstorms of Skaara's home planet.

The mastadges did not like their lot on this new world. They were upset. And they showed their unhappiness, it seemed, by a continual stream of runny excrement. With their size, even emaciated mastadges filled the trash barrels with horrifying rapidity.

Trying to dispose of the effluvia through the human toilets would have quickly overwhelmed the system. Instead, Skaara and his fellow mastadge tenders were detailed to remove the stuff physically, up the elevator.

It was a dirty job, no doubt about it. But, perversely, there was a benefit involved as well. In lugging the barrels of excrement to dump them out the main entrance of the StarGate installation, Skaara and his fellows were the only Abydans to walk the surface of the Earth.

The elevator came to a stop. Skaara sucked in a quick breath as the doors opened. Then he began trundling his barrel out of the cab. A detail of armed marines awaited them. Skaara hid a grin at the warriors' expressions as they got a whiff of the barrel's contents.

But any thoughts of a smile faded when he saw who led his warders. The Earthman called Feretti had been one of the first through the StarGate. He had helped to train the beginnings of Skaara's militia. It hurt to see him now commanding the Abydans' jailers.

Either Feretti was pretending not to know him, or he wasn't paying too much attention to whoever was dragging the mastadge muck. Skaara dragged his barrel past the fortresslike blast doors that guarded the entrance into the huge, man-made cave system.

Involuntarily, he took a deep breath as he stepped out into sunshine—and coughed. Too close to the barrel. A pair of marines trailed him, rifles ready though not quite aimed at him. Both of the fighting men angled to keep a fresh line of fire while keeping upwind of Skaara's burden.

The entrance to the complex was little more than a concrete porch set on the side of the mountain. The lip was ringed with cyclone fencing topped with razor wire. Where the fence met the rocky wall, a concrete chute had been constructed—perhaps to channel rain runoff. Now it conducted the mastadges' wastes to the craggy slopes below.

Skaara heaved against the barrel, pushing it on its side. The contents flowed down the concrete, aided by blasts of water from a high-pressure hose. Skaara slipped off to the side and squatted on his haunches, enjoying the brief few minutes' respite from his disgusting chore. After the drum was emptied and sluiced out . . .

Skaara's reverie was interrupted by an impact that seemed to tug at the homespun robes he wore. The skirt of his outer garment billowed as if it had caught an errant gust of wind.

But it hadn't.

Lying among the folds of cloth, like some sort of exotic egg in a bird's nest, was a shiny pellet.

Skaara casually dropped a hand down while glancing at his guards. Their attention was only half on him as they moved to avoid the water and waste flying around. Had he made any notably suspicious move—say, leaping for the fence—their guns would have swung to cover him.

The arrival of this pellet, however, had not been so detectable. Using the robe to shroud his actions, Skaara examined the container. It was constructed of the clear stuff the Earthmen called "plastic," and there seemed to be a seam in the middle—

Skaara needed two hands, but he got the thing open. A tightly compressed wad of some silky material emerged. Skaara took just long enough to recognize the hieroglyphic symbols traced in indelible black before he crumpled the thing up in his palm.

Indulging in a vigorous but feigned scratching session, he stowed the pieces of plastic and the message they'd contained in various places on his person.

Scarcely anyone on Earth knew that the Abydans had arrived, much less that they could read and write in the ancient symbols. And all those people were supposedly secluded in the burrows of Creek Mountain.

All except one man, the scholar who had accompanied the Earth warriors through the StarGate, the man who'd deciphered the ancient archives of Nagada, who'd devoted himself to teaching the Abydans. The man who'd participated in, and created the turmoil that had overcome the leaders on Abydos. The man who'd been reviled as a traitor, the man who had broken the heart of Skaara's sister.

Skaara hadn't seen him since the night of the great retreat from Abydos, when he'd disappeared in the panicked surge of refugees. Many thought he'd abandoned them.

None now spoke of Daniel Jackson.

Painfully conscious of the message he carried, Skaara picked up his now-cleaned barrel.

He wondered what his brother-in-law had to say . . .

Propelling himself on knees and elbows in the approved commando style, Daniel Jackson crawled back to the tree line of an adjoining crag. Clutched in his hands was an expensive British hunting crossbow that fired pellets instead of arrows.

Daniel wasn't used to the commando crawl, and wound up seeking shelter in what turned out to be a stand of prickle bushes. Swearing through clenched teeth, he finally managed to worm his way out of sight from the entrance to the secret Creek Mountain base. Daniel rose up on his haunches and began pulling thorny twigs off his woodland camouflage outfit.

He sighed. So much of his recent life seemed to be a concatenation of dumb luck spiced with failure. He'd failed to convince his fellow Egyptologists that Egyptian civilization was based on a predecessor culture. When he finally encountered his proof, the Star-Gate, it turned out to be a government top secret. After successfully wangling a spot on the scouting expedition going through the portal between worlds, Daniel had failed to find them a way back until they'd almost gotten killed. He'd fallen in love with a young woman on Abydos, Sha'uri, and lost her to the malice of Ra, a half-human, half-alien being who'd founded Egypt's predecessor culture and still ruled a vast interstellar empire as a god.

Daniel's best winning streak had come when he'd literally brought Sha'uri back to life using Ra's technology, and helped to destroy the god-king. Then he'd married Sha'uri, expecting to live happily ever after.

Instead, he'd had a streak of the other kind of luck. Daniel wound up tangling with humans trying to rape Abydos of its rare elements, with a warrior goddess determined to seize Ra's vacant crown, and with Abydan politics. He'd wound up helping Hathor, the villainess of the piece, find a gigantic killer spaceship that may have destroyed Sha'uri's homeworld. And, along the way, he'd destroyed his marriage.

Although he was Sha'uri's brother, Skaara had shown some sympathy for Daniel's plight—at least before Daniel had bugged out on the refugees in their helter-skelter arrival through Earth's StarGate terminal.

On his return to Creek Mountain, "casing the joint," as Daniel put it, Daniel had seen that Skaara was one of the few Aybdans allowed topside, if only briefly.

Daniel had concocted a scheme, outlined in his note, and spent a lot of money on the delivery system. If his plan worked, he silently promised to hang the crossbow over his mantelpiece.

It would be only fair.

Because maybe, just maybe, it would mean that his luck was turning again.

"Feretti!" a worried voice blared over the transceiver unit, "what the hell is going on down there?"

The short, angular marine turned down the volume of the radio on his shoulder and spoke into it. "It's the Abydans, sir," he reported.

As if the brass couldn't guess that, he thought.

"If they had real weapons, I'd probably call it a riot. But since they're only throwing mastadge shit—"

In the distance he heard a dull *splat* followed by sulfurous blasphemy as a bucketful of muck found its target.

"I guess I'd call it pretty messy, sir."

Feretti had halfway been expecting this for weeks now. He'd never been involved with what the powers that be euphemistically called "immigrant detention centers," but he knew guys who'd served in Guantanamo Bay, where they had a regular stockade full of would-be Cuban escapees.

At least those folks saw the sun on occasion. The Aybdans had been locked down and underground since they'd arrived so precipitately weeks before.

Talk about your illegal aliens.

Feretti wished that Colonel O'Neil were around to handle this problem. But he was in Washington, supposedly for consultation purposes. If the grapevine was right, the brass was probably going to rake him through the coals while juggling the hot potato he'd stuck them with—several thousand refugees who couldn't possibly exist.

And there wasn't even the option of sending the Abydans back where they came from. Feretti had been part of the guard party when the big brains had cranked up the StarGate and lined up the symbols that represented the Abydan connection. They'd dialed the right number, but Abydos wasn't answering anymore.

Could Daniel Jackson have been right when he'd declared that the Abydos StarGate had been destroyed by that big-ass alien spaceship? Nobody had mentioned it after the maverick scholar disappeared. But the thought had given Feretti some sleepless nights.

It would take some shot to destroy an artifact built to contain forces that could hurl somebody a million light-years. But if anything could do the job, Feretti would bet on Hathor's big boat. Which made Daniel Jackson's other prediction even more worrisome.

The professor had said that Earth would be next on Hathor's galactic grand tour.

A sloppy sound from around the corner revealed that another crap-bomb had hit its target. Somebody reached the limits of his restraint.

"Goddamnit!" a voice yelled. Then came the rifle fire. Single shots—at least the guy hadn't set his weapon for automatic. That was all Feretti needed, somebody going rock 'n' roll in these close quarters.

As if the first shots had broken the dam, other marines began shooting, too.

Feretti clicked on his radio. "We've got some isolated instances of fire. I don't think that's a good idea, sir."

"It will get worse if those—those *people* succeed in mobbing the guards."

The derogatory term "Abbadabba" hung unspoken in the air. Feretti frowned. The officers now in charge had merely commanded the support and security sections here at the base. They hadn't been through the StarGate and seen the Abydans battle for their freedom.

There were a lot of brave fighting men and women

down in these tunnels, people who'd gone into combat shoulder to shoulder with the marines. Instead of sanctuary, they'd found a human-sized ant farm, where they'd been locked in, knee-deep in mastadge shit, and left to rot while some alleged brains in the Pentagon decided what to do with them.

It might lead to a bit of testiness.

"We'll send in another rifle company," the voice crackled over his radio.

Oh, great. More people to shoot.

"I think it might be better if we responded with military police instead," he replied.

Supposedly, those were guys who knew how to deal with—and defuse—riot situations.

Feretti gave up on the radio and ran through the corridors, shouting, "Belay that firing!"

Even as he moved, another shot rang out—followed by a scream.

Feretti hoped that hadn't come from a marine. But if it were an Abydan who'd been shot, the situation might just get a lot worse before it got better.

He came on a fire team posted at a major intersection of tunnels. Several men were spotted with malodorous muck.

"Sir!" the team leader saluted. "I think we caught one."

Feretti concentrated more on the noises coming from the cross-tunnel. Crowd noises—angry crowd noises.

"Better hope you didn't catch him bad," he muttered. Then Feretti raised his voice in his best Abydan. "Ho!" he called, "around the corner! How badly is your person hurt? If he needs patching, you can bring him around. There will be no trouble from this side. My word on it."

"A scratch" came the answer. "There will be no more trouble on this side, either."

Feretti stiffened. He recognized the speaker. The voice was still weak, but it could only be Kasuf. Frankly, the guy was lucky to be alive. He'd almost been shot dead by assassins, finally coming out of a coma only to face the trauma of a StarGate transit.

One thing was certain, though. If Kasuf gave his word on something, it would definitely happen.

"I request a truce," the Abydan leader called. "Please do not fire."

Two men came around the corner, stepping carefully to avoid splotches of dung. They carried a blanket, and sitting on the blanket was the thin, pale Kasuf.

"Truce!" he called again, this time in English. His tight, bearded face twitched in a brief smile as he saw Feretti.

"I'm glad there is someone here who speaks my language," Kasuf said. "You worked with my son."

Feretti nodded. He had unofficially helped to teach Skaara's militia recruits the rudiments of soldiering.

Kasuf produced a piece of paper. "We have, however, written this in your tongue."

The marine stiffened. Nonnegotiable demands? He tried to phrase that question in Abydan.

Kasuf shrugged, then winced from his wound. "I

would call them concerns," he replied. "Respectfully submitted."

Feretti took the paper. It was nice to see respect, at least on one side . . .

CHAPTER 2
THE DOG AND
MASTADGE SHOW

Kasuf, the last Elder of Abydos, peered with sunken eyes from the litter on which he was carried. This Earth was a strange place. A single sun blazed in an unlikely blue sky. The temperature in these mountains—what was the name of this place? Colorado?—seemed eternally as cold as the high desert at night.

The hardest thing for Kasuf to accept about Earth was that he was here, part of the handful of refugees who'd streamed through the StarGate to escape the doom of their world.

The StarGate! How he'd feared the emissaries who'd stepped through that oversize ring of golden quartz. Functionaries and powers in the empire of Ra the sun god, they had always emerged with orders for the lowly fellahin of Abydos. Mostly these had dealt with the ever burgeoning hunger for the golden quartz mined at Nagada. And it was up to Kasuf and his fellow Elders that all orders be turned to practical results.

He'd never expected friendly strangers to appear—or the consequences of their visit. Ra had arrived in his golden pyramid-ship, intent on destruction, and the strangers had stirred the people of Abydos, including

Kasuf himself, to revolt. And amazingly, they had destroyed Ra.

But the empire was not done with Abydos. Twice more it had suffered attacks from the goddess Hathor, Ra's would-be successor. Earthmen and Abydans had fought together against these incursions.

Between battles, however, the alliance between the two worlds had been a shaky one. Men of business from Earth had tried to exploit the mines of Nagada. And the riches of Earth had turned the brains of many of Kasuf's compatriots. Factions had grown, subtle fractures had appeared in the traditional governance of Abydos. The old ways had shattered irrevocably with an assassination attempt on Kasuf and Nakeer, the two most respected leaders on the planet. Nakeer had died. Kasuf had lived—but barely. While he lay comatose, Nagada and the surrounding countryside exploded in a chaos of internal strife. And the author of the assassination, Hathor, brought in a new invasion through the StarGate.

Hathor supported her troops on the ground with a space vessel whose mass dwarfed even the pyramid that housed the StarGate. Despite the new weapons they'd brought to the fight, the Earthmen could not prevail. They had retreated through the gateway to their homeworld, accompanied by a ragtag band escaping the chaos of what had been Nagada.

No sooner had they done so than the Abydos side of the connection, the indestructible StarGate, had been obliterated. Kasuf had shuddered at the news, wondering what sort of energies had been unleashed to

complete such destruction. Truly, it would be enough
to kill a world.

Finding themselves trapped on Earth, the Abydans
then endured worse humiliations. Such warriors as
had survived were disarmed. The people were caged
in an enclave of *barbwire*, in the midst of some sort of
warriors' base. Kasuf's demands to speak to the Elders
of this world, or at least to their representative, General
West, had been ignored. The StarGate and the
alliance with Abydos were deep secrets, it seemed,
secrets that no one was supposed to know.

Kasuf twitched a blanket around himself as the
litter-bearers deposited him down in the sunlight. His
daughter Sha'uri stood by his side, her face rigid with
disapproval, even though she had translated the notes
written in ancient hieroglyphics, the messages that
promised an end to secrecy.

He knew why his daughter was angry. The notes
could only have come from one man—her husband,
Daniel Jackson. One of the first Earth visitors to
Abydos, Daniel had not merely befriended the people,
he'd fallen in love with Sha'uri. Although a scholar, he
had fought in the rebellion against Ra. Then he had
stayed on Abydos to teach his adopted people the
hieroglyphics in the hidden archives of Nagada, their
lost history. He also instructed a picked cadre in the
English language, so the Abydans could communicate
with the Earthmen. His greatest student had been
Sha'uri.

But, from the greatest friend of Abydos, Daniel had
fallen to execration as its greatest traitor. Hathor's
assassin had impersonated Daniel, and the Earthman

had fallen into the hands of the disguised Hathor. Together they had gone to the *Boat of a Million Years*, the huge star-vessel Hathor had used to reduce Abydos. Daniel had escaped, to return with dire warnings.

Kasuf thought that it was a measure of the stature to which his son Skaara had risen that he'd managed to ensure Daniel's safety in Nagada. And Kasuf himself had returned to consciousness, clearing Daniel from the charges of treason.

Sha'uri, however, feared that Daniel had committed a more personal kind of treason. They had grown apart during Daniel's first stumbling forays into politics, which had included opposition to some of Kasuf's measures. The rift had grown when Daniel befriended a beautiful young student—who had turned out to be the disguised Hathor. What might have happened while Daniel was in the hands of the legendary goddess of lust and blood?

"We are wasting our time," Sha'uri said. Kasuf had heard gentler tones from the grinding rocks in the mines of Nagada.

"Daniel is the only one of us who escaped in the confusion of our mass arrival. He knew the tunnels carved in the rock."

"He abandoned us," Sha'uri said flatly. "For all we know, he asks us to do as he asks merely to amuse himself."

"That I cannot answer, daughter," Kasuf replied. "But I feel you judge Daniel too harshly."

He gestured to Sha'uri. With a shrug she turned and called out in English, "Lead them out!"

* * *

Never volunteer, Feretti told himself. Action or information, never volunteer.

After calming the riot in the tunnels, Feretti had delivered the list of requests from Kasuf. He'd also read them.

And more than that, he'd supported the petitions in reporting to his superiors.

The two biggies on the list were a request from the Abydans to exercise their tiny mastadge herd, and a plea to let some of their people up to get fresh air.

Feretti was especially emphatic about the mastadges. The big, ungainly beasts, looking like an unholy miscegenation between elephant, musk ox, and miniature brontosaurus, were probably the last of their kind. It didn't help the propagation of the species that these individuals were pining away underground, turning the lower tunnels into a vast, stinking crap ground.

As for the second, even most prisons allowed the inmates out for a little while. Feretti wasn't sure, but that might even be in the Geneva Convention. In any event the powers that be had relented and allowed an experimental airing.

Pairs of Abydan mastadge wranglers were to bring the animals onto the elevator that descended into the bowels of the mountain, moving fore and aft—one leading the beast, the other bringing up the rear with an oversize plastic trash barrel.

Feretti had also interceded that some of the walking wounded be allowed outside, as well. He'd judged that Kasuf could use a little sunshine. It had been a close thing, keeping the Abydan leader alive until they could get him to the medical facilities here at Creek

Mountain. On the whole Feretti wondered if Kasuf considered that effort as a favor. Like all his people, the old man was a virtual prisoner.

However, no good deed lacks its punishment. Feretti had been assigned to lead the contingent of guards who'd oversee the outing. Never volunteer.

With a rifle over his shoulder, he watched as a group of Abydans carried Kasuf into the sunshine. The old man's daughter joined him, then relayed his orders in English. Abydans and their animals streamed from the tunnel cut into the cliff face. They made their way to a clearing among pine trees. In quieter times this had been the calisthenics field for the facility's marine contingent. It was safely tucked behind a chain-link and barbed-wire fence. The armed guards of Feretti's detail stood with their backs to the fence, weapons at the ready.

But there was no attempt at a thundering charge at the barrier. Silent Abydans led the docile if unlikely looking beasts in a slow circle, around and around the knot of wounded, slow, and lame refugees who were sunning themselves.

Feretti let go a breath he hadn't quite realized he'd been holding. The whole exercise had a queerly anticlimactic quality.

Not that he was complaining. The brass would act as if its collective hair were on fire if word of this bizarre parade ever got out. And it would, he had little doubt.

After all, how long could something like this be kept a secret?

*   *   *

Daniel Jackson stood one mountain over, staring at the mastadge parade through a pair of field glasses. He recognized the head of the guard detail as an alumnus of the first StarGate incursion, a bushy-browed, fidgety career marine named Feretti. Daniel let out a long breath. He hoped the poor guy wouldn't get into trouble over this.

Daniel turned to the man next to him in the stand of pines. He'd chosen this shadowy location to avoid any telltale reflective glints off lenses—especially on the tripod-mounted video camera. His companion, how-ever, stood frozen, gawking through the viewfinder at the mastadges.

"Get that damned thing going," Daniel ordered viciously. "They won't be out there all day!"

The cameraman leapt to life as if he'd been shaken from a dream. Daniel had spent precious weeks since his escape finding a reputable cameraman and setting up the show. All the money he had in the world had gone into his caper. He'd cashed in the value of his most treasured possession, a marble bust of a young Egyptian woman, circa 1400 B.C.

That had been surprisingly easy—the delicately carved features now reminded him of Sha'uri—the wife who hated him. He'd spotted her down in the clearing, but resolutely kept his binoculars on other figures.

"Get me an establishing shot," he ordered the franti-cally working cameraman. "Then I want close-ups on the animals. I need this sharp and clear to convince the network news people that what they're seeing is for real."

This videotape would not be a Bigfoot special, a few seconds of a shadowy figure dashing between trees. The mastadges were out in the open, in the sunlight—and they obviously weren't people in rubber suits, animatronics, or wondrous special effects.

They would look exactly as they were—an alien species, being kept secretly on a U.S. military reserve, under marine guard.

Daniel allowed himself a tight grin.

If this didn't start the Big Three and CNN digging up Creek Mountain, what would?

Colonel Jack O'Neil almost wished he were under guard as he pushed through a media contingent in full feeding frenzy. The hall to the meeting room set aside for the closed session of the Senate Armed Service Committee was jammed with cameras and reporters.

O'Neil ignored the microphones shoved in his face, the jabbered questions. At last he reached the doors of the committee room, produced his credentials, and was ushered inside.

The nearly arctic air-conditioning he encountered brought a brief grin to his taut lips. He'd expected a somewhat warmer atmosphere for being raked over the coals.

O'Neil knew what was on the schedule. In previous sessions, he'd watched the senators take long strips of hide off General W. O. West, the officer who'd ordered him into the ill-fated Abydos mission. To put it mildly, the lawmakers were furious that the general had exceeded his mandate—not to mention congressional oversight.

West's testimony had been surprisingly clear of prevarications. "To the best of my memory" was not in the general's vocabulary. He'd been singularly open while explaining his reactions to the dilemma of the StarGate and the decisions he'd made. Perhaps after a career of Pentagon politics, it was a relief for him to be so up-front.

The senators had not been pleased to discover themselves the owners of a successful space program—expecially since it left the United States, and all of Earth, vulnerable to an interstellar empire of undetermined size and proven enmity.

Even the new weaponry captured from the Horus guards hadn't pleased the committee members, who considered them purchased at too high a cost.

For once O'Neil agreed with them.

Today Jack O'Neil would be on the hot seat as the commander on the scene—or was that on the spot?

Senator Albright dissected O'Neil's performance mercilessly, pointing out that in each brush with the enemy, he had somehow been caught by surprise.

Senator Kerrigan showed slightly more sympathy, as might be expected from a veteran of Vietnam.

But it was Senator Foyle, the senior member and committee chairman, who totaled the costs in dollars and sense. "This fiasco has cost us missiles, helicopters, and more Abrams tanks than we lost in the Gulf War."

"The human cost is what concerns me," Kerrigan interrupted. "Over seven hundred casualties—those also exceed the losses from Desert Storm."

"Then, there are all those people you let in," Albright added sourly. "Illegal aliens—"

"People who fought and died at the side of our troops—or their survivors." Kerrigan gave the older man a hard look. "We deserted enough people in Vietnam. I think the colonel did the right thing."

"Those freakish beasts he brought back are the only proof that he was off this world," Albright groused.

"Plus the testimony of all the troops, and the films," Kerrigan put in.

"But in the end, it really doesn't seem to matter," Albright went on. "The doorway on the other side of this StarGate thing has apparently been destroyed. Certainly, our researchers have succeeded in restoring contact."

O'Neil forced himself to take a deep breath. "There is still the matter of the giant starship," he said. "According to Dr. Jackson, that vessel is capable of reaching the solar system within a year."

"I'm sure this Hathor person must have other concerns," Albright began.

Foyle, however, cut him off, reading a note handed to him by a staff member. "I'm told that a Daniel Jackson is outside, with"—he paused for a second, swallowing his fury—"the media people."

O'Neil had to hide a smile. Jackson had torn an irreparable hole in the cloak of secrecy that the Pentagon and Congress had tried to draw over the StarGate and the refugees at Creek Mountain.

But to turn up at the Senate immolation proceedings!

Foyle turned a particularly mirthless smile on O'Neil.

"If you wouldn't mind stepping down, Colonel, we might enjoy putting some questions to this gentleman."

O'Neil gratefully gave up the hot seat and settled in to watch one of the most brutal cross-questionings he'd ever witnessed. The senators seemed ready to charge Jackson with treason and sedition for his activities on Abydos. But they reserved their special fury for the way he'd embarrassed the hell out of them, revealing the existence of extraterrestrial visitors at the complex in Colorado.

"As a contract employee on a military project, you were obliged to sign a security agreement," Kerrigan rasped. "Didn't you realize that what happened at Creek Mountain would be top secret?"

"I just realized *why* it would be," Jackson responded with unexpected coolness. "While catching up with current events in *The New York Times*. I came across an interesting article—it was right when Earth had that close encounter with the asteroid. In the writer's opinion, if the government knew that meteor was going to hit, it wouldn't tell anybody. From your point of view, Senator, it's a better thing that people stay quiet and ignorant—and property values keep stable, even if they'll end up imminently destroyed."

He rode over Kerrigan's roar of protest. "But you've got something worse than a mere asteroid to worry about. There's a warship heading for Earth, a pyramid as tall as the World Trade Center with a base as big as Disneyland. The weapons on board this thing are powerful enough to wreck a planet, if not destroy it. And the person in charge of all that power is not the type who negotiates."

Jackson glared at the senators. "Have you actually talked to the refugees at Creek Mountain? Those people could give you an earful about what it's like to live under Ra's empire. But you should really talk to Kasuf, the Elder. He could tell you what it's like to lead those people, looking over your shoulder at some sort of god-king. The job got him beaten and nearly killed. And he was supposed to be on their side."

Daniel Jackson leaned over the little table where they'd seated him. "You can ignore Hathor only at your serious peril. And if you have some sort of idea about making a deal with her, again, I say talk to Kasuf. If she wins, everyone in this room is a dead man. Some because we fought her. Some because they're leaders."

He shook his head sadly. "Hathor doesn't need leaders. All she wants are slaves."

CHAPTER 3
DREAMS AND NIGHTMARES

The choked scream brought Khonsu to his feet, instantly banishing sleep. He rose from his position at the door of the compartment Lady Hathor had chosen for herself.

The briefest of smiles tugged at his lips. His fellow Horus guardsmen could never imagine Khonsu the Killer acting as a bodyguard, much less guarding the embodiment of lust and death.

But the humor dissipated as he entered the shadowy sleeping chamber. He had not activated the pectoral necklace of biomorphic quartz into its mask form. Better to meet Hathor with his naked face than depend on the mask's darkness-piercing eyes. The lady had been awakening violently of late.

Hathor's nude, perfect body rose to its knees among a tangle of silks. A symphony of sweet, firm, curves rose to a face of startling beauty, the sort of idealized features usually found in a statue.

Although no statue would stare with wild eyes, pupils dilated with horror—and perhaps, fear.

"Lady," Khonsu said, his rumbling voice as gentle as he could make it. "I thought I heard a noise."

For a second she stared at him, uncomprehending, her face naked in its expression.

As he had done for many nights now, Khonsu steeled himself. Hormones pounded at him to take that trembling form in his arms, to offer what comfort he could. But that way led to certain danger—and probable death. Merely by entering, he took his life in his hands. The noble deities of Ra's empire did not deal generously with lesser figures who saw them in attitudes of vulnerability.

Hathor's eyes now displayed recognition, and a masklike stillness came over her features. "You are mistaken, Khonsu. Return to your post."

Her voice held the unspoken threat of one who held the power of life and death over inopportune servants.

Bowing, Khonsu returned to lie across the threshold.

Only when her bodyguard had left did Hathor's facade of calm authority crack. She slumped among the coverlets, eyes closed, fists clenched.

It had been the dream again, the nightmare that had assailed her every night since the *Boat of a Million Years* left Abydos. She had unexpectedly found the key to the ancient vessel hanging from the neck of Daniel Jackson, and had used it to manipulate the Abydos StarGate to an unknown setting. At the far end of the transdimensional portal, she'd found a tool of power beyond any dreams of avarice—the *Boat of a Million Years*.

This titanic spacecraft, built by the elder race that had spawned Ra, dwarfed the cruisers she had used to reduce the planet Ombos, millennia before. Its weapons were more dangerous by at least an order of magnitude, as Hathor discovered when she attempted to use the ship in support of her troops on Abydos.

She had brought the ship in on automatic systems, unwilling to rouse the alien crew Ra had maintained in suspended animation. Arriving on Abydos, she bestrode a computer-generated virtual battlefield like a true goddess, destroying enemies by merely pointing her finger.

Then a supposedly derelict spaceship had fired on her. Automated defenses had targeted the attacker. Before she could give the order, heavy batteries had thundered back. The attacking ship had been destroyed, as was the pyramid it had landed on. Lashing blast-beams raved on to interact disastrously with the subtly balanced fields of the StarGate below the ground.

Cataclysm had resulted—a release of energy that had brought up the defensive fields on the ship. The *Boat of a Million Years* had retreated to the upper stratosphere. When Hathor succeeded in getting an image again, she saw the ranks of her warriors engulfed in a blinding blue radiance, energy emitted by the tortured fabric of space itself. Hathor's army disappeared, snuffed out, as the bedrock of the planet split in a crevasse against which the diggings of Nagada seemed like the merest scratch on the planet's surface.

The crack in the crust enlarged, taking in the mines, the city of Nagada, extending itself across the main landmass.

The *Boat of a Million Years* rose higher to avoid the shock waves from the tectonic catastrophe below.

Clouds spread across the planet with unnatural swiftness, changing its reddish aspect to an ugly, mottled brown. But even through the dust and smoke, the continent-long line of volcanic disturbance glowed like a lurid scar.

In her dream, the disk of the planet had become a face—the red-furred, snouted visage of Ushabti, leader of the alien Setim, who had initially served Ra on Earth.

Even when he had died at her own hand, the first of his race to be exterminated, Ushabti had looked on her coldly, almost dispassionately.

So why was he laughing in her dream?

Hathor sank her face into her hands, rubbing at the flesh as if she could rearrange her features.

On Ombos, she had obliterated the race of the Setim, except for the handful who now slept the sleep of millennia, as she had. Now on Abydos, she had murdered a planet so that it would no longer bear life.

What would she do when she finally returned to her ancient homeworld?

Barbara Shore turned from the noonday news with a groan of disgust.

"Life is definitely not fair," Gary Meyers declared. "That damned Jackson got a court order springing all the Abydans. But what about us, American citizens? We're still locked up in this joint."

"The Abydans didn't sign the standard security agreement," Barbara pointed out. "We did."

For Barbara, signing that form had been a Faustian bargain. The agreement had taken her to the planet

Abydos as the head of a research group scavenging technology from a derelict starship. It had nearly gotten her killed by invading Horus guards. But the crowning insult had come when she'd barely made it back to Earth.

Some genius in the Pentagon had scarfed up all the techno-spoils Barbara and her people had gathered at the cost of several lives. But the research group had been left to rot in the bowels of Creek Mountain.

As imprisonment went, it was fairly painless. Barbara had faced worse privations trapped in the bridge deck of the cruiser *Ra's Eye*, rationing food and water. Creek Mountain had a decent enough mess hall, comfortable quarters, and even access to incoming news— like the broadcast she'd just turned off. She just couldn't talk to anyone, or pick up a phone.

No one knew she was there, that she was even alive . . .

"Dr. Shore?" a young marine orderly interrupted her thoughts. "Someone to see you. Colonel Robert Travis."

"Never heard of him," Barbara said, trying to revive some of her old insouciance. "What does he want?"

"I want you, Doctor." A hawk-faced, graying man in an army colonel's uniform appeared from behind the aide-de-camp.

Barbara's lips twitched in an irrepressible, sexy grin. "How pleasant to deal with true military directness!" she said. "Lately, I've been dealing with swivel-chair warriors."

"You still are, I'm afraid," Travis replied. "I'm with the Special Development Institute."

Barbara gave him a long look. "I don't suppose it's a coincidence that your institute's initials are the same as the Strategic Defense Initiative? Now, that used to be managed by the Defense Applied Research Projects Administration."

"That became civilianized into the plain Applied Research Projects Administration," Travis said.

She nodded. "And Star Wars went to the Ballistic Missile Defense Organization. BMDO—pretty vulgar-sounding initials, I thought."

Travis gave her a lopsided smile. "You're certainly up on your acronyms."

"I'm a research physicist," Barbara replied shortly. "That line of business, you've got to know where your money is coming from, especially if you accept grants from Uncle Sugar." His expression soured. "What little money that's available nowadays usually comes with military strings on it."

Colonel Travis nodded. "I'm a physicist myself. Out of Caltech, with stints at Livermore and the JPL in Pasadena."

"All that, and an eagle, too."

"Reserve commission," Travis said somewhat diffidently, "augmented to deal with the military types connected with the project I've been working on." He gave her a tight look. "My team was the one who reverse-engineered the alien energy weapons retrieved on the first Abydos mission."

"The results of your work saved my butt when the Whorehouse guards invaded Abydos." Barbara coughed as Travis' eyebrows rose. "That's what the marines took to calling the Horus guards," she explained. "Those energy rifles leveled the playing field—until Hathor came along with the *Boat of A Million Years*."

"I understand you were lucky to get away, much less to escape with the volume of technical samples you brought with you," Travis said. "SDI has inherited all of the material you rescued. I'm supposed to make sense of it without the original research team—and no translators for all the hieroglyphic transcriptions you collected. So I finally pierced this nonsensical wall of security and tracked you down. That's why I want you, Doctor. You and your whole team. Can you work with me?"

Barbara gave him a long, unblinking stare. "That depends—what are you working on?"

Travis was taken aback. "What do you mean?"

"I don't know if you've been listening to Daniel Jackson on the TV. I heard him warning us about that killer starship right after he escaped from it. And I was there when the StarGate closed down. Jackson gave us a year before Hathor comes flying down to take names and kick butt. We'd better have something up in space to meet her."

Her face was grim. "That means getting into those antigravity engines I brought back to see if we can copy them."

Even the waiting room outside the offices of Kirkwood and Stiles projected an aura of understated opulence. Of course, Daniel Jackson thought as he sank into a surprisingly comfortable antique armchair. This

is the agency's line of work—public relations . . .
image adjustment.

After sitting just long enough to be impressed with
the seriousness of the firm's business, Daniel saw a
perfectly coiffed blond goddess rise from behind the
reception desk. She wore a simple blue suit whose cost
probably exceeded Daniel's clothing budget for the
past four years.

"Mr. Kirkwood will see you now." Her voice seemed
almost like a caress.

I've been alone too long, Daniel thought as he followed an impeccably undulating rump down a hallway into the inner sanctum.

Miles Kirkwood's office made the reception area
look cheap and gaudy. Daniel had dined in restau-
rants smaller than this room. Kirkwood was a plump,
jowly man with impossibly blue eyes. A fringe of
white hair surrounded the pink, bald dome of his
head. He smiled at Daniel, the image of a rich, favorite
uncle, as the blond goddess vanished out the door.

"I confess it was sheer curiosity that led to this little
talk," Kirkwood admitted. "You've gotten your message out. Why would a man who's appeared on
almost every conceivable media forum now require
public relations advisers?"

"Because I want to keep my message in front of
people's faces," Daniel said bluntly. "I'm fighting to
save a planet, Mr. Kirkwood. My fifteen minutes of
fame were barely enough to spring the refugees. With
luck they may turn out to be ninety-day wonders. But
that's still not enough. I need a year of concentrated
effort from everybody on the planet—especially here

in the U.S. After that, either we'll have succeeded, or we'll be dead."

Kirkwood's sharp blue eyes continued to assess him in silence.

"I made inquiries," Daniel went on. "Your outfit was one of the ones hired by the Kuwaitis to orchestrate our entrance into the Gulf War."

That jarred the measuring glance.

"If you could drag us into a fracas six thousand miles away, I'm sure you could get people moving on a threatened invasion," Daniel finished.

Kirkwood continued to regard him for a moment. "You're quite a communicator, Doctor," he finally said. "A bit on the blunt side, though."

"If I have to sugarcoat the message for *you*, my efforts are doomed right from the get-go," Daniel replied.

Kirkwood's lips quirked. "In spite of your rather slanted take on our efforts, the troubles in the Gulf had a definite impact on our economy and the national defense, not to mention world affairs."

"And you think that my warnings don't?" Daniel burst out. "Forget about sugarcoating. Apparently, I've got to work on clarity, first."

The public relations counselor's face went blank, but his body straightened. Daniel had seen the reaction before—in the goddess Hathor before she started killing people.

Remember, he thought, this guy hasn't signed on with you yet.

Daniel rummaged in the old-fashioned, battered valise that served as his briefcase until he produced a videocassette. Before Kirkwood could speak, Daniel raised a hand. "No, this isn't a rerun of the mastadge parade."

He looked around the room. "I figured you'd have facilities here in the office—no need to call in the AV squad." He gave Kirkwood a mirthless grin. "Strictly speaking, this is supposed to be classified, if not top secret."

Wordlessly, Kirkwood stabbed a finger down on a control panel discreetly recessed into the surface of a desk that otherwise looked like a piece of the last century. What appeared to be a solid-paneled wall split open to reveal the latest in high-tech media.

Daniel slipped the tape into a VCR. "I can't and won't tell you who gave this to me—but it's official Marine Corps footage."

The monitor screen came alive, to show a slightly out-of-focus battlefield scene. For a second Daniel relived the moment, feeling the sand grind under his feet as the chill of the desert night sank into his bones.

It had been a rare cloudy night on Abydos. Daniel was never sure whether the *Boat of a Million Years* had merely reached the planet in the midst of a storm, or if the gigantic ship's drive created some sort of havoc in the upper atmosphere.

"The guy who filmed this didn't survive that night. But one of his buddies on the expeditionary force rescued the tape and got it back. Watch carefully."

Forms moved across the desert landscape—mechanized units, trying to maintain some sort of a perimeter. The bright energy discharge of blast-lances showed in the distance as Horus guards advanced. Then one of the retreating tanks swerved to a stop, and its main armament bellowed, sending a shell toward the enemy. As soon as it fired, the armored vehicle lurched into motion again to escape its pinpointed position—the tactical doctrine of "scoot and shoot."

Up in the sky, the clouds roiled as something tore through them. The image on the screen wasn't clear. There was a sense of sharp lines blanking out some of the revealed stars—whatever it was had to be horrifyingly large to blot out so much at so high an altitude. But the billowing clouds softened those lines, rendering the shape amorphous.

Then the form overhead vanished behind an eye-searing flash—a bolt of energy beside which lightning looked like a pinprick. This was more like the spear of a god—or the released fires of hell.

The blast landed neither on the tank's former location nor on its present course. But that tremendous lash of force didn't require a direct hit. The flash of the exploding tank didn't even show in the maelstrom of ravening energy. But when the blinding discharge ceased, the tank was gone—little more than an irregularity of melted metal in a steaming green-glass caldera of fused sand.

Another vehicle tore by, some sort of half-track. This carried an artillery mount for something that looked like a recoilless rifle—except the barrel was solid and constructed of an alien glassy-gold material.

Frantically, the weapon elevated, tracking across the sky, firing a counterblast toward the ship hanging like doom overhead. But this discharge was like an insubstantial thread of energy flinging upward.

The answering deluge of force was more like a stamping foot. Nothing of the lighter vehicle remained in the fused craterlet, except for a splash of gold in the bubbled, vitrified sand.

"Even I could recognize that was an Abrams tank getting swatted like a fly," Daniel said as the screen dissolved in staticky snow. "And you could see how effective our most powerful mobile energy weapons were against that flying mountain." He impaled the public relations man with a grim glare. "Now, imagine what something like that could do if it came in over Chicago, L.A.—or here in New York. Is that enough of a threat? Does it make a sufficient impact?"

Kirkwood cleared his throat as if unsure his voice would work. "That—that is certainly an undeniable threat. Sufficient to cause mass panic if we revealed it."

"I don't want panic," Daniel said. "I need people motivated to meet that threat. Hathor has a ship the size of a young mountain. But we've got a planet's worth of resources—if we can mobilize them."

Kirkwood seemed to come out of his horror-filled fascination. "There are options that can simulate—and stimulate—public reaction. Letter-writing campaigns to Congress can be started. Media access—there are a number of your refugees who speak English. We could recruit the more telegenic ones . . ."

Daniel nodded, thinking of Sha'uri—and dealing with the sudden, shocking emptiness he felt.

Well, I won't be the one doing the recruiting, he thought.

Kirkwood interrupted his list of options with an almost diffident cough. "However, our course of action is always circumscribed by the client's financial ability . . ."

"Well, I certainly hope you're going to offer me your world-saving rate," Daniel said. "But I don't expect you to do this for free. Perhaps you've heard that I've been nominated the legal representative and financial conservator for the Abydos refugees. I've already been sorting through all sorts of proposals—book offers, TV-movie options, even toy deals. You wouldn't believe how much one guy offered for the official rights to make plush-toy mastadges. Or maybe you do?"

"Even so," Kirkwood said, "generous payments, spread among several thousand refugees . . ."

"I've already spoken with Kasuf and the other leaders," Daniel interrupted. "Other than basic subsistence stipends for those who can't get jobs, all our income will be at your disposal."

Once again Kirkwood stood in astonished silence. "All?" he finally managed.

"Mr. Kirkwood, these are people who lost their planet because of greed—because they couldn't pull together. They learned the hardest way possible. They're willing to suffer if necessary, because they know that unless we get this planet defended, none of us will be around to enjoy that big money."

Kirkwood frowned at Daniel's apparent flippancy.

"As far as Hathor is concerned, everyone who got away from Abydos is an escaped slave," Daniel said almost gently. "Slaves don't escape from Ra's empire. They'll have to be eliminated, and very publicly, as a lesson to Hathor's new slaves—the population of Earth."

He shook his head. "That's what will happen if Hathor wins."

"Admittedly, we didn't expect to be up on war-crimes charges from Iraq," Kirkwood said. "But—"

"I hope you're not expecting to get Hathor's account, explaining the ways of the gods to mere mortals," Daniel warned. "Maybe you should have a word with Kasuf, first. To stabilize the situation on Abydos, Ra's people killed off everyone who could read and write."

CHAPTER 4
GUNS AND BUTTER

Jack O'Neil navigated the halls of the Pentagon, fresh orders crackling in his dress uniform tunic. He was to report at General West's office, for service as the general's aide—probably in preparation for a journey to Thule base in Greenland, or Tierra del Fuego, or some other form of military exile.

O'Neil strode down the last corridor and glanced in surprise at the long line of civilians stretching ahead of him.

The uniformed dragon at the general's reception desk bared her teeth, flicking a glance at O'Neil while impaling an executive-type with her eyes. "You're expected, Colonel. Go right in. The meeting is in progress." She turned back to the executive. "First of many."

O'Neil opened the door, to walk into a wall of noise—snarling engines, the whine of traversing turrets, the blast of primary and secondary ordnance. The sound track came from a laptop computer whose multimedia screen showed a sleek, heavily armored vehicle hurtling over rolling countryside. As the tank came forward, breasting a hill, O'Neil squinted in astonishment.

The fighting vehicle moved on neither wheels nor treads. Instead, its bottom crimped into a plenum skirt, seeming to float in midair.

"A hovercraft tank?" Disbelief was thick in his voice.

"Impractical, given today's power plants," the corporate type stationed beside the little virtual-reality screen began in a persuasive voice. "But General Armaments believes that the quartzose material mined from the planet Abydos—"

O'Neil turned to General West, who had a sort of bemused smile on his face. "Mister, ah—"

"Masterson," the corporate type smoothly introduced himself. He had a bluff, square face, the sort that would seem more at home in a uniform than the suit he was wearing. O'Neil realized that almost all the men outside had the same look—a sales force of majors, colonels . . . probably generals, too.

"Mr. Masterson." O'Neil tried to keep his voice polite, even gentle. "I'm sure you realize our supply of the golden quartz is limited—extremely so. And if we devoted it to ground vehicles . . ."

His voice trailed off as he remembered the udajeets, the antigravity gliders, lashing army tanks, the flying bulk of the cruiser *Ra's Eye* shattering an entire mechanized force. "If we're down to fighting this enemy on the ground, we've already lost the war."

The colonel turned to his commander. West nodded. "I appreciate your design work, Mr. Masterson. Most . . .

imaginative. But at present I couldn't recommend your project to the procurement office."

Masterson's suave expression curdled at this rejection before his presentation had barely begun. "General, in fairness—"

"Indeed," West said. "You saw the number of people waiting to make presentations. It's only fair to try and expedite this process as much as possible. If you wish to leave material for our consideration, please do so. Colonel O'Neil will help you collect your equipment."

O'Neil assisted the outraged pitchman in recovering his deranged presentation. Masterson's jaw kept working as the colonel escorted him out.

Jack O'Neil closed the door behind Masterson and turned to West. "I have to admit, I didn't anticipate this, sir."

"You were expecting to be shipped off on some variant of penguin patrol?" West inquired sardonically. "Head of weather operations in Antarctica, perhaps?"

The colonel shook his head. "No, the powers that be hit on a better punishment than simple exile. They figure I've brought my career down in a spectacular crash and burn. I can kiss any hopes of promotion good-bye, until I'm finally forced to retire—or get bounced. No, my friends in high places have decided to make excellent use of me—while at the same time destroying any hopes I might have had for retirement."

West smiled at O'Neil's uncomprehending response. "Your politics was always as simple as who should be shot next. I, however, was an honest-to-God part of the military-industrial complex. Worked myself up from the crazies in the Pentagon basement." The general's lips twitched. "Maybe if things had turned out differently, I might have been running for Senate instead of Ollie North."

His reminiscent mood abruptly shifted. "I stayed military—until this StarGate fiasco. There've been a lot of guys in the bushes waiting with baseball bats, waiting for me to screw up. Now they've got their chance. They all expect to retire someday and sell military doodads. According to law, they can't sell to their old associates. But it's amazing, the number of friends you make in the service. I knew Masterson. If he were still in uniform, he'd have outranked you."

O'Neil shrugged. "Another friend made."

West frowned. "If that political disaster on Abydos hadn't happened, I could have wound up on the board of the United Mining Cartel. Instead, I had to land on them and make a bunch of enemies. That's why I was put in charge of this study group. Turning down all these suppliers will close more doors for me—if we live through this."

"If I can run interference—" O'Neil began.

The general shook his head. "No. I'll deal with the suppliers. This is politics, and I know where some of the bodies are buried. You have to start arranging a staff—people who can handle the technical end, manufacturing weapons that will make the best use of our limited quartz supply. My secretary has compiled a list, drawing on my contacts. If you can suggest anyone . . ."

Jack O'Neil gave his superior a crooked smile. "You may not like the person I'll suggest."

"Colonel, anyone who helps us succeed at our mission will get my okay."

"All right, sir. Daniel Jackson."

West stared. "Talk about recruiting the enemy."

"He turned around that congressional committee," O'Neil pointed out. "And he's just about become the poster boy for organizing a defense against Hathor. Sounds like his mission is our mission."

The general shrugged. "We'll need a top translator. I've brought in the SDI research group as technical consultants. We have to know how much of that mass of information that came back from Abydos may prove useful in defending this planet."

"So we'll have to bring in some Egyptologists—and definitely the Abydans," O'Neil said. "So we'll have to deal with Jackson. But I don't think we'll be using him as the lead translator."

"No?" West inquired.

The colonel shook his head. "I keep remembering how we got to Abydos in the first place. It was Daniel Jackson. The guy may be a flake, but he's also a genius—that special kind of genius who makes correct intuitive leaps."

O'Neil grinned. "We'd be better off putting him in charge of an Office of Bright Ideas."

Daniel Jackson sat at his desk and massaged his temples. Money management had never been his thing, and here he was, acting as financial agent for the whole Abydan refugee community. He had to find them jobs, balance their living expenses against the costs of his public relations campaign, and keep raising money. It had gotten to the point where he was scheduling mastadge appearances for supermarket and car-dealership openings.

Things were so much simpler when all he wanted to do was die well.

He'd screwed up the political system on Abydos, but not before he'd destroyed his marriage with Sha'uri. Of all the ridiculous clichés, he'd almost let himself be seduced by a student—who'd later revealed herself as the would-be goddess Hathor in disguise.

Hathor had managed to spirit him away as all hell broke loose on Abydos. But Daniel knew that if he hadn't already damaged his relationship with Sha'uri, she wouldn't have believed the phony charges that he'd tried to assassinate Kasuf. And when he finally cleared himself . . .

He remembered a bitter scene on the walls of Nagada, staring from one of the watchtowers as the *Boat of a Million Years* pulverized the marine defense lines around the StarGate.

Sha'uri looked as if she wished he were standing right under those lashing gouts of energy.

"So," she said at last, staring through him. "You're not a *political* traitor."

Amazingly, the conversation had only gone downhill from there. In the end he'd persuaded Sha'uri to get off Abydos and bring her people to Earth. Then Daniel had gone off with the much-reduced Abydos militia on a hopeless diversionary attack. Maybe he could come to a heroic end.

Instead, he'd almost ended up being throttled by a Horus guard in somewhat better shape than he was.

Jack O'Neil had to come up and put a couple of pistol bullets into the guy.

So Daniel had been cheated of his escape and wound up coming to Earth, to work like a dog for what still seemed like dubious results.

Jack O'Neil's visit offered the answer to several problems.

"Jobs for all my Abydan English scholars?" Daniel said.

"At one of the power GS allowances," O'Neil quickly pointed out. "In these fiscally prudent days, we can't go overboard with outside contractors."

"It will let us ratchet up the war of words, while still supporting my people. The last of them are coming out of government custody. Housing and feeding them is turning out more expensive than I thought."

Daniel sat silent for a moment. "You say Barbara Shore is helping out on the technical side? Maybe she'll want to recruit some people directly."

"Like Sha'uri?" O'Neil asked.

"It might—be easier," Daniel admitted.

"Things are still that way between you?"

Daniel shrugged. "Looks like things will always be that way."

"I can't lecture you on that," O'Neil said quietly. "God knows, I had enough of a rocky road in that department myself."

The two men looked at each other. Daniel knew something had been seriously wrong in O'Neil's life when he led the first Abydos expedition. The colonel's death wish had nearly turned the scouting assignment into a suicide run when they'd encountered Ra and his empire. He'd been sent with an atomic bomb to seal the far end of the StarGate if necessary.

Daniel had been horrified to discover that the choice of the distraught O'Neil had been calculated. It was as if he were a piece of equipment—the detonator of the transported nuke.

"I can't believe that you'd work with West after the way he used you." Daniel still maintained a sense of resentment against the string-pulling air force general.

"It's the special ops credo," O'Neil replied. "The mission comes first. If things landed in the pot, they needed someone to pull the plug—if you'll pardon the mixed metaphor."

He cast an appraising eye over Daniel. "Speaking of missions and using people, I've been given carte blanche to recruit people for the general's study group. O'Neil leaned over Daniel's desk and pointed his finger in the best Uncle Sam style. "I want you as our director of nonlinear thinking."

"What?" Daniel said.

"We're trying to come up with ways to defend the Earth from Hathor," O'Neil responded. "Some of the options will seem pretty off-the-wall. I want someone with an open mind to evaluate them. Considering the way you took on the established brains of Egyptology—"

"They'll tell you there's little difference between an open mind and a hole in the head," Daniel said sourly. Then his lips quirked in a grin as he shoved aside the papers on his desk. "Still it beats playing talent agent for a bunch of big, ugly beasts . . ."

* * *

Kemsit growled as he stalked through the aisles of the supermarket. To his Bronze-Age mind-set, food procurement was women's work. But as house captain of his recently settled group of Abydan refugees, he was the only English speaker in the group. Not that he was a scholar. He'd gained his command of the tongue working with the Urt-men in the mines of Nagada. And just in the course of asking directions to a food market, he'd already discovered that his construction-worker's dialect could offend his new neighbors.

This foray shouldn't have been necessary. The house Kemsit and his companions had moved into came with a fully equipped kitchen, with shelves of canned goods and a wondrous box that kept food cold.

The cold food had quickly disappeared, and the canned stocks wasted in an orgy of discovery. Kemsit had at least learned something. The pictures on the outside of the can represented the food within, though the contents were usually much less appetizing than the representations. This was a necessary trick—Kemsit barely recognized hieroglyphics, much less the squiggles the Urt-men used to represent their speech.

In any event, a week would pass before a really fluent English speaker would come to assist in resupply. But the cupboard was bare. So Kemsit had been forced to venture out to the market.

He carried the thin slips of green papyrus that had been left with him for emergencies—some kind of scrip, as far as he could understand. He also carried some jingling cash. For, in his way, Kemsit had been a wealthy man before the fall of Nagada.

When the strangers had begun paying the mine laborers of Abydos with their silver coins, Kemsit had applied himself to capturing as many as possible. He had lent money from his miner's salary to finance various ventures, some of them even legitimate. And he'd added to his store thanks to his position in the Abydan militia. After risking his life against the Horus guard invaders, he felt completely justified selling weapons he'd found in the battlefields around the city in the thriving black market for off-world armaments.

One way or another, he'd amassed eight hundred of the coins before the final battle threatened Nagada and all the humans on Abydos. Marching with the refugees, he'd toiled across the killing fields under the weight of sacks of silver. And when he'd vanished into the maw of the StarGate, feeling as if he'd been kicked all the way to Earth, one of the sacks had burst on arrival. Almost a quarter of his net worth had vanished in a scrabbling rush of refugees.

Kemsit dared not protest, or even claim the errant wealth. Better not to be marked as a man with money in such desperate company. He had hidden his silver, taking five pieces with him now to handle any extra needs.

But as he navigated the shining metal cart before him, imitating the other shoppers, Kemsit felt an interior hollowness that had nothing to do with hunger.

He had begun deciphering the prices on the items so lavishly displayed.

Kemsit gripped the smooth, slightly greasy handle

of the cart to still the trembling of his hands. Had he somehow mistook the Urt-man method of denoting values? In his brief training as head of household, he'd been taught the number system—for such uses as running the *tul-ay-fawn*. Money values had also been shown.

But now, as he examined one of the Susan B. Anthony dollars he held, Kemsit realized that his life savings would only last three months in this insanely extravagant world.

What to do? Should he abandon this place in search of a more economical market? He'd traveled far on foot just to get here.

He could always return home and get the *tul-ay-fawn* from the drawer, where he'd hidden it from poking hands. Kemsit remembered the sequence of numbers he was supposed to punch in.

But that would be admitting defeat. And, perhaps, it might convince people that Kemsit should not have been given a position of authority.

He carefully sorted through the green scrip money. From the numbers written in the corners, this one slip was worth twenty of his precious coins.

"A much more convenient way to carry it around," Kemsit muttered in Abydan.

All right. He would use one of the papyrus slips, and purchase something inexpensive to feed himself and his housemates for tonight. Then he would use the number to call for help.

Kemsit now had a plan, but his heart still sank as he cruised around the store. He weighed cold meat in his hands, poked at cheeses, tried to estimate servings of vegetables. All so costly! Even a simple stew . . .

He turned the cart in search of cans. There had been some soups in the cupboards at home.

Then he spotted the gigantic cans on the top shelf. They were blue, a foot tall and six inches wide. And each showed a complete meal, some sort of fried white meat—maybe *shikken*, an animal that tasted amazingly like roast king-lizard from back home.

And the price was amazingly inexpensive! His twenty-silver piece of paper would allow him to buy five of these buckets!

Kemsit loaded up his bounty after giving one of the cans an experimental shake. Hmm. Solidly packed.

He purchased the supplies and lugged them home.

"Kemsit!" Hetepet greeted him as he came in the kitchen door. "What did you find?"

Hetepet was a pleasant young woman, and the one member of the impromptu community who had learned how best to operate the stove. She'd have the job of cooking whatever Kemsit brought home. A bit belatedly, Kemsit realized he should have taken her along.

"It's a complete meal," he explained, producing one of the blue containers from the amazingly flimsy sack he'd been given. "*Shikken*, I think. See?" He held out the bucket. "I bought enough to keep us for a couple of days. If we like them, I'll ask for extras when we resupply."

Hetepet hefted the container. "Heavy," she said. "One or two of these should feed everyone." She looked at Kemsit. "No need to keep them cold?"

"They're cans—large ones, I guess," Kemsit said. "They were just sitting on the shelves."

"Good. We can keep them for emergencies, then." Hetepet hunted up the can opener and went to work.

The blue can proved remarkably resistant to being opened. It required considerable effort, cursing, and a bloody finger before the pair succeeded in levering up the metal top with a knife.

Hetepet pulled back in disgust at the milky-white contents. "It looks like congealed grease!"

"Must be something they packed the food in," Kemsit said. He plunged his hand—the one without the bloody digit—into the bucket.

By the time he'd finished swirling his fingers around in the vain search for food, Kemsit had slopped most of the solid shortening onto the table.

"Nothing?" Hetepet looked from the gooey mess to the now-empty bucket.

"Let's open another one," Kemsit sighed. "Either these Urt-men cheat their food shoppers, or there's something we're not understanding here."

CHAPTER 5
BATTLE OF THE EXES

Aboard the *Boat of a Million Years*, Hathor stood on a ship's bridge that could have accommodated a regiment. The vista of workstations stretched at least two hundred times the stretch of her arms. Yet the cyclopean vessel proceeded virtually uncrewed, running on automatic systems controlled by an extremely sophisticated computer.

That situation couldn't continue when she arrived on Earth. Like it or not, she'd have to bring the crew out of its sleep of millennia. Some of these control stations would have to be manned. The engineering consoles in the engine room. The weapons systems. And, as she spoke with the computer about the ship's combat capabilities, there were defense and damage control functions to be considered, as well.

Even so, her flesh crawled at the thought of awakening those damned devils stacked in the room of cold sleep.

"How long will it require to bring this ship to a state of full combat readiness?" she asked the computer.

The answer equated with about three months before arrival in the solar system.

"Good. That can wait, then. Now to the problem of internal security. I wish to safeguard against the crew taking control of the ship. Also, I wish to restrict access to certain sections of the ship's memory."

She had to work carefully, defining the wards she wished to put in place. Several times along the way she had sworn, only too aware of her lack of knowledge in the ways of technology. Her husband Ptah had been the artificer of Tuat. He had even built starships, which she had commanded.

But he hoarded his knowledge, using it to maintain his power base. And, judging from the way the systems had failed on the cruiser *Ra's Eye*, either his technology was deteriorating, or her erstwhile mate had sabotaged her.

Hathor felt a familiar stab of fury. No. Now wasn't the time. She had to concentrate on the task at hand. Even Ptah had seemed a fumbler, a student, before the technical expertise of the Setim. And now she, far less skilled in the ways of technology, had to bar access to certain pieces of information in the memory banks.

For the records embodied in the ship's systems had been for the use of Ra himself. They were not the edited histories available even to the successor godlings on Tuat.

It had been a strange experience for Hathor, reviewing the events of millennia ago as seen from Ra's perspective. Even more disturbing had been discovering just how much the god-king knew about the plots leading to the exile and final extermination of the Setim race.

Ra's spy systems had been quite good. Hathor was

shocked to find holographic recordings of events and discussions even in Ptah's quarters, which he had considered absolutely secure.

The recordings also offered an interesting counterpoint to her own memories . . .

Hathor lay in bed with Ptah, enjoying the feel of the silk coverings against her naked body. At the height of what would later be known as the First Times, she had a keen awareness of the pleasures that Ra's technology had brought to her world—the opportunities it had opened for her. It had not been so long ago that the girl who became Hathor had been a collector of plants and berries for a cave-dwelling tribe. As her body ripened, many of the men of the tribe had wanted—and sampled—her. Little wonder this young woman had an anger and a drive to power that had caught Ra's attention.

He had taken her as a warrior-woman among his guards, then elevated her to godhood as cat-headed Hathor. But even then her ambition was not satisfied. The hawk-headed guards—the Horuses—commanded the slave population and the lower orders of troops. Those humans wearing specialized masks—Apis, the bull, Khnum of the ram's head, crocodile-visaged Sebek, and of course jackal-headed Anubis, Ra's champion—these commanded armies of Horuses. These warrior-godlings sparred among themselves for dominance. But there was a naked-faced god in the hierarchy who had chosen a different route to power—a route not blocked by any human beings.

Ptah sought to learn and practice the ways of technology, the management and use of the machines tended by the Setim. Hathor's reaction to Ra's alien helpers was decidedly atavistic. Animals were to be hunted, not spoken with—or deferred to.

Despite this, Hathor had supported Ptah's quest for knowledge, both as an indirect route to power—and because she knew that someday, there would have to be a reckoning between the aliens and the human godlings. No man had sampled her charms since she had learned the ways of the warrior. But now she lay with Ptah, resting against his side, one leg twined between his. The forge god's normally tight visage was softened with pleasure as he spoke of his success.

"Ra has agreed that the ways of technology be put down in writing. And when that is done, my artificers will have all the knowledge of the Setim."

"I think Ra tires of those red-furred . . . *things*," Hathor spat the word. "They feel that their machines should do the work of the slaves."

This struck to the heart of the matter for the human godlings. If the human slaves were to have no purpose in Ra's empire, what then of those humans elevated to control the slaves?

"Certainly, Ra tires of the one who speaks for the damned devils—Ushabti. He keeps prating of a payment from Ra, of a world owed to his race. They overreach themselves, these Setim. One does not bargain with Ra."

Not in such terms, no, Hathor silently agreed. But she saw another reason why Ra could not overmuch like the Setim. Despite their manlike stance, the linen kilts they wore, the interlopers were, in the end, alien.

And, while Ra was a god, Hathor had felt his eyes on her often enough to realize that he also had the needs a man.

The war of influence went on. Hathor tied herself to Ptah, becoming his wife, and they both rose high in Ra's councils. Always, however, the Setim were before them—especially the infuriating Ushabti. Despite their intramural squabbles, the human godlings found themselves making common cause. And the leadership among them went to the one who could meet the Setim on their own ground—Ptah.

Hathor's body had grown used to the silks, even expecting them now as she lay with Ptah ... just as she had grown used to his husbandly duties. Their recently shared pleasure was forgotten, however, as their pillow talk turned to politics.

"Ushabti is the key," Hathor insisted. "Remove him, and it will be as cutting the tongue from the mouth of the Setim."

"I believe you," Ptah replied. "But who will take the risk?"

Her dark eyes bored into his. "Husband," she said, "I will make this happen."

Ra had shifted the court from his villa on the shores of the sea to his great river palace. Few moved among the halls of the villa, set in the eastern delta. As Hathor stalked the corridors, she took care that none of the servants saw her. She had flown back on a udajeet supposedly decommissioned for maintenance, swinging wide over the encroaching desert to avoid detection.

Her target should be alone in the next hall, gathering last-minute records. Unless, of course, he had other reasons for lagging behind the court. Did the Setim dally? Or might Ushabti be up to some sort of plot?

She entered the room, to find Ushabti at a brazier, burning papyri.

"These are odd records you collect, old dog." Hathor produced her knife. She had chosen the blade over a blast-lance because it could more easily be attributed to a mere thief. Some of the household slaves might be executed for neglecting security, but no blame would attach itself to the human godlings.

Ptah had worried that the elderly Setim might struggle or call for help. But if he were in the midst of destroying records, there was probably some business he did not want Ra to know. Ushabti's inhuman hands were quick to thrust more rolls into the flames as Hathor advanced on him.

She had expected the lips on Ushabti's silver-streaked muzzle to ripple. Even a cur will show his teeth when the end came.

But Ushabti merely looked on her as dispassionately as if she was a fly passing by and not his death coming to take him. He even stepped aside from the madly blazing papers to meet her.

"This had to happen sooner or later," he said, with one final glance at the dagger. "Best to get it done quickly, woman."

Ushabti didn't move. But those alien eyes seemed to probe into her very soul as she slit his throat.

* * *

Brilliant sunlight streamed down on the plateau overlooking the great river. In the distance rose the gleaming limestone of the docking port for Ra's flying palace. It had taken years for the slave population to assemble the two and a half million blocks of stone that made up the construction. Ushabti had argued that the Setim's machines could have handled the job in months.

But now there was no Ushabti to speak for the Setim. Ptah, Hathor, and the other human godlings had assembled in a place of honor around their god-king to celebrate the exile of the red-furred devils.

At great expense and effort, the StarGate had been set up in the brightness of day to accommodate the marching throng of Setim males, females, and children. The faintly rippling energy field stretched across the golden quartz ring showed only faintly in the brilliant sunlight. But as the Setim reached the gleaming threshold, they vanished in their dozens and their hundreds.

Around the portal and the gods stood a large detachment of Horus guards, nervously fingering their blast-lances. Udajeets hung overhead. The antigravity gliders swiveled in midair, bringing their larger energy weapons to bear on the constantly moving line.

"At last the time has come," Ptah muttered. He and his artificers were now the sole repository of technical knowledge in the empire—other than Ra.

"Yes, Ra has let them go." Sebek's voice came out as a deep rumble. His warrior's face was tanned as hard and tight as the skin of his namesake crocodile.

"They kept claiming that Ra owed them a planet."

Thoth, the scribe of the gods, had a lazy, drawling voice—at great variance with the knifelike intellect behind the words. "So we found them a perfectly nice world—except for the mountains of ice that cover it. And according to Ra, those will be gone in a few thousand years."

The godlings all glanced at Ra, who merely stood, staring enigmatically down on his first aides and helpers, his features hidden in the golden mask of his godhead.

When the conversation resumed, it was done in whispers.

"I still think it was overgenerous, giving them all that equipment," Ptah complained.

"No weapons, or manufactories that could produce weapons," bull-headed Apis pointed out.

"They'll need some help building shelter against all that snow," Thoth added. "No handy caves near the StarGate."

"Besides, they still have to build the base for my garrison," Khnum added with satisfaction. "A full division of Horus guards, with blast-lances." Hathor could almost picture the smirk on his face. "No, my friends, the problem of the Setim is solved."

And so, he imagines, is the problem of who leads the human gods, Hathor thought in disgust.

On the other hand, Khnum did now lead the strongest armed force in the empire—at least for now.

The silence of Ptah's bedchamber was destroyed by the urgent blare of a communicator. Hathor rolled herself in silk sheets while her husband donned a kilt and activated the holographic connection.

"Lord Ptah." A scared-looking technician's face floated in midair. "This unworthy servant is Dagi, minister to the StarGate."

A third-rate worker, Hathor thought, if he's relegated to monitoring the StarGate in the after-midnight shift. In fact, he'd soon be an ex-technician—or even a dead one—for awakening his lord in the middle of the night.

"My lord," Dagi gulped. "Please forgive my impertinence for disturbing your slumbers. But one came from the world of the Setim—"

"You woke me because of a messenger?" Ptah's voice was quiet, but that just made his mood seem even more dangerous.

"Lord—" Dagi disappeared from the hologram. For a second, the air in that corner of the room seemed to roil. Hathor realized that the technician was redirecting the projector on his end of the connection.

The foot of the StarGate came into focus—as did the still form of a Horus guard sprawled in front of the portal.

Hathor sat up in the bed, forgetting about the sheets. She had been through some fairly rough StarGate transitions, but that was not the reason for the warrior's distress.

A foot-long rod of metal transfixed the Horus, entering through his chest and emerging from his back. Ptah leaned forward. "Quite ingenious," he said. "The pointed head is developed from the metal wood-fasteners the Setim were supposed to use in building shelters. Dagi!" he called to his man.

The technician reappeared in the screen. For a

second he stared wide-eyed over Ptah's shoulder—at her, Hathor realized as she pulled on a warrior's kilt. But Dagi quickly averted his eyes.

"Rouse the guard and interdict the portal," Ptah ordered. "I will take the news to Ra myself."

Dagi's worried face faded. Ptah turned sourly to Hathor as he reached for his pectoral necklace. "Perhaps it will do some good to be the first to report this disaster."

"You think it's a full-blown rebellion?"

"If Khnum can spare only a dying man to send as a messenger, I think we can expect that the farside Star-Gate is already in the hands of the Setim."

"So we'll need a new Khnum," Hathor said. "If the present holder of the title survived the Setim, he certainly wouldn't survive Ra's wrath. "And no doubt there will be an expedition to put down the rebels."

Ptah's lips tightened. "Not that I would be considered for command. Anubis is a certainty—or perhaps Sebek. Both have military experience."

"Admittedly, Anubis is good at crushing slave uprisings—against enemies without technology," Hathor said. "But Sebek? If you consider the way he led the Ramses guards in the last riots . . . the Setim are considerably more dangerous opponents."

"You know I agree, lady wife," Ptah sighed. "But the decision lies with Ra—and whoever has his ear."

"Mighty lord," Hathor murmured as she stretched herself on Ra's bed. The furnishings were even more luxurious than her own. And the attractions of Ra's attention went beyond his eternally youthful body.

His interest in her offered dreams of more than power, but dynasty.

However, Hathor carefully kept such considerations deep in her thoughts as she turned to enfold the god-king in an embrace. He always seemed more like a mortal after lovemaking, as if that basic human activity somehow banished the alien otherness of him for a short while.

Hathor decided to make the most of her opportunity.

"Who will command the expedition against the upstart Setim?" she asked.

Ra favored her with a lazy smile. "Whoever presents me with the best plan," he replied. "Anubis and Sebek have both come forth with variation of a frontal attack through the StarGate. I will not accept such losses. We know the Setim will have prepared unpleasant surprises on the far side."

"Mighty lord, your concern for casualties—"

"I do not care how many Horuses perish," Ra said with a laugh. The *otherness* crept back into his voice as he spoke. "But I object to losing them for nothing!"

He glared down at her. "Khnum has already cost me a strong force—and their blast-lances. I have no wish to supply the enemy with more."

Hathor lowered her gaze from those disturbing eyes, even as her warrior's brain contended with the tactical problem. Never before had the empire dealt with an enemy who had seized a StarGate. It was the only connection to the world where the Setim had been exiled. Coming to grips with the enemy necessarily meant a frontal assault. Unless . . .

A sudden possibility for an indirect approach

occurred to her. Ptah had mentioned that the god-king's flying palace had made the voyage to the exile planet in mere months. Could Ra's flying pyramid carry enough Horus guards to clear and secure the gateway for an invasion force?

No. Too much space would be needed for the months of supplies. But attacking from a star-spanning vessel—avoiding the bottleneck of the StarGate—

She directed her eyes back to Ra's face. "Truly, lord, you would give command of the mission to anyone who offered the best plan?"

Ra smiled. "Even to your honored husband, if he showed the necessary ability."

Hathor smiled in return. "Even to me, lord?"

Frowning as she stood on the bridge of the *Boat of a Million Years*, Hathor ordered the command computer to interdict all records on interaction between the human gods and the Setim, most especially the accounts of her campaign against the rebels—a campaign to extinction.

"Additionally, restrict all history of the empire since the crew boarded this vessel," Hathor commanded. "We will prepare records with an appropriate time line."

Like Ra, she was already beginning to discern the uses of history and myth. The memory banks included holographic records of the growing unrest on Earth. The crew could be told that the planet had rebelled.

They just didn't need to know how long ago that rebellion had taken place.

When Hathor awakened from the slumber of millennia, she'd had access to some of the empire's most secret records. But the Setim would only get her version of history, and must see nothing to contradict that.

Hathor frowned. "Additional order. No crew members except for myself and Khonsu are to have access to Astrogation functions or star charts."

It took a very long time, but given thousands of years, stars move quite perceptibly. Hathor remembered how the constellations over Tuat had shifted.

Who knew how they'd changed over Earth?

Daniel drove a rental car through the guarded gate of a former military base now reclaimed by General West to serve as a home for Barbara Shore's technical research contingent. The general had been quite ruthless in gaining office space for his study group, which seemed to be growing almost with a life of its own.

Daniel was actually based in Washington, but he'd been sent to offer input on the translation facility that would assist the researchers. With his barnstorming tour of the country to lecture about preparedness for Hathor's attack, Daniel had been forced to overcome his fear of flying. He'd even managed to push back his hodophobia, the psychosomatic allergy to traveling.

But his hands shook as he drove to the camp's administration center. Somewhere, very nearby, was Sha'uri.

Gary Meyers was waiting as Daniel parked the car. He was a different man from the Harvard scholar who'd been so condescending when Daniel first appeared on the StarGate project. In those days Gary thought he knew it all. He'd learned a lot more about his ignorance while being manipulated by Hathor and nearly getting killed by her Horus guards.

"The guard told me you'd arrived," Gary said, a smile appearing on his broad, slightly jowly face. "Glad to see you."

"So you're running the translating effort?" Daniel said.

"Bite your tongue," Meyers replied. "This predynastic stuff is your baby—and the Abydans' mother language. I've been *liaising*"—he grinned at the biz speak—"putting Sha'uri's people together with some Egyptologists who haven't suffered from atherosclerosis of their opinions and some science types to help decipher the technical end . . ."

His recitation stumbled at Daniel's sudden expression of pain. "Yeah, well, I'm being about as useful as I ever am—and about as tactful, too, I guess."

"Just something I'll have to live with," Daniel responded. "Do I get a guided tour?"

"Nothing much to see," Gary told him. "The head honcho here is a guy named Travis. He's got most of his people going through the mountain of stuff we got through before the Abydos StarGate shut down. Barbara is working with the pieces from a couple of uda-jeet engines, trying to assemble a working model. For the rest, it's mainly desks with computers on them—looks like an insurance company."

Meyers led Daniel down halls and past rooms that looked pretty much as he'd described. "Here's your office," he said, opening a door to reveal a battered metal desk with a brand-new computer on it. "We've got everybody networked, in the hopes that by cross-indexing what we've discovered, we'll be able to cross-pollinate some of these research projects."

"Sounds like a good idea," Daniel said.

Meyers jerked a thumb to his right. "I'm your next-door neighbor, and Barbara is just down the hall."

"My ambition in life is fulfilled," Daniel joked. "At last I'm close to the seats of power."

"Yeah, right," Meyers responded. "Travis is the one in the base commander's office."

"Could I see Barbara?" Daniel asked.

"Sure, we're still pretty informal around here." Meyers led the way, rapped on a door, and opened it.

"Hey, Barbara, are you decent? I've got a surprise—"

The bodacious brunette was wearing one of her usual jumpsuits, this one a light gray. She looked up wide-eyed from behind her desk as Daniel stepped in.

"Hey, Barbara—oh, sorry, I didn't realize you were with—"

The other person in the room wore a blazer and jeans. As she turned, a nimbus of brown curls surrounded an all-too-familiar face. Sha'uri.

Daniel's words clogged in his throat. Behind him, he heard Gary Meyers mutter, "Oh, shit!"

That pretty well covers it, Daniel thought.

Sha'uri rose from her seat, looking crisp and confident even in the casual attire. "I'll start assigning this right away," she said.

Daniel wondered how she managed to glare at him and ignore him simultaneously. She went to the door, stepping around him as if he were a turd on the floor.

"I, uh—gotta go." Meyers disappeared, shutting the door behind him.

Daniel cleared his throat. "Well," he said brightly, "that went about as well as could be expected."

"We've talked a bit." Barbara gave him a cautious look. "She's still pretty furious at you."

"That hasn't escaped me," Daniel replied. "So I'll make a suggestion—simply to keep things running smoothly." He cleared his throat again. "I'd already pretty much decided to spend most of my time in Washington. But I want you to know that if there's anything—*anything* you need on the translating front, you just get it to me. Do you think I'll be able to patch into your network?"

"I'm sure something can be worked out." Barbara tried to start again. "About Sha'uri—"

"She hates my guts." Daniel sat in the chair in front of Barbara's desk. It was still warm from Sha'uri's body, and a faint trace of indefinable scent remained in the air.

It took every bit of his will to hold on to the calm facade he struggled to project. "I don't like it," Daniel said, "but I really can't let it get in the way. We all have jobs to do."

"Yes," Barbara said. "Don't we?"

Daniel was already on a plane heading back to D.C. when Sha'uri next came into Barbara Shore's office. "He's gone?" she asked the physicist curtly.

Barbara nodded. "And I don't think it's likely he'll be coming back very much."

Sha'uri stood silent for a moment, her face still. Maybe she'd grown a trifle pale.

Damn, Barbara thought, another one I'd hate to play poker against.

Then Sha'uri gave a brief nod. "Yes," she said. "Running away."

"I think it's more like running things," Barbara gently contradicted. "I'd say he's been about as busy as a one-armed juggler lately. But he left himself on call."

Barbara described the system she'd set up to use if they needed to tap Daniel's translating expertise. At least Sha'uri didn't try to suggest he'd never be needed.

Daniel Jackson was probably Earth's greatest expert on the archaic system of hieroglyphics used in Ra's empire. He'd taught Sha'uri and her Abydan translators, setting them on their way.

No, Sha'uri was a professional. She'd even admit that Daniel might be indispensable—at least in certain things.

CHAPTER 6
TECHNICAL DIFFICULTIES

The Florida sun beat down on Barbara Shore as she walked to one of the outbuildings in the Kennedy Space Center. Back on Abydos, the two local stars had shed more heat. It was the stickiness in the air that got to her—that, and the tension.

Barbara's destination was a massive structure where rocket engines were usually prepared for the space shuttle.

If this works, she thought, we'll retire that entire industry.

For weeks, she and a crew from Colonel Travis' Technical Advisory Group had combed through the mass of high-tech spoil rescued from the two earlier battles on Abydos. They'd been searching for wreckage from Ra's udajeets, while Sha'uri sifted through transcribed records and yet-untranslated hieroglyph manuals for information on the antigravity gliders.

The results of that work awaited Barbara in the cavernous building—an effort to reconstruct the gravity-defying engine that allowed the udajeets to perform their incredible aerobatics.

It hadn't been easy. The wreckage had been taken

through the StarGate in pieces—the portal wasn't large enough to accommodate an intact udajeet, even if they'd captured one. Most of the antigravity gliders had been shot down or crashed.

Still worse, a number of the technicians who'd disassembled the components for shipping had died in Hathor's final invasion of Abydos. Barbara had undertaken her restoration job on the basis of notes, photographs, annoyingly ambiguous diagrams from the hieroglyphic instruction manuals, and enough jigsaw pieces to build three aircraft.

It had *not* been easy.

But, by dint of ruthless pushing, hard work, and a few inspired guesses, they had assembled what Barbara hoped was a rough approximation of the antigravity drive.

She had only the vaguest conception of the physics behind the engine. Ra's manuals were designed to protect his technology while keeping his machines running. They were frustratingly short on theory and long on telling the mechanics which bolt to tighten. The symbols for power ratings and constants were difficult to translate, too. Whatever symbols Ra's civilization used to represent volts, watts, joules, or thrust had no meaning to the succeeding nontechnical culture. Or they had been adapted, as Gary Meyers had found, into theological equivalents, referring to the manifold powers of the gods.

Unfortunately, knowing that the manuals rated an antigrav output at fifteen hundred godpowers didn't tell very much. All Barbara knew for sure was that the golden quartz that made up so much of Ra's technology had a very strange effect. Power pumped into it produced an incredibly high energy output—orders of magnitude greater than what went in.

That result had already been proven with the Star-Gate, which had eaten Earthly electricity through huge, heavy leads—but expended immeasurably higher energy levels drilling a hole through space to the Cir-rhian galaxy. It was also implicit in Ra's threat to destroy the Earth—or at least, a good chunk of it—by channeling a nuclear blast through unrefined quartz fragments.

Computer simulations on input and output from the cobbled-together engines had proven useless—so now Barbara was trying the empirical, brute-strength approach. The antigravity engine had been enclosed in what she irreverently called the "beer keg"—a gleaming cylinder tapering at both ends.

This metal skin was braced and securely attached to the engine—and then secured even more stringently to the concrete floor of the testing ground. Chains usu-ally employed in anchoring aircraft carriers were attached to bolts sunk yards into the ground. Cables as thick as Barbara's arms entered the beer keg from an impressive power system.

Power controls were set at the far end of the enor-mous space, behind safety barriers that looked stronger than the Alamo. As Barbara took her place with the project engineers, she wondered if that would be enough, should the test rig fail.

Well, she'd sat right beside the StarGate when they'd first tested it.

"So we gonna take this sucker for a test drive today?" she brashly inquired of her team.

Mitch Storey's bearded face flashed her a grin. "Hope you brought the ignition key." He adjusted the lucky beret that made him look like Che Guevara from a touring company of *Evita*.

"Let's warm this sucker up."

Storey's fingers caressed his console, and power began to flow into the engine.

The beer keg didn't move. Barbara's eyes flashed back and forth between the power readouts and the dead-on-the-floor mounted engine. "Increase the power," she ordered, hiding her own misgivings.

Had they missed something in the manuals? Was it a case of technician's error? Perhaps a faulty component had gone into the engine—hell, they were working from junk, stuff that had either been shot down or hit the ground pretty hard in combat maneuvers. Even if all the pieces worked, something might have gone in backward.

A low whine came from the container as Storey upped the power. In counterpoint a low hiss came from Barbara's lips.

The damned thing was moving!

It was like watching the Indian rope trick—or rather, like a mechanical cobra being charmed. The beer keg, like the head of a gigantic snake, seemed to waver on the huge chains holding it to the test bed.

"Okay, we've got a minimum," Storey said, checking his outputs.

"Perfect, if we want to shift something around for a keg party," Barbara muttered. Louder, she said, "Push it up. We've got to find out how much thrust this bad boy can develop."

Storey advanced the power controls minutely, and the metal cylinder no longer wobbled in midair. It stood at the end of the chains, hauling them up tight. A warbling whistle filled the huge room. Barbara remembered after-action reports with the udajeets. Yes, the engines were working.

"Big difference from that first power surge," Barbara commented. "Slowly, now. Up one more—"

The technician manipulated his console controls with delicate fingers. But Barbara's eyes were on the beer keg. It strained like a living thing, trying to tear free of the chains. The whistle turned into a shriek.

Then a new sound intruded, a flat, metallic screech. Barbara stared as one of the thick steel links sheared in half. She ducked despite the blast barrier, as metal fragments flew. Almost in slow motion, the beer keg swung around, tethered only by three chains now.

Another chain gave before Barbara could even open her mouth to give an order.

"Cut—" she began, but the beer keg had already burst out of its shackles. As Storey moved to cut the power, the antigravity cylinder rocketed to the ceiling and ripped through.

Barbara stared up at the newly torn opening, round as a bullet hole from some monstrous pistol. "Well," she finally said, "we learned that the power changes appear to be geometric. Our control systems will have to be pretty finicky."

Mitch Storey was still staring at the hole. "Will it be coming down?"

"Of course it will. No more juice is going into the circuitry." Barbara gestured to the torn power cable lying on the floor. "I just hope it doesn't land on anybody. For the rest—"

She shrugged. "Well, we kept our notes, didn't we?"

Hundreds of miles to the north and west, in an area of the Atlantic known to oceanographers as the Bermuda Rise, sensors detected a discharge of energy unknown on the planet Earth for five thousand years. An emplacement in the ocean bed shuddered to semi-alert status.

The mechanisms were balky—they had been installed in haste and never tested. Automatic systems had maintained them, keeping them going for millennia, though the test cycles had to be run more and more often to keep the equipment in working order. The devices hidden in the undersea emplacement were still operational, but worn. Their creators had not expected a continual stop-and-start cycle that went on for thousands of years.

The devices were not in optimal condition—but their programming was definite. More units were now roused. Sensor nets winked into existence, to provide data for the local control systems.

And, much farther away, central control units slipped into cognizance . . .

Jack O'Neil looked at his boss in some surprise. General West had conducted hundreds of briefings in his career, even at the White House level from his days as one of the "crazies in the basement." Back then he'd brashly offered the president all sorts of notions for counterthrusts to the Communist threat. So why was the man running his palms along the seams of his dress uniform trousers as if he were wiping sweat away?

O'Neil admitted to himself that he'd be a little apprehensive at facing the Joint Chiefs. Certainly, the plan West was advocating would be immensely more expensive than any of his covert missions. It was also immensely more crucial.

The colonel busied himself with a last-minute check of the presentation effects. They had ruthlessly stolen the best effects of the pitchmen who had besieged West's office. The briefing would present the bad news on the wings of multimedia, with slick computer animation. But would it elicit the necessary reaction?

During the Cold War, military men rarely saw a weapons system they didn't like—especially if it could be aimed eastward. In an era of fiscal constraints, the battles to defend budgetary turf had only heightened interservice rivalries.

That was the worrisome part of the West proposals. Defending the Earth would not be a navy project, or an army one, nor even an air force job. It would take an ungodly amount of cash, with damned little credit for any of the existing services.

The Joint Chiefs and their staffs filed in and took their seats. West cleared his throat.

"One month ago, I was tasked with evaluating the best defense that could be mounted against an extraterrestrial attack," he began, "bearing in mind an implementation window of less than one year. After examining a number of options, I propose a space-borne defense as the most promising.

"Essentially, the approach is to use off-the-shelf systems, plus whatever we can develop from the technology captured from the enemy's wrecked cruiser vessel."

West tapped the remote in his hand. A blunt, cylindrical construction in golden quartz appeared on the large screen facing the generals. "This is a salvaged energy weapon. It operates on the same principles as the enemy's personal weapons, commonly called blast-lances." He glanced at his audience. "We successfully reverse-engineered those for use by our ground troops. My science advisers assure me the same can be done for these blast-cannons."

Several officers sat forward in their seats, taking in the size and scale of the heavy blaster.

"These weapons will provide the energy component of a constellation of 144 orbital weapons platforms," West went on, tapping the remote again. An image of the Earth appeared, the Western Hemisphere going into the night zone. The lights of major cities glittered in the darkness. "These will be distributed in twelve orbital planes to provide total coverage around the planet."

Another tap on the remote, and the world was suddenly surrounded in a webwork of fine lines, with bright white dots spaced along them like pearls.

"The blast-cannon on each platform will be supplemented with chemically powered nuclear missiles." Still another tap, and an artist's conception appeared on the screen. The term "platform" was a bit of a misnomer, but the term was already familiar from the Star Wars program. The image showed a spindly construction with ten rocket cradles and the distinctive snout of the energy cannon, with small attitude jets to handle aiming.

An army general with distinguished service in the Gulf and a potential political career looked pained. "Nuclear missiles? Our allies won't be pleased with that—nor will the rest of the world. Orbital weapons are banned—"

"By the Outer Space Treaty of 1967, sir. But this is a contingency that treaty never considered. There are provisions under Section IX for consultation with the signatories. Given the emergency facing the world, the United Nations must consider amendments."

The war hero's expression would have had lesser officers scrambling to save their careers. But West seemed to ignore the glare. "In any event, the energy needs for the blast-cannon will demand a nuclear power source—"

"This thing is going to run on atomic power?" an admiral interrupted. "You're just asking for trouble from the tree huggers. They've kept reactors out of space on our side since the Sixties."

"Nonetheless, sir, there are presently fifty-five nuclear-powered satellites in orbit."

"And an explosive reentry that caused an international incident," the admiral recalled. "Our reactors are either obsolete or still on the drawing board. Where do you figure on getting an off-the-shelf power source?"

"Our calculations show that we can use the latest

design of the Russian Federation," West replied. "It's serviceable, and has had a good track record on their ocean-observing satellites."

"*Very* good." A Cold Warrior smiled grimly at the thought of an old enemy providing the power for U.S. space hegemony.

"The OWPs will be unmanned, but controlled from space. We propose two manned platforms, in Low Earth Orbit."

Dollar signs danced over the Joint Chiefs' heads as West went on. "We can adapt an already existing construct—the *Mir* space station." At a touch of his remote, the image of the Earth englobed in protective OWP orbits reappeared. Now an additional red dot formed on a much lower orbital level, at the left-hand side of the planet.

"You'd let the Russkis get a finger on this button?" the Cold Warrior demanded in horrified disbelief.

West continued. "The other platform would have to be constructed—we proposed a modified version of the present space station *Freedom*." Another dot, this one blue, appeared at the right-hand side of the schematic.

Then the screen flashed through quick before-and-after views of *Mir* and the theoretical *Freedom*, then detailed the additional fire control and weapons systems components.

"The space station is supposed to take seven years to build," an air force general objected.

"We do not intend to build the complete facility," West replied. "If we can get it to the status known as 'human-tended,' we'll be able to maintain a crew aboard—in admittedly spartan conditions."

"Even so, that would require—what? Doubling the original construction schedule?" the general asked. "You're asking a lot of NASA and the shuttle program."

"Which brings us to another breakthrough in reconstructing the enemy's technology," West continued, working the remote.

A laugh greeted the next picture, which looked like a beer barrel with a very noticeable dent in one side.

O'Neil had warned his superior that would happen, but West continued smoothly. "Our Technological Assessment Group succeeded in producing a working model of the enemy's antigravity drive. Their proposal, which I think makes considerable sense, is to refit the space shuttle fleet with these engines."

A flurry of images ran across the screen, detailing how the shuttles' rockets could be replaced.

"This would give us a much more . . . *dependable* launching schedule, daily if necessary, and allow us greater lift capability for the more sensitive components."

An image of a shuttle with the Spacehab module appeared on the screen. Beyond was the growing truss work of a space station in construction. Half a dozen space-suited figures came out of the shuttle's air lock, while another shuttle in the background extended its manipulator arm. "In addition, we'd be able to field more shuttles simultaneously for construction, to serve as crew quarters in orbit, and to supply the *Mir* station."

A new picture appeared. It showed a shuttle with its

cargo bay open. A blast-cannon poked its snout into the vacuum of space, surrounded by a ring of missile tubes.

"When the construction cycle is finished, the upgraded shuttles can be outfitted with weapons to act as a mobile reserve."

"Fighters," the air force general said greedily.

"Although they won't be as nimble as the udajeets we've seen in filmed record," West quickly warned.

The Earth-defense schematic was displayed again, now with an arrowhead of seven golden sparks over the Atlantic.

"Wait a minute," the admiral spoke up. "There are only four shuttles presently available."

"Yes, sir: *Endeavour, Atlantis, Columbia,* and *Discovery.* But there is one out of service—*Enterprise*—on display in the Smithsonian Institution. And there are two prototypes of the Soviet shuttle—*Buran* and *Ptichka.*"

"Okay, so you nearly double our initially considered lift ability," the admiral conceded. "What is all this going to cost?"

"Even with antigravity flight, there's considerable tonnage to be lifted," West pointed out. "Beyond the space station components and the OWPs, we'll have to launch long-range sensors for the earliest warning possible. My technological assessment people assure me that Ra's stardrive, like the StarGate, creates detectable gravity distortions. The tonnage to be lifted looks like this."

He flashed figures on the screen. The generals groaned.

"Chemical rockets will be required to bring the simpler, more robust components into orbit. Using our facilities at Cape Canaveral and Vandenberg, the Russian facilities at Baikonur and Plesetsk, the European Space Agency, Japan's launching capacity, and if possible, China's, the job can be done."

"But it won't be done for free," the admiral said grimly. "What kind of expense are we talking about?"

Silently, West hit the remote. An even louder response came from the military men—and these were people who were used to throwing huge amounts of money around.

"That—that represents an appreciable part of the world's gross economic profit," the Cold Warrior said in a hollow voice.

"It represents the best defense we can mount with existing technology," West replied impassively.

"But you can't assure us that it will successfully repel this goddess-woman and her ship," the admiral shrewdly pointed out.

"No, sir. I can only assure you of what will happen if we don't try."

West's finger twitched on the remote. The world again appeared on the screen, without the defense system he'd just proposed.

Then West hit the button again.

One by one the lights of the world's cities began to go out.

CHAPTER 7
THE NATURE OF THE ENEMY

The office building was generic. A quick elevator ride brought Gary Meyers to the third floor, where, after a brief search, he found a door marked ABYDOS FOUNDATION. The waiting area could have fronted anything from an insurance company to a gambling operation—more or less the same things, Meyers thought.

At last a secretary appeared from behind the young receptionist. Daniel Jackson's personal assistant reminded Meyers of his third-grade teacher—rather plain woman who didn't take much nonsense.

Harsh experience had apparently taught Daniel something about young, beautiful associates.

"Dr. Meyers," the secretary said, making Gary feel that he'd been woolgathering when he should have been answering the problem on the board. He followed the woman down a corridor that fronted other offices—none of them extremely luxurious. The desks didn't match, except that they all looked worn. The decor was definitely bankruptcy auction. A couple of people—number crunchers by the looks of it—had new computers. The whole place gave the impression of being run on a shoestring.

Where most corridors in the executive sanctum would have been carpeted, this one had tile. The secretary's sensible shoes echoed with each footstep. Four steps from her desk, six to the final office, and the door to the sanctum sanctorum opened. Daniel Jackson grinned at his colleague.

"I couldn't believe it when I saw your name on today's appointments," he said. "What brings you to the nation's capital? I hope everything's going well with the technology assessment."

Meyers gave an empty nod in return. "It's all fine." He paused for a second. "Sha'uri is well."

"Yah," Daniel said succinctly. "I can see she told you to pass that bit of information along."

The big, slightly bumbling man made a gesture of distress. "She's certainly not happy, and neither are you. Lord knows, I'm not one to give advice. Faizah—"

"Hathor," Daniel quietly corrected.

"That woman made a fool of both of us," Gary said. "And she's still making you and Sha'uri miserable."

"Sha'uri hates my guts for what she thinks happened—could have happened," Daniel amended. "Very easily. She may be wrong about my personal life, but she's right to blame me for creating such a godawful mess on Abydos. I can only ask for her forgiveness, and she obviously isn't ready to give me that."

He managed a smile. "Somehow, I can't bring myself to believe that you're here as love's messenger. What's up?"

"I wanted to see what you're doing," Gary replied.

"It's a regular three-ring circus," Daniel said. "Part

of the time, I'm the poster boy for Intergalactic Invasion Preparedness, trying to line up support for General West's defense proposals. When I'm not being tapped to appear somewhere as an expert on aliens, I'm still managing the Abydan's affairs. Actually, that's what most of the staff here does. It's getting a bit easier as the people settle in. Sha'uri is one of the lucky ones. She's got a job. We're still trying to get the immigration questions straightened out. Representative Grinch and his conservative friends want the Abydans out—or, at least, not collecting any government benefits. I try to balance whatever money comes in from licenses and such with sordid economic needs."

"I'm more interested in this Office of Bright Ideas," Meyers said as Daniel led him to a seat.

"That certainly has the most entertainment value," Daniel admitted, plopping behind his desk. "It's another public relations job, courtesy of General West. Sometimes I think he just set me up as a sort of lightning rod so he could get on with his work. 'If you have an idea that sheds light on our situation, or which will assist in defending the Earth, take it to Daniel Jackson at the Abydos Foundation.' "

He shook his head. "The appointment before yours was with the Mothers of Daughters Impregnated by Space Aliens. They wanted to know what legal recourse they had in Ra's empire. Apparently, their new theory is that Horus guards were coming through the StarGate to frolic with their daughters."

"Not the most helpful," Meyers said.

"That's putting it mildly. Still, it beats dealing with

former colleagues looking for jobs." Daniel put on an obsequious voice. " 'Of course, I always knew your theory had merit. It's just that in the face of such a strong prevailing opinion . . .' " He made a gesture of disgust. "They laughed me off the stage when I tried to raise a couple of questions. Now, though, they think I can do them some good, recommending them for translating jobs—"

He broke off. "I suppose you get enough of that, too."

Meyers nodded. "Most of them I couldn't recommend. They're worse than I was. But a few—the young ones who aren't already fossilized in the brain pan—I've brought aboard. Lately, I've been teaching them what we've learned rather than translating stuff myself."

"Good going!" Daniel said. "If we get through all this, there'll have to be a general reevaluation of the whole field. If Ra was a real person, how much else of what we once considered mythology is actually garbled history?"

"It sounds as if you've been doing some thinking on that already," Meyers said.

Daniel nodded. "The battle between Set and Horus. Good and bad. Satan versus the angels. The climax of the whole Osiris myth. Modern opinion says that the Horus-falcon was the fetish of lower Nile tribes who conquered the Delta and unified Egypt. Set—though nobody was ever able to figure out what animal he was supposed to be—was the fetish of the losing side."

"That's the theory," Meyers agreed. "In an early

example of propaganda, Set was turned from a beneficent god into the god of evil by the winners."

"The problem is," Daniel said slowly, "there may have been an actual Set—an alien. Maybe a whole *bunch* of aliens. I saw some aboard the *Boat of a Million Years*."

"And we've both seen lots of Horuses," Gary Meyers said. "Most of them were shooting at us."

"So what if this legend of a battle between Set and Horus isn't about fetishes, but refers to an actual struggle in Ra's predecessor state?" Daniel leaned across his desk, eagerly speaking. "You should have seen Hathor's reaction when she found that chamber packed with frozen Setim. That's what she called them. She made the name sound like a curse."

"Factions," Meyers said with a grin "Reminds me of university politics—who'd run the department, and all that."

"What else do the legends tell us?" Daniel went on. "Set is originally depicted as a warrior on board the *Boat of a Million Years*, defending it against the monsters of the night. Suppose Ra picked up the Setim before he arrived on Earth? Once he got here, he elevated certain humans to quasi-godhood. Maybe he even got the idea of using the animal heads to set them apart, as the humanoid Setim were set apart from the ordinary humans."

"Makes sense," Meyers admitted. "But then the Horus and the other-headed demigods didn't want to share their status with the aliens. They eliminated the Setim. So in history, and mythology, we get the Set-Horus war."

"Genocide?" Daniel frowned. "There are some pretty bloodthirsty Egyptian legends—for instance, about Hathor. She's also referred to in the hidden archives of Nagada—they say she exterminated an entire colony."

"You think she's the one who killed off the Setim?" Gary Meyers asked.

"She certainly looked surprised to see them," Daniel said. "Surprised . . . and something else."

"An ancient story with modern implications," Gary Meyers said. "This ties in with the proposal I came to make—to the Office of Bright Ideas."

Daniel gave him a quizzical glance. "Fire away."

"It came to me while I was teaching the proto-hieroglyphics to my student translators. I may be hopeless at turning those tech manuals into English, but I know the symbols—especially the techno-glyphs. My proposal is to see if there are any more samples here on Earth. Maybe we can clear away some more mythology from the history." He glanced at Daniel. "Set was still a popular god in the Delta and the Upper Nile. Maybe the Setim befriended the plain, ordinary humans. There may be secrets to be found."

"And you'd be the guy to find them," Daniel said. "If I asked, I'd always be that troublemaking crackpot. But you have an international reputation."

"Yeah, as a nice, safe and sane scholar. I always knew a Harvard education would come in useful." He laughed out loud. "At least I know the enemy."

Aboard the *Boat of a Million Years*, Khonsu stood impassive in the large chamber Hathor had chosen for a briefing room. The revivification had gone well, and the great ship's alien crew walked the halls again. Seeing the beast-men made the Horus guard's hackles rise, as a dog's might at meeting a strange animal.

But his response was not as virulent as the Lady's. Judging from her unguarded comments before the crew was taken from stasis, she had fought and feared the Sons of Set.

Yet none of these venomous emotions showed as she faced the silent, red-muzzled crew. The face Hathor exhibited to the Setim was a mask as carefully crafted as the briefing she was about to present.

"Warriors of Ra!" she spoke suddenly, hidden mechanisms augmenting her voice to fill the chamber. "I allowed you some little time to recover yourselves from the rigors of revivification. But I knew you wished to hear why you are brought forth—and why he whom you follow is not here."

Hathor's voice grew solemn as she faced her audience. "The reason is simple—rebellion!"

A holographic image appeared in the air over Hathor's head. It showed an unruly crowd of humans confronting some of the empire's Ramses guards. The Ramses, Hathor had explained to Khonsu, dated back to the First Days, a lesser order of peacekeepers subordinate to the Horuses. They wore a linen head cloth, the *khepren*, instead of the hawk-mask. And they were armed merely with heavy batons instead of energy-weapons.

The angry crowd pushed against their line, the faces of the fellahin distorted with rage as they shouted and jeered—all in silence. Hathor had removed the audio portion of the presentation. She didn't want the Setim to hear the cause of the disturbance—that the guards had been out seizing "volunteers" to be sent to a new colony-planet.

The Ramses guards struck out ruthlessly, engendering counterviolence from the crowd. Fists, sticks, and stones were raised against the guards, who nonetheless fought savagely until their formation was broken. Then furious rioters overwhelmed them.

It still shook Khonsu to see mere fellahin assail officers of the empire. The notion seemed as alien as fur-covered beasts who walked on their hind legs and conversed in the imperial tongue. But Khonsu had seen rebels on Abydos who had killed even trained Horuses.

Hathor, apparently, had seen too many rebels to pay them much mind. Riots like the one recorded in the ship's library had been a frequent occurrence in the years after the extermination of the Setim—and the great rising that had cut off Earth's StarGate.

"We will turn this record to our purposes," she'd said.

And as he watched Hathor's performance, Khonsu had to admit that she was very convincing.

"The rebels had a certain low cunning," she told the Setim. "They waited until a large number of guards and artificers had gone through the StarGate to work on a new project. Then they rose, attacking the guards and seizing the StarGate itself so reinforcement was impossible. Many of our Horuses—and many of your own people—have already been slaughtered."

That struck the until-now silent crowd. Short, barking whispers ran among them. "How can this be?" one of the Setim asked. "Our people have always been well-disposed to the lower orders."

Khonsu had to force himself not to flinch at the alien accents. But Hathor replied smoothly.

"Treachery," she said. "The low ones used the goodwill of your people to further their attack. Our forces now hold only a few strong points, protecting the civilian survivors of the initial rebel attacks. Mighty Ra dispatched me with the necessary amulet to open the StarGate to this destination." She gestured to the golden Eye of Ra hanging between her breasts. "I set out with a company of Horus guards. Only we lived to pass the StarGate, which the rebels were already preparing to bury."

She faced the silenced throng. "Contact has been broken with the StarGate of Earth. But already we hasten back to that planet at the best speed this vessel's engines can deliver. Our dread lord and your own people await rescue. Prepare your weapons, brave Setim. Our enemies will be numerous and powerful."

Standing among the revived Setim, Nekhti, son of Ushabti, felt his lips instinctively rippling to reveal his fangs—a sign of suspicion among his people. He trusted this warrior-woman not at all. Too many bargains with the empire of Ra had proven to be empty promises.

When the dying being that had become Ra arrived on their homeworld, the Setim had faced ecological disaster brought about by their own technology. Ra had promised them passage to a new world if they would serve him.

The bare remnant of the race had boarded this gigantic vessel and gone into stasis. When they emerged, they found themselves orbiting another world, rich, untouched . . . inhabited by primitives.

Nekhti had been one of those operating the vessel's launch when Ra had flown down to examine a tribe of hunter-gatherers who had fled at the sight of the ship. All but one.

Ra had melded his psyche with the young Earth-human who had responded with courage and curiosity to Ra's dramatic arrival. In his new, quasi-human guise, Ra had ordered his Setim followers to prepare armaments and strange equipment, which he had bestowed to selected humans. Nekhti had even participated in charades of power before the awed tribes folk of this world. Ra was using his technology to present himself as a god, the apex of a vast pyramid of slaves.

Nekhti and his people had tried to keep their word to Ra. But Nekhti knew that his father was concerned at the outlines of the society they were shaping. More to the point, Ra always had additional projects to be attended to, additional needs before he could requite the Setim with a new world.

Ushabti had come to doubt Ra's promises. And Nekhti feared, his father might have begun to take action. Ushabti had not confided in him—Nekhti was one of Ra's chosen bodyguards. But Nekhti had noticed little things, movements of materials and supplies.

He had no idea what his father had in mind. But apparently Ra also had suspicions. That was why Nekhti had found himself in a commander's position among the "trusted crew" who had gone into stasis aboard this great vessel. He and his people here had been as much hostages for the good behavior of the majority of the Setim as honored guards.

But it now seemed that rebellion had come, not from Ushabti and the Setim, but from the great mass of human slaves whose labor supported the empire.

Ushabti had always argued that the fellahin need not be treated so harshly, that the careful introduction of technology might allow them to become something more than speaking beasts of burden. His proposals had always been stymied by the mask-wearers—the ones like this bitch warrior—who feared that the end of slavery would also end their status as slave masters.

Nekhti recalled the distorted faces of the rioting humans. They had the look of people goaded beyond endurance. In such madness they might indeed attack those who meant them well—even Ushabti.

The Setim commander had noticed that Lady Hathor had been curiously silent as to the cause of this rebellion. One thing was sure. There was much more to the situation on Earth than the "trusted crew" was being told.

Nekhti promised himself to redress that state of ignorance, in any way he could . . .

"Please sit down, Dr. Moench," Daniel Jackson invited, though without any great enthusiasm. The beautifully dressed professor arranged himself on the guest seat with brisk, precise gestures. He seemed like a combination of Hercule Poirot and Santa Claus, a small, egg-shaped head and body distinguished by piercing blue eyes, pink cheeks, and a full white beard.

Daniel Jackson had encountered the name of Julius Moench before. The professor was one of a long line of "Masters of the Obscure"—i.e., crank scientists—to whom Daniel had been compared when he first outlined his theory of a predecessor culture on the Nile.

Actually, Moench had at least a tinge of academic respectability. He'd started out as a philologist, and then involved himself as an early champion of the theory that humankind had originally spoken one language. A number of language specialists now examined the matter, but Moench's popular work on the subject, *Before Babel*, had captured public interest because of its more extravagant speculations. Moench had then turned his pen to alien abductions, UFOs in history, mysterious disappearances of people, airplanes, and ships, several improbable interpretations of archaeological finds, and a number of volumes of "Unexplainables"—reports of occurrences which defied scientific solutions. In this way Moench had inherited the mantle of the late, great Charles Fort, who for decades had propounded such mysteries.

In fact, the more cynical pointed out that very often, Moench actually recycled Forte's discoveries in his own volumes.

Daniel was not a fan of "Unexplainables," nor had he read any of Moench's fractured archaeology—although he'd been somewhat incensed to discover that one of his papers had been quoted in several of the good doctor's works.

"It's good of you to see me," Moench said, his

eyes twinkling. "I know you must be annoyed at the way I seem to have misused your research in my little manuscripts."

"Widely published manuscripts, especially in Europe," Daniel replied.

The eyes twinkled more brightly. "But I should be jealous of *you*, Dr. Jackson. You're that rarest of all seekers after truth—the crackpot who's proven correct. I predict—or is that warn?—that your name will feature largely in occult literature of the future. You'll be another Galileo or Semmelweis, reviled by the so-called experts of their day, but proven correct. And not only were your theories shown to be right, but you were still alive and sane to enjoy the fame. Quite commendable."

"Thanks for your good wishes, Dr. Moench. But if we could move along . . . ?"

"I'm a professional crackpot," Moench said with engaging candor. "I know fifteen languages, but was barely managing to get along with translating jobs before I wrote *Before Babel*. I still get royalty checks from that. The publicity was good, and I was able to set myself up as a gadfly on the rump of know-it-all science. My specialty had always been asking questions rather than producing answers. But the questions *your* success has raised . . ."

Moench shook his bald head. "If the Ancient Astronauts theory was, at least in some points, correct, what other truths may have been swept under the academic rug?"

"I appreciate your interest, Doctor, but I've already

got a competent Egyptologist looking for clues to the predecessor culture."

Laughing, Moench raised a hand. "Oh, I have no aspirations to legitimacy. Serious academics lock the doors when they see me coming. No, I was going to suggest something a bit more my speed. Consider me the crackpots' consul-general. You're sure to be swamped with all sorts of cranks by now. Why not use someone who speaks their language?'

The little man's eyes twinkled again. "Besides, you never know what we may come up with. There's a mountain of fascinating rough data lurking in the notebooks of Charles Fort."

CHAPTER 8
BEHIND THE SCENES

Walking along the Mall in Washington—that axis of greenery stretching from the Washington Monument to Capitol Hill—Colonel Travis could see thirteen major buildings. Nine of them, all important museums, worked under the aegis of the Smithsonian Institution.

"Just shows you what a rich bastard can do with his money," the colonel muttered to himself.

Travis wasn't being pejorative. James Smithson was an illegitimate son, the child of a man who later became a duke. In fact, Smithson was nearly fifty before he went to court to use his father's last name. But he had become wealthy, and at his death, he left his fortune to the United States, a country he'd never visited, to establish an institution to advance human knowledge.

Travis had heard that Smithson's tomb could be found in the red-brick castle he now approached. This was the original home of the Smithsonian Institution, a combination exhibit gallery and lecture hall. But the Smithsonian collection now spilled out all over Washington and even to other cities. "The Castle" was now home to a tourist center . . . and the administrative offices of the institution.

Here, at last, Travis hoped for an end to his quest.

The curator had an office furnished with antiques—appropriate perhaps for the man in charge of a collection nicknamed "the nation's attic."

His greeting was gracious, but with a definite undercurrent of perplexity. "Our collection is always open for research, but I'm not sure I understand your request, Colonel Travis."

"It's the same I made to the Air and Space Museum," Travis said. "We wish to reactivate Orbital Vehicle 101—the *Enterprise*."

The curator blinked, as if he were hearing a foreign language. "I've heard some popular reports about using the space shuttles for defense purposes—but surely there are sufficient mock-ups available for training."

"The *Enterprise* will be entering active service," Travis said.

The curator's blinking increased, as if he were sending a distress signal in Morse code. What next? his unhappy expression seemed to suggest. Would the government demand *The Spirit of St. Louis* for airmail duty?

"But—at least as I understand it—the *Enterprise* was only a test vehicle, dropped from an airliner to evaluate the craft's gliding abilities. As such, a number of vital systems are, ah, not on board."

"All the better," Travis said. "We'll be refitting the propulsion system. The less that's there, the less we'll have to tear out."

A natural conservator, the curator flinched at the engineer's blithe description.

"I sincerely hoped that this could be arranged at your level," Travis said. "If we have to go to the institution's chancellor and board of regents, we will. I don't know how the chief justice will appreciate being asked to rule on this. But I do know the vice-president is on our side."

"As a matter of national defense ... if you really need it ..."

Travis tried to soften the blow. "As our test vehicle, *Enterprise* will set all sorts of new standards. She'll embody even more history when the time comes to turn her back to you."

If she survives the antigravity tests and the battle to come, he thought.

"I'm sure the piece we seek is down here." The curator of the small Munich museum was a stork-like individual, almost a caricature—all legs and nose. Gary Meyers had to keep reminding himself that caricatures don't rise to curatorial positions—even in small museums. Herr Doktor Schmitt was an expert in his chosen aspects of Egyptology—and he also had a photographic memory.

Meyers remembered an international conference where Schmitt had demonstrated his ability, writing down a hieroglyphic inscription sign after a brief look at a photograph. Gary held that memory tightly as they navigated dusty stairs to an even dustier sub-sub-basement.

"It was many years ago," Schmitt said in his heavily

accented English. "These storerooms have seen no real use since the days of the Allied air raids. Only the most dubious or least useful items are kept down here . . ."

They arrived at the storeroom in question. A flick of a switch activated an extremely anemic ceiling bulb, which gave off just enough radiance to put most of the objects in shadow.

Still, as Meyers looked around, he could concede the aptness of Schmitt's description. There were swarms of scarab beetles, apparently picked up at generations of Cairo markets. Copies all, though Meyers saw the raw material for an interesting exhibit on post-dynastic fakery.

Schmitt quested about as if his large proboscis were sniffing out the exhibit he sought. "Even so, we conducted an inventory."

Meyers gave thanks for Teutonic thoroughness.

"There was one doubtful find, a stele, which carried some of the glyphs you showed me."

Gary Meyers had only been passing through in his continuing quest for Daniel Jackson. He'd visited Schmitt only as a courtesy, not expecting anything from the museum's small collection. But the curator's eyes had lit as Meyers displayed his photos of the predecessor culture's technological symbols. Gary had been spreading them around to academics and those in charge of large Egyptian collections, but Schmitt's instantaneous response had sent them down on this glorified junk depository.

"Ach! Here!" Schmitt cried, pointing to a jumbled

pile of stone fragments. He fumbled in his jacket pocket and produced a small flashlight.

In the improved illumination, Gary made out the inscribed hieroglyphics. They seemed to be an invocation to Sutekh, another name for Set. Then came an unlikely reference, to the god's center of power to the east, where his strength was measured—then came one of the elusive technological symbols that Gary had dismissed as "godpowers"—and then the symbol Ra's empire used for energy weapons!

Schmitt reclaimed the flashlight to read a notecard attached to the wall. "According to this, the find was made by an expedition that went to the eastern delta of the Nile back in the Thirties," he said. "The location seemed to be the ruins of a temple, but they were unable to place the dynasty. And, after discovering the dubious glyphs in the inscription, there was some suspicion of fraud."

"I'd be very interested in seeing whatever records remain from that expedition," Meyers said.

Dead files were one basement up. Meyers found not only photos of the shattered stele, but also descriptions and a sketch map of the site.

"You think this would interest your friend Dr. Jackson?" Schmitt asked.

"The delta was one of the strongest areas of Set-worship," Meyers replied. "And, because it's low-lying, often flooded, and still the seat of Egypt's agricultural production, proportionally less has been found there in terms of archaeological sites."

He looked through the photos until he found the odd inscription, seeming to point to some actual seat of Set's power. Traditionally, Set was seen as the god of the East, the god of the desert.

But after Daniel's experience on the *Boat of a Million Years*, it seemed that those traditions might have a basis in fact.

Gary scanned other photos, trying to pick up the broken inscription. Yes, Daniel would be *very* interested in this, he thought.

A very harassed-looking premier faced the American ambassador. "You wish to consult on the Outer Space Treaty? Perhaps the time for that should have been months ago, before you decided to violate it."

"There's been no violation," the diplomat protested. "Only contingency planning. But those plans must be implemented quickly, if we're to defend ourselves."

"Defend ourselves against what? Something from a science-fiction film?"

"My government has shared all the footage we've shot of this inimical empire in action," the ambassador said. "We've also invited any and all experts to examine the people and animals that came from the planet Abydos. They are real—as is the menace facing this world."

"It's easy enough for your president to speak of menaces and countermeasures. He has only one party to deal with. And for some reason, it seems your voters always approve of vast military expenditures— even when they serve no purpose. Our political system has *dozens* of parties, and the measures you suggest attack the core beliefs of half of them."

The politician extended a hand, cutting off the

ambassador as he was opening his mouth. "For myself, I do not think of your president as a mad power-monger. But he will not be president forever. Can he speak for the will—or ideology of future governments? For such power to be in the hands of one—perhaps two nations, it is too concentrated."

"And if it's spread, it may turn out to be too ineffective," the ambassador finally spoke.

"So we must support you in this crisis. But for how long? With what limits? Giving you such power is too much like releasing the genie—and then smashing the lamp."

Hot desert air wafted through the window. But the mullah was a strict traditionalist. None of the lesser Satans—like air-conditioning—for him.

The official, however, took a more agnostic view of creature comforts. Sweat stained his uniform as he stood before the ascetic holy man.

"So it is not enough for the Great Satan to count his bombs and send forth his aircraft as he likes to chastise the righteous," the mullah proclaimed. "Now he must bind the world in a web of destruction, polluting the heavens and threatening the just?"

"Yet, revered one," the official replied, "the recording of this strange world—and of the attacking strangers—have been found to be genuine."

"There is no truth except for what is to be found in the sacred writings," the old man rapped. "Still, if this doorway to other worlds exists, it means there are other peoples to whom we must bring the Word."

"And what of this invasion against which we are warned, holy one?"

"If invaders come to bring down the Great Satan, it is a good thing. When the unbelievers contend among themselves, our cause prospers."

"But, holy one, the invaders may also threaten us— and the holy places."

"If the infidels do such, then . . . jihad!" The mullah made an abrupt gesture.

"Yet the invaders have weapons that can level entire cities!" the official cried. "We have seen the films of them at work. There would be no way to defend the holy cities against this blasphemy."

"We must learn more of this doorway between worlds," the mullah declared. "Search among those strong in the faith for ones with the necessary knowledge. It would be a great thing to bring the Word to new worlds."

The old man brooded for a moment. "For the rest . . . even the Prophet went upon a Hegira."

Daniel Jackson had become quite used to the talk-show circuit in the past few months. He'd come to accept the broiling lights, the touch of makeup so he wouldn't look like a zombie, the ill-prepared hosts with the handful of inadequate note cards.

But he never got used to the so-called "public affairs programs" that better resembled shark tanks. Toss in the visitor and see who chews his leg off.

Daniel had gotten a lot more requests for guest appearances since the Military Study Group's recommendations had become public. Daniel hadn't done that. It had been the work of Kerrigan and a group of senators—surprisingly in favor of the proposals. Some seemed to be of the *Amerika Uber Alles* type. But many, like Kerrigan himself, were veterans who knew what a war could do to a country—or a planet—on the receiving end.

Oddly enough, Daniel now found himself taking flak from people on the end of the political spectrum where he'd more or less given allegiance during his days as a revolting student. He'd be the first to agree with Pamela Throckmorton's environmentalist concerns—except that she was trying to freeze all work on what had become known as the Space Shield.

"With the Outer Space Treaty of 1967, we managed to keep the heavens, if not demilitarized, at least free of weapons of mass destruction," Ms. Throckmorton gazed appealingly at the camera. "Now you want to cram them into orbit."

Daniel rolled his eyes. "I'd hardly consider 144 weapons platforms cramming. Not when each platform is responsible for defending about a million and a half miles of the Earth's surface. For myself, I wish we could get more up there. But this is the best we can do in the amount of time we have remaining. And the time is always running shorter."

Throckmorton shot him a dagger glance. "I can't see how you can talk about our government doing its 'best' when we're breaking a commitment that we've held for thirty years."

"We're not breaking a commitment, as some people choose to say," Daniel responded. "We're discussing the response to a situation that was never considered at the time the treaty was drawn up. That's why Section IX was included in the first place. If one of the signatories thinks things have to change, they're supposed to consult with the other signatories."

"It's still a unilateral decision—with unknown consequences. Part of the treaty is an agreement not to change the environment of space—or the planet beneath. Suppose this killer spaceship you're always talking about *does* come—and we shoot it down. If it's the size you say it is, the resulting impact would leave something like Meteor Crater—a three-mile-wide hole in the ground. If that happened in a major city, millions would die."

"This begins to sound very much like the Chicken Little theory of environmental impact," Daniel riposted. "We'd better not defend ourselves, or the sky will fall."

"Very clever, Dr. Jackson, but there is one case where a nuclear-powered satellite—thankfully without warheads, like the ones you want to send up—*did* fall. It was the Soviet Kosmos 954, which reentered the atmosphere in 1978, blew up, and scattered radioactive debris across almost 48,000 square miles."

"Of generally barren tundra in Canada's Northwest Territory," Daniel finished. He'd done his homework.

"What if it happens again, but this time on irreplaceable rain forest—or perhaps on a city?"

"Let's stay in 1978 for a moment, to see what happened," Daniel said. "Negotiations took place between the USSR and Canada, handled under an international convention. The Canadians were paid a good six million dollars for cleanup expenses."

Ms. Throckmorton stuck to her point. "Rather a cold comfort if New York were dusted by something worse than Chernobyl. Even less than that if the city were ground zero for a falling nuclear bomb."

"If wars could only be waged after environmental-impact studies, we wouldn't have the mess that the First World War made of northern France—or what the Luftwaffe did across Europe in the next war. We wouldn't have had the Dresden firebombing, or Agent Orange in Vietnam, or whatever is causing Gulf War Syndrome. We wouldn't have had Hiroshima or Nagasaki."

Daniel looked at the environmentalist with pain in his eyes. "Those were all awful things, but they took place in struggles to stop worse things. The Nazi death camps—the horrors in Cambodia—as terrible as they were, they were at least directed by human beings. The people coming here to conquer us consider themselves as gods. For all your distrust of government, at least we have systems that often work. Talk to the survivors of Abydos about the ruling elite who oppressed them.

"I know it sounds like typical military hyperbole, but this really *is* an evil empire, with a tiny collection of quasi-gods living off a vast preponderance of slaves. Do you think you'll get any environmental impact statements from them?"

Daniel leaned forward before Throckmorton could reply. "Let's take a look at what we know of Hathor's environmental record. She's accused of planetary genocide. On Earth, her ruler made the slave class transport two and a half million blocks of stone, sized between two to fifteen tons, *by hand*. That's enough rock to put a ten-foot wall around the boundaries of France. And what was the purpose? To provide a parking spot for Ra's spaceship!"

"You refer to the Great Pyramid—" Throckmorton began.

"I refer to its original use," Daniel shot back. "There was a similar pyramid on Abydos, also built by hand at the cost of God knows how many human lives. It was a perfect fit for Ra's flying palace—and for the warship that Hathor later turned up in."

Again, he didn't allow the environmentalist a chance to interrupt. "While we're at it, I'd like you to read a report by a mining engineer who examined the diggings at Nagada. Apparently, the ore was reached by having heavy-duty energy weapons blast big holes in the ground. Hundreds of feet deep, miles long. This was done all over the planet. Do you think that benefited the environment?"

"I can't—" Throckmorton began.

Again, Daniel cut her off. "I have one other piece of evidence."

He pulled a small, lumpy object from the pocket of his rumpled sports coat. Placing it on the moderator's table, he asked, "Can you zoom in on that?"

The studio monitors showed the image of a twisted shard of shimmering, almost translucent gold—the famous energy crystal of Nagada. But smeared over it, like the stone droppings of an obscene troll, were lumps of black rock.

"This is probably the last thing that came through the StarGate from Abydos," Daniel said. "The shiny part there is the gold quartz that was mined on the planet—the basis of Ra's technology. We can't tell what this was a piece of—it went through some pretty awful stress before being blown through the StarGate."

He tapped the shard, staring into the cameras. "But we know what the black stuff is. It's basalt—lava. The chamber of the Abydos StarGate was apparently undergoing a very sudden and severe bout of volcanism an instant or two after the last escapees arrived. I think there's only one thing that can explain that. The gigantic vessel under Hathor's command had already attempted to seize control of the StarGate. Failing that, I believe she fired on the StarGate—with weapons powerful enough to reach the magma level of the planet."

Daniel flipped the black-and-gold shard in the air, caught it, and returned it to his pocket against a background of dead silence.

"How'd you like *that* to happen in the middle of a major city?" he asked. Then he turned to Pamela Throckmorton. "Or perhaps you'd agree with me that such an enemy should be fought as far from our planet as possible."

CHAPTER 9
HARD WORDS

Larry Ingalls swore under his breath, his clumsy gauntlets losing their grip once again on the construction tool he was using. "Of all the goddamn stupid ideas," he growled. "They've got us constructing the space-going version of the Eiffel Tower."

The truss-work construction grew slowly under his fumbling hands. One gauntlet gripped a cross-strut, helping to brace his feet against the deck. His other hand pushed the tool into the connector and, as usual, missed. Larry shifted his gripping hand, and began to float away.

He grabbed for the strut, the damned gauntlet bouncing off. With his feet floating, he managed to clamp onto the strut again, pulled himself around, regained his stance, and tried to re-aim the tool.

The whole astronaut corps was being pushed in space-construction techniques, what with the proposed stepping-up of the space-station schedule. The truss work would serve as the backbone of *Freedom*, with solar panels, a crew module, weapons components, and a nuclear reactor.

If they couldn't get this goddamn thing put together, however, the rest of the station would be useless.

Larry jammed the tool in, twisted . . . and began to lose his grip again. His comments on tools, gauntlets, and space suits in general began to grow sulfurous.

"Larry," a voice echoed in his ears, "we'd prefer not to be recording this."

"Sorry," Ingalls replied. "I don't think this suit really fits me. Guess I'm thirty years out of place. For the Apollo project, they custom-built every suit for each guy. These off-the-rack things, I don't think 'one size fits all' really goes for smaller guys."

Larry was on the short side, which was one reason he was being pushed into construction. One team was based at space station *Mir*, which had height limitations on its crew.

"Just don't break the damned thing," his project leader responded. "It cost us about ten and a half million dollars."

Larry tried again with the stupid tool, which rewarded his tenacity by flying out of his hand and floating away.

"At least you didn't unscrew your faceplate," the project leader mocked. "I think you might as well give it up."

Sighing, Larry released his grip as his spotter came up.

That was the costume he wished he could wear. The spotter had a pair of swim trunks, a mask, and a scuba regulator.

Gently, they began swimming to the top of WET-F, the Weightless Environment Training Facility in the

Johnson Space Center. The surface was a good twenty feet above them.

Larry could hardly wait to get out of the weights that left him perfectly buoyant in the water, simulating the microgravity of Low Earth Orbit.

He could also barely wait to get out of the stupid suit.

"I hope the station isn't going to depend on *your* construction skills." The voice on the other end of the earphones laughed.

Larry sighed. "Maybe I can drive the shuttle."

Barbara Shore looked from the model of the space shuttle to the control panel, where Mitch Storey was putting in the last-second adjustments. This was a copy of the Digital Autopilot Panel from the actual shuttle, with the addition of a joystick, and would be operated by a trained shuttle pilot.

"I hope you can do this," she told the astronaut who stood by the panel. "We're running out of models."

"Maybe this time we've got the impellers located and calibrated correctly," Storey said hopefully.

Having successfully gotten the antigravity drive to work, Barbara and her team had been concentrating on how to control the damned thing. The salvaged udajeets had been fitted with impellers at various points to provide thrust, impart a braking impulse, boost lift, and to control pitch, yaw, and roll—or to induce these characteristics for some impressive aerobatics.

Using a drastically scaled-down version of the drive, they had managed to get a model of the shuttle to float. Then came the job of determining impeller placements to steer. It had been a frustrating mix of theoretical aerodynamics and trial and error. How do you make a fairly lumbering aircraft, nicknamed "the flying refrigerator," float lightly as windblown thistledown?

The first answer had been to place impellers at the usual control surfaces, to see if the model would fly like an airplane. Mitch Storey was a competent small-aircraft pilot. He'd given it a try—and crashed miserably.

Then they'd decided to treat the shuttle model as a spacecraft, placing impellers in place of the craft's RCS—Reaction Control System. That had resulted in several wobbly flights—and hard landings.

This time, they'd decided to try and wire the system exactly to the shuttle's controls. How would it turn out?

"Field on," Storey said.

The model wobbled into the air.

"Going manual." The astronaut flipped a switch on the control panel. "I'll try some mild acceleration while trying to bank it around." Working with the autopilot computer, he entered data and jockeyed the stick. The model stopped wobbling. It accelerated forward, upward, then went into a shallow turn.

Squinting from the panel to the model in flight, the astronaut tapped in new parameters and the model banked again. With some more work, he coaxed the model into an "orbit" of the huge hangar bay. "This isn't quite what these controls are supposed to do," he said. "The autopilot isn't programmed to play ring-around-the-rosy. And this isn't the control system we use for landing."

The astronaut went back to the controls, entering new instructions. The model slowed, its nose rising. "That would be the setup for the descent glide. Where do I cut the power?"

Storey did the honors. The model fluttered a bit in midair as gravity and momentum brought it down. It hit the concrete floor with a clatter of plastic, skittered along, and came to a stop. But it hadn't smashed.

The astronaut, however, winced. "Hard landing. And no landing gear."

"We'd never gotten that far before," Barbara admitted. "Thanks to your piloting, we know that controlling the shuttle this way looks practical. We can try to refine the calibration and control with computer simulations."

"I'll tell you one problem right off," the astronaut said. "You've got a rough approximation of the shuttle. With a little cleaning up, that should be good enough to get whatever you want into orbit."

"Right." Barbara grinned. "After I figure out how to adapt the system to lift ten tons of actual shuttle, plus crew and cargo."

The astronaut shrugged. "You got this far. I worry about what comes after that. You've got a transport there, sure. Orbit-capable. But it's a long way from a fighter craft."

East of the Florida testing ground, on the submerged Bermuda Rise, augmented sensor nets again detected the unmistakable pulses of antigravity impellers—faint, but definitely engaged in maneuvers.

Reports had been logged regarding other such readings, which had quickly died out. These were more sustained. Ancient programming went into effect. Processing units that were only awakened at decade-long intervals winked into full alert status.

Instead of the passive net, active sensors were brought on-line. They detected heavy traffic both on and above the ocean in the ancient emplacement's area of cognizance. New demands were made on hidden core taps as energy flowed to more processing units. Weapons systems were activated.

As the mothballed processing units reached ever higher levels of awareness, they began correlating isolated data from earlier testing runs.

Gaps became apparent in the record. Auto-diagnostics were carried out, detecting failure in several memory-storage areas. Redundant systems were brought on-line as the emplacement's command centrum began a more painstaking review of equipment status. Molecular circuits hummed in the mechanical counterpart of dismay at the deterioration that had set in during the long downtime—and at the *length* of time the systems had been maintained at lowest alertness.

Retrieval programs were launched to retrieve the damaged data. New patterns emerged in the mass of information recorded during the deteriorated equipment's more frequent self-tests.

Surface and air traffic had been steadily increasing in the emplacement's area of cognizance throughout the last century. Several times, passing vessels and aircraft had been incorrectly identified as target drones—and destroyed.

Security subroutines kicked in, examining the risk that the emplacement's secrecy had been compromised. Given the infrequent nature of the discharges and the continuing traffic, the probability was classified as unlikely.

Nonetheless, the data had to be forwarded to Central Control, thousands of miles to the east . . .

The central workings of the ancient system had slumbered deeper and longer than the unit on the Bermuda Rise. Alertness had been stimulated only by earthquakes that had threatened remote units . . . and the occasional outbursts of thermonuclear force which had occurred in the past half century, starting with the two so close to its remote station off the eastern coast of the Greater Landmass.

With the input of the new data from the Lesser Landmass station, Central Control began to read all the records from the remote stations. Some, like the Northern Greater Ocean, recorded almost no contact with artificial constructs. Others, like the ones placed off the western coast of the Greater Landmass, at the mouth of the inner sea, displayed data on occasional tracking and destruction of passing vessels.

Growing traffic all over the globe had not been considered in the original programming. Volitional units came on-line, triggering new activities.

New sensor capabilities were awakened, tracking the traffic around the world—and beyond.

The data was immense. Thousands of vessels above and below the oceans, myriads of aircraft, hundreds of devices in orbit. . . . Enhancing the sensitivity of its passive receptors, Central Control began to track the traffic.

So many artifacts—and not one transmitting the accepted recognition signal . . .

General West appeared in Jack O'Neil's office, a glint of triumph in his eyes. "Good news!" he announced. "The president has finally made up his mind to go ahead with Space Shield."

"His polls finally came in?" O'Neil inquired.

"He can't afford to be seen weak on defense," West's enthusiasm faded. "And he can't afford to be wrong. Faced with credible proof of a threatened interstellar invasion, he *had* to do something."

O'Neil nodded. "What about Congress?"

"We've got strong bipartisan support. Kerrigan has done some strong preaching on the issue. And there's been considerable activity from what Foyle calls 'our natural constituency.' "

"The big defense firms?" O'Neil didn't like the sound of that.

"It's an arena they're used to playing in." West's voice took on an acid tone. "I suppose we'll have to look out for amendments and riders tacked onto any Space Shield appropriations."

O'Neil sighed. "In addition to anybody whose sacred cow gets gored by these budget-busting proposals."

Sitting on the set of yet another public affairs forum, Daniel Jackson did his best to contain his anger as the Honorable Marcus Chaffee turned accusing eyes on him. Representative Chaffee was the congressman for a poor urban district. He was now a loud voice against the appropriations for Operation Space Shield.

"You talk about putting this country on a war footing. But there's been a war going on against America's cities for more than twenty years! Mr. Reagan and Mr. Bush never lost an opportunity to chastise poor Americans for being poor. Their congressional successors have turned the word 'welfare' into a political obscenity. We had hopes of improvement from the present administration—until you started beating the drums for this pointless exercise in outer space—"

"I don't think that defending all the humans on Earth—including the ones who live in cities—is a pointless exercise," Daniel replied. "Your attitude oddly reminds me of a speech by another great New Yorker, Ed Koch."

Chaffee's face went from accusation, to blank amazement—then to fury.

"Oh, I know," Daniel went on, "Mr. Koch became regarded as the enemy in your community, especially during his later service as mayor of New York. But in his days as a congressman, he once spoke against the Apollo project. I can't swear this is an exact quote, but he said, 'I can't see spending money to put a man on the Moon as long as there are still rats in Harlem apartments.' "

Daniel shrugged. "Well, we did go to the Moon, although there are still rats to be found in every big city. We thought there was value even in a symbolic victory in the space race. The struggle we face now has already killed more American troops than Saddam Hussein ever managed, not to mention the loss of countless civilian lives on Abydos itself against a predatory empire. We represent a very desirable playing piece in a deadly political game. If we don't defend ourselves, millions will be shanghaied as cannon fodder, while our techno-logical base is raped to produce weapons. We won't have to worry about rats in Harlem, because they'll be everywhere—and we'll all be slaves."

Now Daniel looked accusingly at the congressman. "It's one year's spending, Mr. Chaffee. Temporary pain for a lot of people—against servitude for *everyone*."

Foster Harleigh was the second secretary in the Moscow embassy of the United States. A career diplo-mat, he'd handled numerous negotiations on the gov-ernmental level—if the fact were to be acknowledged, he much preferred working with the *apparatchiks*— fellow travelers in the bureaucratic life stream—than with the new entrepreneurs who had arisen in the former Soviet republics.

But the man Harleigh was waiting to see was defi-nitely an entrepreneur—as well as being a member of the Russian parliament and a former cosmonaut.

Pavel Chartorynsky was a short, stocky man who had, in his space-going career, spent six months on the *Mir* space station. Harleigh had heard how, to fix damage to one of *Mir*'s components, Chartorynsky had ventured where no human had been for years— onto a part of the space station not equipped with handholds or tethers. The last people to touch that area had been the construction crew back on Earth. Any excessive motion could have sent Chartorynsky off onto his own orbit, to die miserably when his air supply gave out.

No, Chartorynsky was not a man to be easily frightened, as his new business venture showed—the venture that Harleigh had been sent to buy.

"Mr. Chartorynsky," Harleigh said as soon as the ex-cosmonaut had him seated in his office, "my government has been negotiating with yours for the use of the two *Buran* shuttles available. But governments move slowly. Our technical people need a shuttle airframe to test. We know that six test frames had been made, but several have been scrapped, and the only one we know of is yours—Vessel 011."

"You want my *Buran*?" Chartorynsky said. "That is the heart of my enterprise."

"I know," Harleigh said. "I've even ridden on it."

The space shuttle test frame had been moved to the banks of the Moscow River, in Gorky Park. There it served as a flight simulator, a ride in the midst of an exhibition on the Russian space program. For the equivalent of thirty-five dollars, Harleigh had enjoyed a forty-minute virtual flight, a multimedia extravaganza complete with launch, various orbital emergencies, and space food distributed by stewardesses in flight suits.

"It's a pleasant simulation," Harleigh said, "but now there is a real need for the space frame, to assist in our planet's defense."

"That was why *Buran* was developed in the first place," Chartorynsky interrupted. "The Soyuz capsules were a mature technology, more than sufficient to move crew into space. But your space shuttle frightened our military. They feared that the shuttles could be used to drop bombs from orbit. Determined to contest the high ground, they ordered us to develop our own orbiter, even while we were deriding the American efforts as useless and wasteful."

"The results will be useful now," Harleigh suggested.

"The results were to create a launching system and an orbiter that have flown exactly once," Chartorynsky replied. "In the meantime diverting funds from other, more useful projects."

The look he directed at the State Department man was little short of a glare. "Do you know how much those two mothballed shuttles cost us? At least ten billion of your dollars. That is the amount you now budget for building this new space station. Directed to other projects, it could have taken us to Mars."

"Lost opportunities, to be sure," Harleigh admitted. "But conditions have changed. The shuttles will serve a legitimate defense purpose, protecting us from invaders. Surely, you can see the responsibility—"

"I have a responsibility to my investors," Chartorynsky pointed out. "In addition to the billions the government lost, people have put a good three million dollars into the space exhibit. Surely, I must make good on the money they have put into this project."

"You can't seriously expect my government to pay you three million dollars!" Harleigh gasped.

"It is a mere—how do you call it?—'drop in the basket—' "

"That's 'bucket,' " Harleigh corrected.

"It is a small amount, compared to the billions you

will be spending in the rest of your buildup." Sitting behind his desk, Chartorynsky steepled his fingers together. "Your people have picked over our aerospace industry, taking whatever you wanted. Did you know that even Premier Khrushchev's telegram congratulating Yuri Gagarin as the first man in space was even auctioned off—as a collectible?"

The ex-cosmonaut favored Harleigh with a smile that held no geniality at all. "You wanted us to be good capitalists. It seems only fair that you should pay appropriately for something you really want."

Foster Harleigh sighed. Was it any wonder that he hated these new entrepreneurs? Settling himself in his seat, he prepared for a long, hard—and expensive—negotiation.

CHAPTER 10
RISKS AND LOSSES

Oleg Kuzma, one of two cosmonaut caretakers aboard the space station *Mir*, floated into the main module, where his crewmate, Nikolai Galitsky, had anchored himself by the table.

"Gone," he reported, helping himself to a tube of borscht.

Kuzma nodded toward the instrument consoles at the far end of the module. "I watched," he said, helping himself to a portion of rehydratable scrambled eggs. "It's almost frightening, how smoothly the shuttles travel with that new drive. Now we have ten hours to ourselves while the Americans work on their station."

Galitsky shrugged, propelling himself over. "I thought I would get used to them, after two months."

"One thing, having eight Americans aboard," Kuzma said, "when they go off to work, we seem to have so much room."

"But more smells." Galitsky wrinkled his nose. "They work like pigs, and can hardly bathe."

"They do their best," his roommate said. "Even with

the upgraded supply schedule, we can't bring enough water for showers."

"They strain the very fabric of the station," Galitsky complained. "We had to give up most of our experimental facilities to give them living space—"

"The Europeans screamed louder when the Americans gutted the space lab modules," Kuzma said.

"But the Europeans don't have to *live* with them," Galitsky replied. "Always underfoot. Tall, short—"

"They don't need to fit our criteria, Kolya," Kuzma replied, releasing himself from the table. "When all we had were the Soyuz capsules for an emergency escape route, we all had to fit the acceleration couches." He raised his knees until he floated in almost a fetal position, then reached down to catch the table and pulled himself to a standing position on the deck. "Now we don't need to travel in such tight quarters. Otherwise less than half the American astronauts could have worked here."

"Too bad," Galitsky grumbled. "Then we would not be bursting at the seams." He took a brief sip-squeeze from his borscht tube. "Pah! Tastes like nothing."

"*Everything* tastes like nothing up here," Kuzma reminded him. "The scientists can't tell us why. I think it's the thinner air." He gestured to the tray on the table. "You could try one of the American meals. I never thought I would miss chicken and stewed prunes."

"That reminds me. Another of the American shuttles will be bringing supplies today. More of their imitation food."

"And daily newspapers, and oranges," Kuzma said. "They do bring what we ask for."

"I'll be happier when they finish the flight tests for *Buran*," Galitsky continued to grouse, then smiled. "At least that would let us get imitation food from home."

"Our work here could be the truest accomplishment of our space program—if we succeed," Kuzma said. "Saving the world from an invasion—"

"Yes, yes," Galitsky replied impatiently. "It would be an entire justification for our existence—just as the Great Patriotic War was for the Party." He took another sip of borscht and made a sour face. "But Stalin was officially 'forgotten' twenty years later, and twenty years after that, the Party collapsed."

"Surely, we can offer more than a group of drunken *apparatchiks*." Kuzma gave him a sharp look. "You don't want the Party back, do you?"

"Ah, Oleg Denisovitch"—Galitzky gave him a fine, Russian smile—"there is a question wise people could never find an answer for."

The smile faded, however, to a look of worry. "Freedom has meant many wonderful things. But it also means leaders who must always worry about pleasing the people who may vote for them. In the emergency of the Great Patriotic War, our government was often quite cold-blooded—condemning people to starve, or die. But they won that war, in part, perhaps, *because* they didn't have to worry about popularity."

Galitzky turned to take in the newly added control consoles for the weaponry units being added to the space station. "We barely got an agreement for those weapons over there."

He then glanced out the porthole in the wall, nodding to the blackness beyond. "And if something should happen to one of the Americans out there, how would the people on the ground take it?"

Larry Ingalls tried to forget that he was moving at probably a bit more than five miles per second, on what normally would be considered an extremely precarious perch. He was positioned at the tip of the space shuttle's remote manipulator, in what the astronauts called "the cherry picker." A pair of foot straps held him in place as the crane-like arm swung to place him over a new workplace on the rapidly growing space station *Freedom*.

Ingalls had slipped into the queerly bunny-like rest position that human bodies assume in zero gravity. His arms were half-cocked at his sides, and his legs seemed to have stopped at the beginning of a deep knee bend. It would have been a damned uncomfortable posture on Earth. Larry's thighs had hurt just watching people maintain that stance on training videotapes.

But after two months up here, it seemed not only natural, but restful.

The space-medicine wonks had their explanation for it—apparently in zero-g the flexors, the bending muscles, worked to bring the extremities closer to the body's center of mass. But the extensors, the muscles that helped one stand erect, actually deteriorated. He'd have to log more time on one of *Mir*'s exercise bikes before he returned to full gravity next month.

Home . . . it had seemed like an agonizingly distant

vista during his first painful days aboard *Mir*. The hard-diving stunt plane that simulated free-fall conditions had been nicknamed the "Vomit Comet," which should have been a warning about entering a zero-gravity environment. At least the powers that be had the sense to dispatch an experienced crew of forerunners up to the station and then dispatch the newbies at three-day intervals. Space sickness was usually worst in the first couple of days in orbit. In the crowded quarters, it was best to have only *one* new crew person puking his or her guts up.

That was well past for Ingalls now. He could look forward to returning home, exercising to replace lost muscle mass, lecturing the next generation of zero-g construction workers, and then joining the "day shift," the building crew that lifted up from the surface every day.

At least, Larry had to admit, the reality of space had proven pretty close to the simulations of his training. But water had a resistance that didn't exist in the vacuum of space.

Standing at the end of the manipulator boom, Ingalls had the weird feeling of "surfing" atop the shuttle—except for the lack of wind in his hair.

Well, he was a veteran now. He'd arrive at his destination, open the toolbox already bolted in place, and get to work . . .

The nut was a tiny thing, barely a quarter-inch square. It had been a fitting on the Hubble Space Telescope, removed during the *Endeavour* astronauts' recent repair job. Their space suits were called EMUs—Extravehicular Mobility Units, not Extremely Maneuverable.

Heavy gauntlets designed to protect against hundred-below temperatures make lousy catcher's mitts. The small piece of metal had flown free, and had spent months describing its own orbit, heading down to Earth, the atmosphere, and destruction.

It was only moving about four miles per second, a bare crawl on the celestial scale.

But it was moving almost head-on with the vector astronaut Larry Ingalls was following. It struck the faceplate of his suit with a force equal to the combination of their speeds—nearly eight miles per second, almost twice the speed of sound, or about the speed of a Hawk missile.

Of course, this unguided missile didn't have the Hawk's 100-pound warhead.

But the nut's kinetic energy was more than enough to shatter the faceplate and drill Larry Ingalls through the left eye.

The EMU is equipped with a secondary breathing apparatus in case of tears or holes in the suit. But the shattered faceplate meant that Ingalls was effectively unzipped. And the impact and shock waves traveling through his brain meant he was effectively dead.

The first warning that something had gone catastrophically wrong on the orbital construction site came when Larry Ingalls suddenly seemed to tear himself loose from his cherry picker perch and began to follow a slow, somersaulting course into deep space.

Christy Manville, the shuttle's payload specialist in charge of project safety, caught the empty footrests as she ran through the various surveillance cameras covering the workers. Quickly, she whipped around to the shuttle's commander, Neil Antonelli.

"Trouble," Manville announced. "Ingalls is off the cherry picker."

"Find him!" Antonelli replied, already preparing to relay the news to Dick Conway, who piloted the other shuttle orbiting the station. With the improved engines going into all the orbiters, two shuttles were always detailed to accompany the work crews in space.

Radio calls to Ingalls brought no response. But radar pulses found him. Following the vector, surveillance cameras zoomed in. Christy Manville sucked in a deep breath as she saw the jagged hole where the faceplate had been—and the frozen red crystals that had boiled out and now occasionally showed against the white chest of the suit.

"He—he can't have survived," she gulped. "Do we recover, or will *Atlantis*?"

"Neither." Antonelli's voice was tight as it came over the intercom. "Orders from the top. We're to let him go. They don't want people to see what happened. And you'll have to erase those tapes." He paused, as if the words he was saying left a bad taste in his mouth.

"As far as official records will show, he was buried in space."

Daniel Jackson interrupted his report to Jack O'Neil so they could both watch the noonday news. As the car ad came on—incredible values for three-year leases—O'Neil shook his head. "One of the stories you *won't* hear on the news is the sudden ballooning of credit. Lots of people have decided to go on an end-of-the-world shopping spree." He looked disgusted. "I remember the Cuban Missile Crisis. Everyone thought that was the end, so they went to church. This time, everyone's going to the mall."

Daniel looked sick. "I don't know why the hell we watch this stuff," he said tightly. "It's like picking at a scab. You know there's going to be pain and probably blood, but you keep on doing it."

"It would still be going on, even if it weren't being covered," O'Neil pointed out. "I'd rather know what the other side is up to."

"This isn't the other side," Daniel sighed. "That's Hathor and company. These people"—he pointed at a bunch of rioting Belgians on the screen—"are just poor, scared idiots . . ."

"Who would leave us completely unprotected if they had their way," O'Neil finished for him.

The next cheering news item was the rise in suicides.

"I wonder if it was the same in Nagada toward the end," Daniel said in an altered voice. "Maybe it was lucky that we didn't have the media to 'help' us."

O'Neil figured he'd better head off that line of thinking. But the mention of Nagada brought an image of various friends from Abydos. "I haven't seen Skaara lately," he said, "or—"

Daniel glanced over at the colonel's sudden silence. "Or Sha'uri?" His lips stretched in a rough approximation of a smile. "She's still working with Barbara Shore, translating the *Earthling's Guide to Ra's Technology*. We had a couple of meetings, trying to determine whether this stele Gary Meyers found was actually from the predecessor culture or priestly gobbledygook. Sha'uri was polite, but . . . well, I've seen warmer expressions on Mount Rushmore."

Now it was Daniel's turn to try changing the conversation. "Skaara is my strong right arm at the Abydos Foundation. He troubleshoots among the people we've settled, and he's the star of our little speaker's bureau. Not only does he propagandize for the cause, but he helps bring in some speech-making fees."

O'Neil nodded. But his next words showed that he hadn't been turned away. "You still have feelings for Sha'uri."

Daniel's face tightened. "Is that really any of your business?"

The colonel just shrugged. "The welfare of your subordinates is supposed to be part of the job. Although," he admitted, "I wasn't really good about listening to tales of woe and 'Dear John' letters or romantic entanglements with cantina girls. Hell, I wasn't all that great in my own life. After we lost our son, I shut Sarah out. She was scared to death that I would . . . do something stupid."

Daniel remembered the Jack O'Neil he'd first met, almost a caricature of the military man, clinging to duty to avoid suicide—so, of course, he was sent on what almost turned into a suicide mission. Oddly enough, his adventures on Abydos had brought O'Neil back to life . . . and back to his marriage.

"I'm glad you managed to get back together with Sarah," Daniel said, "but I don't think it will happen with Sha'uri. She blames me for betraying her, but her father—I nearly got him killed. And then there's Abydos . . ."

"You saved her," O'Neil pointed out.

"Yeah, I got her out," Daniel admitted. "After destroying her hometown, and probably killing her planet. With that between us, I don't see much hope for a happy reconciliation, do you?"

He turned his back on the television, which was showing yet a new series of riots someplace. "Maybe you shouldn't have saved me back in the mines. Maybe if I'd died heroically, it would have balanced— something."

"You think she's seeing someone else?"

For a second Daniel's eyes held the same spark that had burned in them during that last, forlorn hope battle on Abydos. "I don't know," he finally replied.

"But you can't say you don't care," O'Neill said. "For me, that was a reason to stay alive. It's better than trying to hide in your work."

"*If* we survive." Daniel's gaze went back to the screen, which showed Asian protesters this time. "If we can hold things together. We can't let it fall apart, the way it did on Abydos."

His eyes were haunted, conjuring up scenes from months ago and a million light-years away. "We can't let it happen again."

Mission Control at Cape Canaveral was busy— perhaps busier than it had ever been. But there was a subtle difference in the air. Instead of the linchpin of the nation's space efforts, the Cape had become the freight yard for Operation Space Shield.

Technician Richie Kaye grimaced as he went through the prelaunch checklist. Oh, sure, they were engaged in more launches, pushing a staggering amount of tonnage into orbit. But the manned missions were going up in the rejiggered space shuttles, which nowadays could land and take off from anywhere. Tracking stations was becoming more like air-traffic control. And anyplace that had a decent launch facility was being pressed into the Space Shield's service.

But here they were mainly launching the bulk stuff, prefabricated components, the airtight modules, supplies. "Sensitive materials," like nuclear reactors and warheads, traveled on the safer shuttles.

At least, Richie thought, until one of the shuttles blows a circuit or something.

Richie pushed that thought from his mind. His job was to make sure that the present launch wasn't scrubbed. That there were no embarrassing incidents with frozen O-rings, or improperly programmed onboard computers.

This was a heavy launch, using the Shuttle-C configuration. A cargo carrier occupied the space that only months ago would have been occupied by a shuttle. Important construction components were aboard, and they had to get them up.

So far everything had been picture-perfect.

But Richie was sweating right through the final countdown.

"Ignition," the report came over his ear set.

Richie sank back in his seat. Well, at least it was out of his hands.

Somewhere in the Bermuda Rise, self-diagnostic tests were underway at a newly alert installation. An entire defense sector seemed to have circuitry problems. But just as those circuits were activated, unusual activity was detected in the installation's operational area. A large craft of unknown design was apparently heading for Low Earth Orbit. Although there was no threat, and no detection of antigravity drive, the damaged circuits flared to activate targeting and weapons circuitry.

Inhibitory commands flashed from the newly awakened Central Control complex. But they were too late to undo the commands of the damaged control nodes.

Ancient weapons fired.

Betsy Sharrington sat in the front seat of the old Buick with her husband Bert. They had ridden the car down to their Florida retirement eight years ago. Bert took care of the car like his baby, washing and waxing it. It shone like some of the brand-new cars they saw at line-dancing.

They hadn't driven simply for enjoyment very much lately, not with the price of gasoline rising so sharply. But they had to do the marketing, even if the cost of food in the stores was pretty shocking nowadays, too.

Betsy didn't know how her daughter got along, with a mortgage and a family and a husband out of work. She and Bert had debated pretty seriously whether it was worth the gas money to drive around and comparison shop for better prices.

As they pulled up at a stoplight, she raised her eyes to the Almighty through the windshield—that was when she noticed the bright light rising above a vapor trail.

"Look, Bert, another launch at the Cape!"

"Another heaping helping of money going off into orbit," her husband responded sourly. "Our tax dollars at work. Not to mention our cost-of-living increase, our health-care premiums—"

His words cut off as a searing brilliance seemed to lance across the sky. It intersected the rising rocket, which went off like something on the Fourth of July. The space vehicle turned into a miniature sun, throwing off gobbets of flaming debris to trail downward.

Husband and wife both stared, openmouthed, until the horns of the cars behind brought them back to Earth.

"Damned fools," Bert fumed as he threw the car into gear. "Managed to crash two of their rockets together."

"Didn't look like a rocket to me," Betsy said, replaying the incident. "It was more like the terrible swift sword."

CHAPTER 11
RUINS

Even though it was mid-morning, the living room was dark. That was because a plywood panel covered the picture window that should have looked out on the front lawn. Skaara sat with Kemsit and a local policeman, looking at the brick that had shattered the glass.

Kemsit couldn't read the note that had been wrapped around the missile. Skaara could. Four simple words: "Go back to Abbidose!"

Four words that demonstrated someone's ignorance and fear.

Times are bad, Skaara thought. A half-dozen refugees appear in their community, and this is their reaction.

He turned to the law enforcer. "I know that Kemsit should have contacted you immediately last night. But his English—"

Kemsit and the others had been planted down here for months, but still they didn't fit. Hetepet, one of the other housemates, explained how they had taken to watching television programs for children to try and improve their English. But these were people decades older than Skaara. A new language did not come easily to them.

On Abydos, Skaara suddenly realized, he'd have deferred to Kemsit because of his age. But here, Kemsit and the others were more like children or the brainstruck, dependent on those who were more conversant in what Kemsit still called "the Urt-man tongue."

But the Abydans who spoke English best also read hieroglyphics, and were off working for the government in its attempts to understand Ra's technology. It just happened that Skaara was in town to handle this particular ugly outbreak.

The lawman, an Officer Novick, simply shrugged. "Not much we could do in any case. Whoever heaved that brick would have been gone by the time we arrived."

Skaara glanced at the wrecked window. "It will be expensive, replacing that. My friends here would like some reassurance that it won't happen again."

Novick's response was another shrug. "All we have is a brick and a note that everybody here has probably touched. It could be kids, it could be somebody else— *anybody*. I expect it's a onetime thing, but I can't offer any guarantees."

"Does your police have a—what do they all it—a hate crimes department?" Skaara asked.

Novick stiffened, probably seeing more paperwork than this case deserved. "What else?" the police officer growled. "You want to go to the feds because their civil rights are being threatened—by a brick? For people who aren't even citizens, I'd say you get enough government help—"

"And we don't pay enough taxes, merely renting a house?" Skaara demanded. "For your information, Officer, that 'government help' doesn't exist. These people live here on a stipend from the Abydos Foundation. Those of us who have jobs contribute most of our salaries—after taxes—to help support them. No welfare, no unemployment." He glared at the policeman. "Or do you think it would make things better around here for Kemsit and the others to try taking jobs from the local people?"

Novick gave a quick, convulsive shudder at the results *that* line of action would stir up in town. "I'll look into things," he finally said grudgingly. "See if we can get people to tone it down."

But, Skaara thought, he probably agrees more with whoever threw that brick.

As they watched the law officer leave, Kemsit touched Skaara's arm. "Do not worry about us," he said. "We're ready if they try more." He opened the closet near the front door. Skaara's eyes went wide as he saw two clubs—no, they were sporting goods—baseball bats.

Kemsit took him upstairs. Inside another closet were a couple of hunting rifles. "They don't shoot as fast as the ones we had on Abydos," Kemsit said. "But they shoot well enough if anyone comes after us."

"How—?" Skaara started to ask.

"We've been very careful with our food allowance," Kemsit said. "And some of us came with a little money."

Skaara looked at the house captain with new eyes.

On this world, Kemsit might be comparable to a child. But back home, he'd been a dependable member of Skaara's militia, patrolling the factionalized ruins of Nagada to keep the noncombatants safe.

I didn't realize we'd have to do the same thing here, Skaara thought with a chill.

Daniel Jackson sat with Gary Meyers, staring over a desk mounded with copies and photos of the stone fragments and their enigmatic hieroglyphs. "I wish those Germans had recovered the whole stele," he said for about the fiftieth time.

"Don't you think you're making a little too much of this?" Meyers asked.

"In light of what happened at the Cape . . . I don't know. Besides, the Office of Bright Ideas should have some sort of notion to explain what happened there."

Meyers shrugged. "I thought there were enough theories already. We've been pressing NASA pretty hard. They've had more launches in the last couple of months than they'd completed in the past five years. With all that wear and tear, maybe one of the engines gave."

"Or it could be sabotage—somebody objecting to his tax dollars going into orbit," Daniel had heard the litany already. "Fortunately, an onboard computer aborted the launch before the rockets got completely out of control and landed that load in downtown Miami. What worries me is the streak that's supposed to have hit the launch vehicle."

"Nobody's sure about that," Meyers said.

"Enough people had gathered for the show," Daniel said. "And it's not just the casual observers. There's film showing the launcher getting hit."

"Or something blowing off it at right angles," Gary pointed out. "Though," he admitted, "it's hard to say what that might be."

"Then there's the school that suggests it's a ground-to-air missile, fired from out at sea," Daniel said.

"Pretty far out, to hit at the angle it did," Meyers replied. "Or are we postulating an enemy submarine?"

"Better that than an attacking UFO." Daniel pointed to a pile of tabloid newspapers.

"I think you're hanging out with that Moench guy way too much," Meyers warned.

"I'd just be happier if we had a better under-standing of this 'fastness' referred to in the hiero-glyphics here." Daniel pored over a photo of one of the stone fragments. "Is it a religious center, so that this godpower reference refers to a mega-holiness? Because if it's a real technology reference, the power output is—well, it's scary. Especially when you con-sider this fragment, where it talks about girdling or binding the earth . . ."

"Come on!" Meyers' voice began to sound annoyed. "You can't believe that launch was zapped from some-where in Egypt. Any missile would have been spotted and tracked. And it's too far for an energy beam—"

The irate voice of reason was interrupted as Dr. Julius Moench came through the office door.

The guy must have practice in dodging secretaries, Daniel thought as his own assistant dove through the door just a second too late.

"This disaster in Florida," Moench puffed. "I've pinpointed the source of the beam."

Daniel waved his secretary off. "Where?"

"Apparently, it originated from a spot several hundred miles off the coast of Bermuda—"

"You're not going to drag in the Bermuda Triangle!" Meyers began beckoning the secretary and pointing at the crank scientist. "That's all we need."

Moench, however, began unloading a bulging briefcase. "Whether you like it or not, Dr. Meyers, that is an area where air and seacraft tend to disappear— or discover anomalies in time, magnetism, and other phenomena."

"It's a heavily trafficked area right off our coast—" Meyers began.

"And there's been a huge upsurge of anomaly reports in recent months." Moench took an inch-thick stack of paper from his case. "These hardly qualify as the lunatic fringe. I'm talking about experienced airline and military pilots. But that's not all."

He brought out more stacks of paper. "Suddenly, it seems we're getting similar reports in other areas of surface and air traffic. A nuclear submarine coming out of Gibraltar experienced control problems. Pakistani jetliners losing their way—a squadron of fighters from the Japanese Defense Forces led astray by their compasses. A supertanker almost going around off South Africa . . . an Australian pilot being forced to ditch in the ocean because he missed Tasmania."

"The police blotter of the bizarre," Meyers muttered. "It's probably a typical week for somebody who runs a series called 'Unexplainables.' "

"Believe me, I'd have lots more books out if I had weeks—or months—like this," Moench replied. He looked somewhat the worse for wear—Santa Claus at the height of his busy season. "It was the locations of the anomalies that caught my attention."

He took out a map of the world and began marking it. "Bermuda." He made an oval around the island. "Gibraltar." This oval took in a good deal of the Mediterranean. "Pakistan. The Sea of Japan." Glancing at Daniel, he asked, "Notice something?"

"The way you draw them, your anomaly spots seem to lie in a straight line," Daniel replied.

Moench nodded. "Between thirty and forty degrees, north latitude. And as one heads east, they crop up approximately seventy-two degrees of longitude apart."

He went back to the map. "I've had reports from South America, South Africa, and Australia." The ovals he made here were spaced farther apart, but all fell in the same latitudes—between thirty and forty degrees.

Moench regarded the map. "All this reminded me of a theory developed by Ivan Sanderson, another delver into the unknown."

"A rival?" Meyers inquired.

The little man ignored him. "Sanderson suggested that there were anomaly spots—'vile vortices,' he called them—equidistantly situated around the globe." He added ovals in the north and south Pacific and the Indian oceans. "These are less heavily traveled, and thus, fewer anomalies have been observed."

Daniel looked at the two rings of anomaly zones

Moench had outlined and all of a sudden, a line from the stele translation came back to haunt him.

"Girdling the Earth," he muttered. Then, louder, he turned to Meyers. "Get out those maps from the old German expedition. We really have to re-excavate where they dug."

Skaara looked surprised to find Daniel Jackson in the offices of the Abydos Foundation. "We don't see much of you here these days."

"And you'll wish you hadn't by the time I'm done," Daniel replied. "I'm looking for money." Quickly, he outlined the story of the Set stele and the need for an archaeological expedition. "The problem is, I can't find anyone to pay for it. Jack O'Neil can arrange transport and supplies, but that's all. The universities who normally bankroll archaeological research are feeling the current financial pinch. So I've come here like a beggar, hoping the market for plush mastadges was better than we expected."

"Money here is tight, too," Skaara said. "We're barely supporting—"

He paused for a second. "You have yourself and Gary Meyers—couldn't you raid the translating project for some more Egyptologists? Then all you'd need were diggers."

Picking up the phone, Skaara said, "Send Kemsit in."

The Abydan refugee looked a little nervous as he entered the office.

"Kemsit has a problem in common with a number of resettled refugees," Skaara began. When he explained

Daniel's need, the house captain smiled. "Digging is something we know how to do," he said. "The people with me were miners of Nagada."

He looked at Daniel. "We'd rather work to earn our keep—and we'd be happier away from people who hate us."

Daniel needed a boat to reach the world's most rapidly assembled archaeological expedition. The Germans' maps were sixty-plus years out of date in the ever shifting lands of the Nile Delta. Though the yearly floods had been controlled by the Aswan Dam, the river still carved new routes for itself through the low-lying, loamy soil. This was the breadbasket of Egypt, the fertile "black earth" of the ancients, as opposed to the red earth of the desert.

The island where the old German dig had taken place was much bigger than their maps showed, and was part of a farm. Daniel had already paid off the farmer, as well as engaging in expensive negotiations with the government for permission to dig.

He'd left Gary Meyers marking out the most promising areas with a grid work of stakes and string. O'Neil had lent Ferretti's services as transport liaison. Skaara was acting as the foreman for the diggers, and Sha'uri was along as head translator. Perhaps that was one reason Daniel had spent so much time in Cairo, wending his way through the bureaucratic labyrinth in the huge institutional office buildings.

He'd received reports on the technical problems to be overcome. There was a reason why less work had been done to uncover the history of Lower Egypt. It was buried deeper, and the job was much, much messier. The yearly floods didn't just rearrange the geography: They deposited the silt picked up along the river's four-thousand-mile course at the Delta. Even in the course of Egypt's three thousand years of dynastic history, old towns had disappeared. If they were searching for something even older than that, how far down would they have to go?

That raised another problem. Digging in the Delta's marshy soil quickly became a battle against water and mud. Thankfully, modern technology had just come up with a solution. The German Archaeological Institute—cultural descendants of the 1930s excavators, perhaps?—had just recently begun digs in the Delta region with the help of new pumping equipment. With a diplomatic assist from Gary Meyers, that machinery was also helping Daniel's diggers as they began working their way down.

When Daniel returned from Cairo after a new (and prolonged) round of dickering, he stared around in disbelief.

"What have you guys been doing?" he demanded, "giving an exhibition of smash-and-grab archaeology?"

"Your Abydan friends are more into digging than sifting," Meyers admitted.

Daniel surveyed the cleared forecourt of a small temple. "I wouldn't say this represented Set's fastness," he said.

"There are a couple of inscriptions on the building there." Meyers pointed. "To Sutekh."

"The Asiatic avatar of Set," Daniel explained to Skaara. "People from the Near East often wound up settling in the Nile Delta. Sutekh was an important god in the XV and XVIII dynasties."

He shook his head. "But that's thousands of years after the time we're interested in."

"Maybe," Meyers agreed. "But we found the base where the stele had been erected. It says some pious Hyksos pharaoh brought it from down south—a town called Nagada."

Daniel's lips quirked. Somehow, he wasn't surprised to hear that name crop up. Earth's Nagada was one of the most ancient predynastic centers on the Nile, a settlement on the loop of the river later dominated by Thebes. Way back when, it had also been a center for the worship of Set.

"So. A reerected monument. That explains something."

Meyers nodded. "As far as we can figure out, this place was leveled when the Hyksos invaders were defeated. The stele was knocked down, and the pieces were shifted around in the floods. The Germans were lucky to find as many as they did."

"And how did we do?" Daniel wanted to know.

"What we've found is all in here." Meyers led the way into a nearby tent. Chunks of rock were arranged on a table like an archaeological jigsaw puzzle.

Standing over them was Sha'uri, looking excited. "We've just fit these together," she announced. "It's at least the beginning of a place reference."

Daniel looked over her shoulder, barely noticing her

as he read the inscription. " 'Beyond the Mountains of Bekhen.' Well, it's a start."

Entering the mullah's presence, Kasim Firdusi felt a psychic tug-of-war. Firdusi was a born rebel, an important and useful trait in a terrorist. Yet here he was, offering fealty to this withered old man.

"What news on these ... 'scholars?' " To the old man, the only true learning was to be found in the Koran. Other disciplines, from rocket science to nuclear physics, were the realm of false scholars. This was especially so with anyone expressing interest in the pagan ruins of the past.

"Wise one, we have kept watch on these archaeologists since they arrived." The mullah's believers offered many trickles of information to the movement. Government workers in the Institute of Antiquities had quickly given warning of the arrival of Daniel Jackson.

"And what do the minions of the Great Satan seek?" the mullah demanded.

"It has not been easy to infiltrate their camp," Firdusi admitted. The foreigners brought their own workers—these people of Abydos. They speak their own language, and it had been hard to get information. But the local people, who expected work from the foreigners, are all the more willing to tell us whatever they hear. The Americans seek a lost inscription. They seem to be searching for some other place."

The mullah nodded. "You have done well enough,

Kasim Firdusi. Continue to keep your eye on these foreigners, and prepare your band. Whatever these unbelievers reach for"—he extended a clawlike hand, and clenched the fingers—"we will seize."

CHAPTER 12
THE SECRET IN THE SANDS

The remorseless excavation at Daniel's dig had enlarged the collection of rock shards on the table. Every evening, Daniel joined Gary Meyers and the other translators as they tried to fit the shattered carvings together. It was reminiscent of a family evening over the old jigsaw puzzle, although working with Sha'uri made for a somewhat chillier experience.

"Beyond the mountains of Bekhen," Daniel repeated the section they had joined together and translated. "In later days that was the location of the granite quarries for the pink stone in the Thebes temples. They were along the Wadi Hammamat, the route the ancient Egyptians used to reach the Red Sea."

"That seems to narrow down the choices for the location of this 'fastness,'" Gary said. "There's not much of Egypt left beyond those mountains."

"Spoken like a true Egyptologist," Daniel growled. "Even the ancient Egyptians were trading beyond the Red Sea. And we're talking about the predecessor culture. If they had udajeets on Abydos, they must have had antigravity here on Earth. Look, if Professor

Moench's theory is right, these Set people were setting up things all over the world."

"You don't have to attack Dr. Meyers," Sha'uri interjected.

Daniel felt his lips tighten. "And you don't have to defend him just because *I* opened my mouth!" he retorted.

"Look!" one of the other Egyptologists said hastily. "This piece could fit in here."

More fragments came together, and a new corner of the wrecked stele took shape.

"We're missing a section in between," Meyers said. "But this gives us a direction. 'To the south and east, on—' something."

Daniel forgot his sharp words with Meyers. He even forgot his estranged wife as he looked at the fragments. "We should be glad the Rosetta stone didn't come in this many pieces. Otherwise, we'd still be wondering what the hell these hieroglyphics mean."

More bits of shattered granite were fitted together.

"On the great peninsula," Meyers read. He glanced at Daniel. "The Sinai?"

Daniel shook his head. "The directions are wrong. The Sinai is *north* and east of the Mountains of Bekhen. We've got to find the bit that goes between these two sections."

"Looks like that's the part that took the hit from the battering ram or whatever they used to knock the stele down," Meyers muttered.

Sha'uri fingered her way through the smaller fragments, almost gravel. She might not be a trained archaeologist, but she was a miner's daughter—and a miner herself. She knew stone. "Here's a weathered face," she exclaimed. Holding up the smaller chunk, she revealed part of an inscription.

The others joined in, looking for dented chips smashed from the stele. It was a far more delicate job of jigsaw work, but they gathered enough pieces to suggest what the missing inscription might have been.

"I make it out as 'Beyond the Mountains of Bekhen, 160 schenes to the south and east, on the great peninsula.' " Daniel scowled. "That would make a lot more sense if the Egyptians had refined their system of measurement a bit more. They went from cubit, which is less than a yard, to the schene, which is a lot more than a mile. The Greeks estimated it as sixty stadia. Depending on which city-state's stade you choose, you could wind up with as many as 630 feet to a stadium. The most commonly accepted is the Attic stade, 607 feet, which makes the Egyptian schene something like 6.9 miles."

Raising his eyes to the featureless tent roof above, Daniel tried to do the math in his head. "More than a thousand . . ."

"One thousand, one hundred and four miles," Sha'uri said. He glanced at her, and she suddenly realized she had helped him. Sha'uri almost broke her neck turning away.

Daniel stifled a sigh. "Looks like we'll need a map."

One of the archaeologists produced a map of ancient Egyptian trading routes, prompting another sigh from Daniel. "A map with a scale of miles," he amplified.

Feretti, in his roles as quartermaster and transportation officer, had an entire sheaf of charts, but most were military maps, local scale, covering Cairo, or the route from there to here. "Nothing bigger?" Daniel asked.

The marine left the tent and returned a couple of minutes later, bearing a large book.

"An atlas?" Daniel said in surprise.

"Be prepared," Feretti replied with a grin.

Daniel paged through until he found a fairly detailed representation of the Middle East. He set the atlas on the table, marked a sheet of paper with the distance they'd calculated, then swept it in an arc around the map. "Due south would put us somewhere in Ethiopia. Due east leaves us in the Persian Gulf off the coast of Kuwait. South and east . . . well, it would definitely be on the Arabian peninsula—"

"The great peninsula," Meyers said.

"We're either in Saudi Arabia or Yemen." Daniel squinted at the map. "I can't tell which, because there's apparently no defined boundary. We'll be searching through something called the Rub al-Khali—the Empty Quarter."

"Biggest sandy desert in the world," Feretti amplified. "I was along for the ride in Desert Storm. Although our part of the war was an amphibious attack into Kuwait, we got lectured about everywhere on the peninsula."

"A long, dry search," Daniel said. "Unless we can figure a way to narrow down the haystack—or is that the sandpit?"

Colonel Travis was surprised to see his visitor. "Jackson! I thought you were busily digging up half of

Egypt. You've already stolen all my best translators. What more could you want?"

A severely jet-lagged Daniel raised both hands. "I come in peace," he said. "All I want from you now is a good word to some of your colleagues at the JPL."

"A funny request from an archaeologist," Travis replied. His eyes narrowed. "You didn't find something new out there, did you?"

"Right now I think we found a riddle wrapped in an enigma." Daniel quickly summed up the results of his dig, then went on. "When I began to read about the archaeology of Arabia, I found this interesting story about how some people found the lost city of Ubar in Oman."

"Sounds like something out of Edgar Rice Burroughs," Travis quipped. Then his face grew serious. "Wait a second. That strikes a note—"

"The searchers zeroed in on the location with the help of some people from the Jet Propulsion Laboratory and something called Space Imaging Radar."

Travis snapped his fingers. "That's right. They used orbital imaging from the *Challenger* in 1984."

"Plus a couple of other satellites." Daniel nodded, producing a map from the briefcase he was carrying. "I'd like to get some new pictures—of this area here." He indicated a huge crescent scrawled across the desert area. "It may not be as easy as Ubar. They were able to trace old caravan routes through the desert. Whoever built this site probably flew in. But if there's anything out of the ordinary down there, I want to know about it."

He kept his mouth firmly closed on the next words

that went through his head. *I just hope we don't get any-thing shot down while we're looking.*

The professor at Boston University's Center for Remote Sensing examined the map that had been faxed to him. "We may have several series of photos covering the areas that interest you." He squinted for a moment, comparing the map in his hand to a mental image.

"There's a large, extinct river that cut across the whole of the peninsula, perhaps as recently as five thousand years ago. It intersects part of your search area. I'll send you our plats. You might want to con-centrate there."

"Little side trip this morning," Neil Antonelli spoke into the intercom from the pilot's position on the space shuttle. He diverted the orbiter on its way to the *Freedom* construction site so that it overflew the Ara-bian peninsula.

Christy Manville activated the SIRS equipment, which took image after image of the sands below.

Computers blended the images taken by the space shuttle with series from two other orbiting satellites and enhanced them.

A NASA space archaeologist began examining the swaths of desert for any anomalous images. "Hmph," he said, rubbing his eyes. "If this river really was flowing five thousand years ago, who knows what we'll find? There may be traces of all sorts of settle-ments along the banks. This may be the start of a whole new page in archaeology—the discovery of an entirely new culture."

His roving eyes suddenly stopped. "That's odd."

"What?" Daniel Jackson leaned over the scientist's shoulder, trying to see whatever had caught the man's attention. He couldn't make heads nor tails of the computer-enhanced images.

"This is—or was—the river." The NASA expert ran a finger along a shadowy line in the middle of the picture. "As I was saying, you'd expect to find remains on the shore. But this ..." He pointed to a blob—a blob, however, with sharp angles. "That's an artificial structure—man-made."

Or made by *somebody*, Daniel thought. "What's so odd about it?" he asked.

"That would be smack dab in the middle of the river. In the deepest channel. No signs of any other settlements nearby. It doesn't seem to be a dam, or part of any irrigation system—"

"I think it may be just what we're looking for," Daniel said, squinting at the enigmatic blotch. "Can you get us some coordinates?"

Kasim Firdusi felt severely out of place as he lowered himself to a cross-legged squat on the camel-hair rug. He was an urban guerrilla, used to conducting attacks from alleyways and rooftops. Others fought in the countryside.

But the mullah had ordered him forth with a small band of followers, into the desert of the Rub al-Khali, to meet with this chieftain of sand fleas. Firdusi had known various bedouin who had come—or been forced—to live in the cities. Unable to wander with their camels, most had become truck drivers—the nearest technological equivalent.

Firdusi had a low opinion of these transplants, and tended to use them as cannon fodder in his tactical plans. They could usually be worked up into a fine religious frenzy to pilot their truck, now full of explosives, and do away with unbelievers or backsliders.

But here in the deep desert, after jouncing for miles in a badly sprung truck, he had to treat this bedouin chieftain as a colleague, an equal, if they were to seize whatever it was the American devils were seeking.

He had bowed deeply to Sheikh Faris Aban and used the usual flowery language about God giving him a long life and prosperity.

"When a city man speaks to a bedouin about prosperity, that is the time for the bedouin to count his teeth," the chieftain had replied.

Annoyed, Firdusi had changed his tack, discussing his mission as one of religion. "We have word from various believers, both in Egypt and in the government here, that agents of the Great Satan are coming to your deserts, mighty chief. What will you do to put them down?"

"Many foreigners travel the sand nowadays." Sheikh Faris shrugged in his robes. "Believers and unbelievers, Arabs and feringhee. They search for oil, and it is the will of the king that they not be molested. In your grandfather's day, young Firdusi, the tribes of the west went against the king, attacking the land-grubbing farmers. Where are those tribes now? Gone—

crushed. I understand some of their young men live at the tails of the cities, driving trucks."

The sheikh pointedly glanced toward the entrance to the tent, beyond which stood the three trucks that had brought Firdusi and his men to the encampment.

"We keep to the old ways, as much as those who rule will let us," Faris went on. "They have overlooked us—for now. But if we call attention to ourselves by attacking the oil workers . . ."

He shook his head.

Firdusi launched into a long speech while the sheikh looked at him with distaste. To his desert-bred sensibilities, city men were not true men at all, enslaving themselves with walls and machines until they could never roam free. And this one had the nerve to come into his tent and lecture him!

If it weren't for the fact that Firdusi came as the emissary of a very holy man, the sheikh would have simply eliminated him and his followers. The sands could hide many secrets.

But to take all his young men on an attack, to put the whole tribe at risk, even at the behest of a holy man . . . the sheikh hesitated.

"Understand, great chief, these outlanders will commit sacrilege!" Firdusi went on.

"And how will they commit sacrilege in the empty sands?" the sheikh inquired. "This might be something these old eyes would wish to see."

"The infidels dug in Egypt to reveal the dwellings of the ancient pagans who lived there," Firdusi said. "No doubt they will do the same here."

"They seek to open the vaults of the djinn?" Faris

demanded. This went beyond mere sacrilege. The djinn had ruled the deserts long before Mohammed and Allah had come to the bedouin. Who knew what disasters these crazy foreigners might unleash?

Sheikh Faris leaned forward. "Tell me more, esteemed Kasim Firdusi," he ordered.

CHAPTER 13
VIPERS AND OTHER STRANGERS

Daniel stepped into Jack O'Neil's office and executed his idea of a snappy salute. "Office of Bright Ideas, reporting in before I head off to the new dig."

"I understand you've moved on from Egypt to Saudi Arabia. Do you intend to turn this into a tour of the Red Sea states?"

"We dug, and got pointed in a new direction," Daniel replied. "Maybe we should be glad we were out of the country, with this martial law being declared. I don't know if we were too busy or what, but I never heard about it till I got back here."

"Perhaps it didn't seem like such a big deal in Egypt," O'Neil said. "Martial law is sort of a political fact in a lot of the Middle East."

"But it's got to be a big deal here." Daniel's face was tight. "Were things getting that bad?"

O'Neil nodded grimly. "Idiots were advocating everything from overthrowing the government to killing off the Abydans."

Daniel's expression became more set. "I just hope we aren't starting something we'll come to regret."

The colonel suddenly grinned. "Come off it, Jackson. This is real life, not *Seven Days in May*."

"I wish I could take that at face value," Daniel retorted. "But aren't you the guy who went off on spook missions all through Latin America? Taking out people who disagreed with our country—or rather, with your commanders?"

O'Neil lost his smile. "Would you rather see things fall apart the way they did on Abydos?"

Daniel went as white as if he'd been suddenly stabbed in the heart. "Anything would be better than that," he said hoarsely. "At least I hope so."

A severely jet-lagged Daniel Jackson gazed out the helicopter window at the desert below. His rump had ached after his transatlantic flight to reach Riyadh. Now his ears and his whole body were assailed by the vibrations of the jet helicopter's engines as they cruised over endless reddish sands.

The red lands, he thought, bringing up the ancient Egyptian term for the desert. Set had been made god of the infertile reaches after he'd been ousted from the ranks of the good gods and made into a blustery cosmic villain.

Although, if the reports he'd read made any sense, this hadn't been desert when Set's fastness had been built. A river had run through this land. Hard to imagine now, he thought, looking down at the undulating landscape. Sand dunes stretched out around him like an ocean of frozen whitecaps. Lumps of sand—

The helicopter began heading down, and Daniel revised his estimate. These were sand hills.

They passed over the crest of one of the piles, and Daniel saw what looked like a scattering of toys in the lee of the dune. Trucks and tents huddled in the relatively quiet area at the base of the hill.

With the human artifacts before him, Daniel again had to change his scale. Make that a sand *mountain.* The pile had to be more than eight hundred feet high, tall and wide enough to hide the Transamerica Pyramid in San Francisco.

The downdraft from the rotors raised a cloud of granules as Daniel involuntarily shivered. How long would it take for such a mass to assemble itself? It seemed flatly unbelievable, but here he was in a helicopter, scudding past the downslope. Below him, he saw a pause in the work in progress. A Humvee removed itself from the clot of earthmoving vehicles tearing into the depression in the ground beyond the sand mountain.

Daniel realized that the declivity had to be the bed of the long-lost river. He glanced back at the towering sand drift. However long it had taken to pile up, he was glad the archaeological team had arrived now—it would be a real pain in the butt trying to cut through all that stuff to get to the fastness.

The helicopter settled, and the hummer pulled up just outside the rotors' dust cloud. Gary Meyers emerged in sweat-stained khakis. "Hey, there, Chief!" he called.

Daniel stared off into the deepening excavation. "I'm impressed you got all this stuff out here into the back of beyond."

"That's Feretti," the archaeologist admitted. "He managed miracles as transportation officer. The Abydans were very good, too. We were able to locate ourselves using satellites. Then Kemsit and the others dragged the ground-penetrating radar all over the place to pinpoint the fastness."

Daniel flinched a little as a bulldozer came roaring up, creating a ramp way out of the enormous dig. "Looks like the Giovanni Battista Belzoni school of archaeology."

Gary Meyers flushed at the reference to the earliest days of Egyptology, when diggers were more like tomb robbers than scientists. Belzoni was a former circus strongman turned archaeologist who smashed his way into tombs for gold and objects of art, wrecking grave goods that later scholars would have given their eyeteeth to uncover.

"This isn't exactly a case of straining the sand for potsherds," Meyers replied with asperity. "This thing was built in the middle of a frigging river, for God's sake! Whoever constructed this place had to have used techniques that were faster and more advanced than anything we know about."

He glared at Daniel. "If you had been around here instead of back in the States, you'd see why we have lots of reasons to get finished here—the sooner the better. We've got poisonous snakes in the neighborhood who are otherwise so rarely seen, no one has gotten around to developing an antivenin. Then there's the spider that stretches six inches from the tip of one leg to the other. But that's not the most charming part. Its bite is anesthetic—it deadens the feeling as the beastie eats your flesh while you sleep."

Involuntarily, Daniel glanced down at the sand around him. "Some tourist spot. Any casualties?"

"None so far," Meyers admitted. "But none of us will be brokenhearted to clear out. We figure another day or so, and we'll have dug down to the fastness."

"I hope we don't have to pull a Belzoni to get in," Daniel said glumly.

Aboard the *Boat of a Million Years*, Nekhti, son of Ushabti, stalked down one of the vast corridors. The ship had once held thousands of his people in the great migration from the world of Tuat. As one of the leaders, Nekhti's father had been responsible for getting this huge number to the new world without friction. Ushabti had shown how to do that—working the travelers unremittingly until they were too tired to cause problems.

Nekhti suspected that the "Lady" Hathor was using the same technique with the much smaller caretaker crew. All of the Setim on board were set to the grind of computerized gunnery practice.

Nekhti was dragging himself back to his quarters after another session in virtual reality. His eyes ached. Although they had tuned the equipment as best they could, it was evident that Ra's lost race saw in a different spectrum than the Setim—or, probably, the humans. Because of that, prolonged work at the gunnery screens was tiring to the eyes.

It was also infuriating to Nekhti. This was not his area of expertise. He had been trained as second officer and astrogator. But Hathor and Khonsu were not using his competence. For some reason they were depending on the ship's computers to control the course back to Earth.

Nekhti had found himself banned from the enormous control room's Astrogation center. He knew there was no hope of appeal. These human would-be gods had a definite antipathy for his kind.

Khonsu's response was odd enough. The warrior always seemed to be guarding his back, being sure to face Nekhti whenever they encountered one another. If Khonsu had been one of the Setim, Nekhti would have expected to see his hackles rise and his teeth to show. Instead, the alien's flat, muzzle-less face seemed even more expressionless than most humans.

With Hathor, the response was more straightforward. Nekhti could smell the hate.

As he headed to his cabin, Nekhti encountered one of his erstwhile Astrogation officers, a trim female named Ankhere.

"Sir!" Ankhere braced herself in the Setim salute, hands at her side, head back to reveal her throat.

Nekhti made a dismissive gesture. "It seems we're all crewmen together now."

Ankhere's muzzle wrinkled. "Sir, I knew I was prohibited from the Astrogation computers. But you—?"

Even against his better judgment, Nekhti felt his lips rippling back from his teeth. But he also felt a decision crystallizing. "Yes, Ankhere, even I."

His subordinate was obviously looking for an opportunity to complain about the humans and their un-Setim work schedule. But Nekhti cut Ankhere short. He was tired, too. But now he had something to do.

The crestfallen fourth officer trailed off to more gunnery practice. Nekhti, however, passed his cabin, heading instead for the ship's library.

Passing out of the crew's quarters, Nekhti found the huge hallways seemed even more empty and echoing. His ears kept cocking at even the faintest sounds. Instinctively, he found himself sniffing the air. The odors wafting about revealed that no Setim had been through recently. He did detect the spoor of Hathor and Khonsu. And there seemed to be the faintest trace of another human.

But all of these were mere vestiges. No one was in the large, shadowy room as Nekhti entered. Normally, physical contact wasn't required to access the library. Every cabin had a flatscreen and a miniature console. But since Hathor had awakened the crew, these connections had been read-only, featuring some insipid "entertainment" capabilities, including several so-called games that seemed to be thinly disguised gunnery exercises.

Nekhti stepped to a corner of the room, using the gestures and verbal commands that invoked a console. A twin to one of the command deck units seemed to congeal out of the misty atmosphere. Nekhti sat at it and began a series of queries on course corrections. But neither the flatscreen nor its holographic counterpart lit up with information.

Hunching in his seat, Nekhti allowed his lips to writhe in the snarl that passed among the Setim for a deep frown. So, even from here, access to Astrogation had been prohibited!

Ushabti's son was not one to give up easily. He tried

various logical side roads, indirect approaches to the information he sought. But his mechanical prevarications all failed. Astronomy was blocked, as was astrophysics—at least those portions that would have dealt with real-life course experiments.

A low growl rumbled deep in Nekhti's chest. Perhaps, in the name of security, Hathor might have blocked access to the conning of the *Boat of a Million Years*. But these additional prohibitions had nothing to do with running the ship. They were strictly informational.

So what information was Hathor hiding when she barred the crew from the computer memories?

There was another way, perhaps to get at the course data. Using his special coding as second officer, Nekhti invoked the ship's log. His unnoticed growl turned into a bark of pure fury. Access denied!

Truly angry now, Nekhti attacked the console, using the experience of years of operation against the newly erected safeguards. Ptah had been the only one of the human godlings who'd had any real understanding of advanced technology. Sure Hathor wouldn't have been able to lock him out *completely.*

In the end, however, Nekhti rocked back in his seat, snapping down a whine of frustration. Whether by luck or by craft, Hathor had issued just the right orders to the master computers on board the vessel. Nekhti had not been able to pierce the security barriers. The closest he'd come was to call up a directory that listed the files making up the ship's log.

He glared at the shimmering ideograms on the flatscreen. For this he had lost hours of sleep! All too soon he'd be expected to awaken and make his way to the ordnance sections for more of this Ra-be-damned gunnery practice. The figures on the screen seemed to dance before his tired eyes.

Then Nekhti sharpened his gaze. The size of the file . . . certainly, the *Boat of a Million Years* was a prodigious vessel, with a tremendous volume of information to be processed at all times. Much of that information was stored in the General Log file, dating back to the unimaginably ancient time when the ship had first gone into space. Smaller files were scattered throughout the vessel's computer system as backups, but this was the main record.

As second officer, Nekhti had input reports into the log. He had a rough idea of the file's size. It was much, much larger now.

Abruptly, Ushabti's son vacated his seat and made the console vanish. His nose twitched as those of his far-off ancestors' might have, when the spoor of prey had mysteriously disappeared.

Systems on stand-down would not have added so much information as the size of that file indicated. The *Boat of a Million Years* would have had to go to war to account for such an influx of data.

Not for the first time, Nekhti wondered exactly what had been going on while he and his fellow crew members had rested in the arms of Ra . . .

High, thin clouds wisped across the setting full moon, like the thinnest of veils across the face of an Arab beauty. Not that Daniel Jackson had seen any such beauties during his lightning visit to Riyadh. The few women he'd seen had looked more like giant truf-

He pulled his eyes a
turned to the Gibraltar-li
them. So huge, so solid .
as he watched, the wind
the monster dune's cres
slope leading down to th

A moment later very fi
tent, gusted through th
aimed straight for his ey
water bottle, his toothbru

The earthmovers h
burden of sand so that
the bare rock where th
course. Now it was do
and the other Abydan
sand from the mound
excavation. Daniel bega
a flat roof, sloping wal
Set's fastness looked al
blockhouse, like the la
in a 1950s sci-fi movie
an atomic bomb.

Except the walls wer
vitrified rock, plain and

Daniel joined in the
maw of an earthmove
blockhouse brought h
indentation—a doorwa

Working like fiends
the sand. "Looks like a
"The opening is a bi

McCay

ay from Sha'uri's tent and
ke hulk of sand overlooking
. yet so impermanent. Even
took a billow of sand from
and laid it on the rippling
e camp.
e grit rattled against Daniel's
e open flap, and seemingly
es. Blinking, he turned to his
h, and the business of the day.

d cleared away the over-
he bottom of the pit reached
e long-vanished river cut its
wn to hand labor as Kemsit
, wielded shovels to remove
emaining in the center of the
a to discern regular outlines—
s. In the sandy surroundings,
nost like an oversize concrete
unch center for a rocket ship
. . . or detonation control for

en't concrete, but some sort of
undecorated.
igging, shoveling sand into the
r. A cry from one side of the
m over. Kemsit had found an
y?
. they cleared away the rest of
n entrance," Gary Meyers said.
too narrow to send a bulldozer

against it." Daniel turned to Feretti. "Did you bring any demolition material?"

"You're going to blow your way in?" Sha'uri demanded in disbelief.

"And you were the one complaining about the way *I* was digging," Meyers said.

"I don't see a doorknob, and there's no keyhole— even if we had a key," Daniel replied. "What else is left?"

The other man shrugged. "Well, there's this."

Raising his fist, he brought it down, on the huge, inset slab of vitrified stone. "Knock, knock," he called. "Open sesame."

The panel began to tremble. Inside, ancient machinery groaned in protest. But the slab was definitely moving, rising up till it appeared almost as an awning sticking out from the sloping wall, providing shade for the opening it provided.

Not that the big black doorway needed any shade.

" 'Step into my parlor,' said the spider to the fly." Meyers said dubiously.

Sha'uri continued to stare at the outthrust awning-slab. "I imagine that thing could swing down much more quickly than it went up."

Daniel simply looked at them in annoyance. "As someone keeps reminding me, we don't have time to fool around. So with that in mind—"

He stepped into the dark doorway. But even so, he was holding his breath.

The air inside the fastness was cool and stuffy with millennia of dust. But it was breathable. Daniel was now joined by Meyers and Sha'uri, and a couple of the diggers. Deeper inside now, Daniel seemed to make out a faint light—or was it merely an afterimage on his retinas?

"Halt!" The voice boomed from the darkness, freezing Daniel in his tracks. It spoke in the high accents of ancient Egyptian, in the many-tongued roar of Ra's voice. "Do you come from Ushabti? What is the word of recognition?"

Daniel, Sha'uri, and Meyers stood where they were—whether through bravery or being frozen in fear, Daniel couldn't tell. Most of the Abydans recoiled at the sound of that horribly familiar voice, used to elicit instant obedience.

"You do not respond," the voice boomed again. "Measures must be taken. All subsidiary installations now energizing. Unless the word of recognition is given, every construction in the high heavens will be destroyed."

"W-wait a minute," Daniel said in English. Then he switched to ancient Egyptian. "Stay your hand!"

His plea got not farther. Gunfire erupted in the sunlight behind him.

CHAPTER 14
SHUTTLE DIPLOMACY

It was a mixed force of raiders roaring down the dune. The ones on trucks were mostly Kasim Firdusi's troops—followers of the mullah and ready to die. They fired their automatic weapons with wild abandon. Sheikh Faris Aban's people mainly rode camels, screaming at the top of their lungs. But their rifle fire was more deliberate—single shots, conservative of ammunition.

It had been difficult enough to find this camp in the trackless waste, especially without giving the infidels any suspicions that they were under surveillance. The mullah's intelligence assets on the coast had warned when the enemy cavalcade had set off. But even so, they had lost the intruders several times in this sea of sand. When they had finally located the camp, they'd nearly been spotted themselves by a low-flying helicopter. Firdusi had organized his men and the sheikh's at the nearest oasis, then struck cross-country to launch an attack.

The situation looked promising. Most of the strangers were in the huge hole they'd been excavating in the sand. If the attackers could only keep them trapped there, the enemy would be in the palm of Firdusi's hand.

The thin picket line of guards had been breached easily. Firdusi allowed himself a wolflike smile as the camp's satellite dish—and the frantic radio operator—were erased in mid-message by a small rocket.

But the remaining guards and diggers proved to be made of sterner stuff. At the first shots, earthmoving machinery came boiling out of the excavation while Firdusi's trucks were still plowing across the sand to take up positions to command the site.

One bulldozer raised its blade as an improvised shield against his people's fire as it moved to intercept the lead truck. The earthmover came on like a tank as one of Firdusi's truck drivers panicked, trying to swerve away. Instead, he merely presented a broadside target to the bulldozer operator.

Engine roaring, the heavy construction machine leapt forward to ram the truck, overturning it. Firdusi ground his teeth as the crowded truck toppled, tossing men like toys and crushing many of them.

Biting back an imprecation, Firdusi ordered the driver of his command jeep to halt, snatching up one of the precious rocket tubes they carried. He stood in his seat, aimed, and fired, ignoring the yells of the camel-riding bedouins behind him as they scattered to avoid the back-blast.

Firdusi's antitank rocket hit the curved blade of the bulldozer and detonated. The shaped charge spewed a bolt of white-hot gases through the steel blade and into the engine beyond. A second later the bulldozer went up in a fireball.

But another earthmover lumbered up behind it, with diggers clinging to every possible handhold. At first Firdusi thought they were trying to escape. Instead, they spilled off at his stricken truck, seizing up the AK-47s from the dead, dispatching the wounded and stunned survivors with pickaxes and stealing their weapons as well.

In seconds counterfire shattered the windshields of two more trucks. In one, the driver managed to duck and swing the truck away. The other driver lolled out the window as his vehicle, laden with men, rolled to the lip of the dig and disappeared.

Gunfire and screams erupted in the pit, out of Firdusi's sight. Then came ominous silence—until more sweat-stained foreigners appeared, also carrying Soviet-made assault rifles.

A bullet whistled past Firdusi's ear, eliciting a scream from one of the bedouin, who toppled from the back of his camel.

The attackers were suddenly backpedaling as the diggers and a few uniformed guards turned the area around their camp into a killing field. Firdusi swore in disbelief. The supposed day laborers moved and fired as well as any regular troops, quickly finding defensive positions behind earthmovers, the wrecked truck, even dead bodies.

Their marksmanship was even more disconcerting. Bullets whined off the frame of the jeep as the defenders began aiming at an apparent leader.

Firdusi's driver gunned the engine abruptly into reverse, nearly tossing his leader onto the hood.

"Who are those sons of Shaitan?" the terrorist leader swore as he jounced in undignified retreat.

Feretti sighed in relief as the attackers pulled back. They'd made a shambles of his security arrangements, killing off his squad of guards on the sand mountain. Luckily, the night crew sacking out in the camp had turned out with rifles at the ready. And the bad guys apparently hadn't expected the Abydans to get involved.

But all of the diggers were members of Skaara's militia, alumni of the fierce fighting on their home planet. They hadn't run—they'd struck back.

Kemsit had just about blunted the attack single-handedly, ramming that truck. Feretti shook his head. That rocket was damned bad news. They could have used Kemsit in round two of this match.

The marine fed a fresh magazine into his M-16 and examined the tactical situation. Those attackers who would move had headed back up the sand mountain.

Feretti's marines and the Abydans were mopping up in the camp, where a couple of unhorsed (un-cameled?) guys in flowing robes were trying to hold out among the tents.

On the plus side, the defenders had accounted for two out of five of the attackers' trucks. They'd recaptured the camp, with its supply of ammunition, food . . . and water. Feretti drew a breath through his teeth as he saw the pattern of bullet holes across one of the tanker trailers, precious water leaking away into the thirsty sands.

We all may end up pretty thirsty before this ends,

the marine thought. Item one on the debit side, along with their casualties and their lost radio link. Had they been able to get out word of the attack to the satellite above?

If not, no one would know they were in trouble until their evening call-in time. That just might be unacceptably late.

The good guys had won the first battle, but the enemy still had the advantage in numbers—and position. From their vantage points up on the sand mountain, they overlooked the entire camp, and even the punch bowl depression the expedition had dug.

They could snipe us mercilessly, Feretti thought, and launch another attack whenever they wanted.

And there definitely would be another attack. Feretti already knew that this was no mere bedouin incursion. The guys on the trucks were all in Western clothes—city Arabs. They were well armed with assault and hand-carried rockets.

Terrorists, no doubt about it. Feretti had no idea which faction they represented. He did know the bastards had taken it on the chin when their surprise attack turned out more surprising than they'd expected.

Feretti stared up the sand mountain, where movement showed that the other side was setting up observation and sniper positions.

Definitely round two coming up, he thought. Whoever was in charge up there must want whatever we found pretty badly.

The marine ran a tongue along already dry lips. One thing was certain. Things would only get worse before this was over.

* * *

Jack O'Neil stepped into General West's office without even knocking. A sheet of flimsy paper shook in his grip. "Radio message from our people in Saudi Arabia. They're under attack—then the transmission broke off."

The general frowned. "In that part of the world, there are only about forty-seven groups that could be responsible. Terrorists, counterterrorists, or maybe even some locals playing cowboy and bedouin."

"What are we going to do, sir?"

"I don't see there's much we can do, Colonel—except send it up through channels."

Daniel Jackson tried to push away the tumult behind him—God, was that an explosion?—as he confronted the mechanized guardian of Set's fastness. No, not just a fastness, but the apparent nerve center for a world-girdling set of unimaginable weapons installations. Professor Moench will be delighted to have his theory validated. Too bad it would be at the cost of Earth's defense system.

Taking a deep breath, he spoke in ancient Egyptian—the tongue of Ra. "I do not come from Ushabti—but his name remains—'He who speaks.' But who is he? For whom does he speak?"

The voice was silent for a moment. "Ushabti speaks for the Setim."

"There are no Setim on this planet," Daniel replied. "The only Setim I have ever seen were on the *Boat of a Million Years.* How long has it been since *you* heard from them?"

"No communication for eight thousand, three hundred and thirty-nine solar revolutions," the emotionless voice admitted. "Overheard communications suggest they were sent to the planet Ombos."

"Ombos?" Daniel exclaimed. "That's where Hathor exterminated the colonists!"

"Signal intelligence seem to indicate so," the voice agreed.

"Then, how could you expect—?" Daniel abruptly broke off. This had to be a computer, for lack of a more accurate term. Some kind of relic left to wait. It merely followed its programming. If that programming called for it to wait for Ushabti, well what was eight thousand years, more or less?

"Does your signal intelligence also indicate other revolts?" he asked.

"Local inhabitants rebelled some two hundred years later," the computer replied. "Electromagnetic transmissions ceased until approximately one hundred years ago."

"But those were not in any language you knew."

"That is correct."

"That is because the empire of Ra ceased to exist on the planet Earth." Daniel could feel sweat trickling down his back. How could he convince this blasted relic not just to spare the ironmongery in orbit, but to join the battle on the Earthlings' side?

"What is your function?"

"To maintain the weapons systems, and, upon orders from Ushabti, coordinate their use for defense against the hostile spacecraft commanded by Ra."

"Ra is dead," Daniel said. "But there is a hostile spacecraft coming to Earth." He paused. "Did your signals intelligence name who exterminated the Setim colonists?"

"Transmissions indicated the Lady Hathor," the computer answered.

"That's who's coming—aboard the *Boat of a Million Years*. If Ushabti was against Hathor, shouldn't you help us?"

"Probabilities are high that Ushabti was murdered by Hathor."

"How do you compute that?" Daniel demanded.

"Signal—"

"Intelligence," Daniel finished. "Very well. Logic should dictate that you help us battle the enemies of Ushabti."

The voice was silent for a moment. "Insufficient information," it finally said. "I wish to know more about the history of the human inhabitants of this planet."

Daniel sighed. "This would be a good time to turn up a laptop computer with an encyclopedia CD-ROM."

General West put down the phone with an audible bang. "Those State Department bastards never use one word when a dozen will do," he growled at Jack O'Neil. "Boiled down, they've encountered diplomatic problems. The Saudi government has told us that this is an internal affair. But they're not doing anything—either they're dithering, or some faction has hamstrung their response. I think it's choice B—

several other countries have suddenly refused to let us use their airspace."

O'Neil frowned. "So we can't even get anybody over there to help."

"Not unless you can just drop them out of the sky."

"Drop . . ." Jack repeated. "Suppose I could, General?"

West stared as if his subordinate had suddenly gone out of his mind.

"It would require our special unit at Vandenberg. And some volunteers from NASA."

Sudden comprehension dawned on the general's face. "I'll see what I can do in the way of string-pulling at NASA. You see Kawalsky. It will have to be a strictly volunteer mission."

O'Neil shrugged. "Feretti is one of the people in trouble. I don't doubt that Kawalsky will volunteer."

Lieutenant Kawalsky's face took on an extra glow as he saluted for O'Neil. "Welcome to Space Marine headquarters, sir!"

"That's not the official name for this outfit, Lieutenant."

"No, sir," Kawalsky agreed. "It's just what everybody calls us. We've been going through the same preflight training that the astronauts get. Including repeated aerobatics rides on the KC-135—"

"Better known as the 'Vomit Comet,' " O'Neil finished. The aircraft would climb, then go into tight parabolic turns, offering a taste of free fall on its downward dives. From what O'Neil had heard, that first "taste" was of somebody's last meal, coming back up.

Kawalsky and his unit were being trained for deployment in space, in case shuttles or orbiting stations needed to be defended—or boarded. The marines were learning to use pressure suits and the energy rifles developed from weapons captured from Ra's Horus guards.

"What have you learned, working in zero gravity?" O'Neil asked.

"That it's amazing what the leads from blast-rifle can get snagged on when they float around like loose spaghetti," Kawalsky answered promptly. The energy weapons were powered by a heavy backpack battery, connecting by wire to the business end—a unit about the size of a sawed-off shotgun. Kawalsky had used the weapon on Abydos. But he'd obviously had a lot to learn when floating with the weapon in midair.

"How would you and your people like to put what you've learned to practical use?" O'Neil asked. He proceeded to outline the situation in Saudi Arabia. "It's strictly a volunteer mission," he warned. "And it will all depend on whether we can get the use of a shuttle to avoid the banned airspace."

"I'll talk to the others." With his weight lifter's body, the lieutenant could probably elicit voluntary service just by looming over his chosen victim. "If Feretti has gotten his ass in a crack, it's the least we can do."

"Daniel Jackson is down there, too," O'Neil added.

A muscle quirked in Kawalsky's face. "Why am I not surprised to hear that, sir?"

* * *

Shortly afterward O'Neil called Washington to report that the Space Marines had all volunteered for a rescue mission.

"You're in luck, Colonel," West's voice came over the phone. "One of the new shuttles has just been fitted for combat, and they're about to start testing. The commander is an ex-navy pilot and might be willing to lend a hand. His name is Antonelli—Neil Antonelli."

Daniel and Sha'uri clung to one another, their breath coming in tight gasps as their bodies writhed in passion. Sha'uri's pale skin seemed to glow in the darkness, her flesh soft but sturdy . . . and very, very active.

There was a frantic quality to their coupling, as if they feared interruption at any moment. No time for encouragement, endearments, or words at all.

The blood pounded in Daniel's temples as they raced together toward climax. Then the moment came—Sha'uri gave a great, wounded cry—

And Daniel awoke with a convulsive shudder, his body sitting bolt upright seemingly without his conscious command.

He looked around in the darkness, momentarily confused. Then the memories of the day came flooding back. Daniel put a hand to his throat, which still ached from his ever hoarser discourse on human history. The ancient system had been particularly interested in the rise of Islam and the crusades.

In brief side conversations, Daniel had also heard about the present-day march of Islam against himself and his companions. He'd asked the relic if it had local defenses, but if the machine did, it had refused to activate them. Perhaps it was waiting to see who won.

Daniel lay back in the darkness, trying to compose himself for sleep. From somewhere nearby came the sound of deep feminine breathing, not quite a snore, which Daniel immediately recognized. Once upon a time he'd heard it every night. Sha'uri.

Perhaps that was the subliminal cue that had precipitated the erotic dream. Or perhaps it was catching a trace of her scent. Daniel released a sigh that was more like a groan. Thank God he'd awakened before he'd disgraced himself!

Daniel closed his eyes, then heard bumbling footsteps—and caught a size twelve desert boot right in the short ribs. He flung himself upright again as Gary Meyers stumbled back and apparently managed to kick Sha'uri, too.

"What?" her sleep-fogged voice demanded in Abydan.

"Sorry, sorry," Gary responded in both Abydan and English. "I had to step out for a moment, to . . . uh . . ."

"To answer nature's call," Sha'uri finished for him in some annoyance.

"Um, yeah. Figured it would be better to do it late at night. I remember reading an old Byzantine military manual that the Arabs didn't like to fight at night—"

The silence outside the vitrified stone walls was abruptly shattered by automatic weapons fire.

"Sounds like things have changed since the fall of the Byzantine Empire," Daniel dryly observed. "Now, could we *please* get a little sleep? Or maybe *you'll* be the one to try and describe the Industrial Revolution using only ancient Egyptian tomorrow."

From his observation post high on the sand mountain, Kasim Firdusi scanned the defensive positions in the camp below.

"The infidels must have been busy all night," Sheikh Faris Aban said as he stood beside the terrorist leader. "I could hear their earthmovers. Look at the walls of sand they've raised."

"It will do them no good," Firdusi said confidently. "We still have them outnumbered. A determined attack, and we could push them back to the excavation and capture that building they've uncovered."

"We?" the sheikh asked. "Your followers took terrible losses from these defenders you disparage. An additional attack will be borne by my people. Besides, if the king's troops arrive—"

"That will not happen, Sheikh. The mullah has followers in the government. They will ensure that neither the military nor the troops of the Great Satan will intervene—"

But the sheikh was no longer listening. "What is that up there?" he asked, pointing.

Commander Neil Antonelli spoke into his microphone. "Okay, we're coming down. Believe me, reentry was a much bigger deal before antigravity drive."

Beside him, the copilot was calling up images from the spy satellite they'd deployed before beginning their descent. "There's some sort of activity by one of the trucks." He focused in. "That's a handheld missile!"

"Looks like we get a serious field test." Antonelli hit the controls to open the shuttle's payload doors. "Hold on tight, back there." He sent the shuttle nose-down.

"Aiming," Christy Manville reported. She'd volunteered for this mission the moment she'd heard of it. From her position on the mid-deck, she watched a TV monitor, moving a set of crosshairs with a computer mouse. The crosshairs centered on the truck. Out in the payload bay, a skeletal construction that looked more like a crane than a weapon swung to cover the target.

The blast-cannon spat a foot-wide bolt of energy. The cab of the truck exploded, and a second later, so did the vehicle's gas tank, taking out both the missile crew and anyone else in the vicinity.

Even so, a few intrepid souls began firing rifles up at the advancing shuttle. In the mid-deck Jack O'Neil got on the intercom to Antonelli. "We're down far enough that the air is breathable. Why not open the air lock and send out a fire team?"

Seconds later a quartet of Space Marines emerged into the payload area, all armed with blast-rifles. Climbing onto improvised fire steps on either side of the air lock, they hitched themselves to crew restraints and began firing downward.

Kasim Firdusi still stared at the apparition swooping down at his position, spitting fire. Who'd have thought that the infidels would risk one of their space shuttles. His lips writhed in silent curses.

* * *

Behind him, Sheikh Faris Aban slipped a knife from the sash around his waist. "We are too late," he declared as he shoved the blade into the terrorist's back. "The djinn are already loose."

CHAPTER 15
A DOOR CLOSES

After being officially debriefed, Daniel Jackson sat in General West's Washington office. Beside him, Jack O'Neil stood at rigid attention, as if he were expecting to get called to order for his own court-martial.

For a long moment West simply observed them from behind his desk. Muscles quirked at the sides of his usually expressionless mouth. "Between you and your friend here, you've given the State Department enough work to round out the century," he said to Daniel. "Words like 'saber-rattling' and 'gunboat diplomacy' are flying around. Even our nominal allies are alarmed."

"I guess they would be, sir," O'Neil said.

"On the other hand, certain persons in the Pentagon are just about creaming their jeans over what you found in that dig."

"So I gathered while I was getting debriefed," Daniel said. "The general reaction was that we wasted a lot of money putting your orbital defenses into space."

"That initial euphoria will dim a little when they start to realize that none of those planetary defense installations are on our soil," West replied evenly. "Some of them are located in or near countries that aren't that friendly to us. And the controls are in Saudi Arabia, for chrissake."

He tempered his tone. "You did a good job there, Jackson, talking to that computer."

"It got easier, once the cavalry arrived and cleared out the bedouins and remaining terrorists. We were able to ferry in supporting documentation for my brief history of Earth's culture. And it didn't hurt to have the shuttle land in the vicinity. The control center's sensors could see that it *definitely* wasn't an udajeet."

Daniel hesitated for a moment.

"There's something else you want to say?" West prodded.

"Everyone is delighted with the additional fire-power, and I can't knock that," Daniel said. "But don't you think we're getting a little overconfident here?"

The skin around West's eyes tightened. "What are you saying?"

"As far as I was able to get from the computer, the system was set up to take out Ra's flying palace— which, as we now know, was just the ship's pinnace for the *Boat of a Million Years*."

Daniel glanced at the two military men. "I don't want to rain on anybody's victory parade. But Hathor is coming in a ship that's physically larger, with more powerful engines and unknown weaponry. Are you sure we can handle it?"

General West looked him in the eyes. "Frankly, Dr. Jackson, I don't know," he said in a formal voice. "But I won't say that outside of this room, and I hope you won't, either. I think you'll agree, we've been doing the best we can. This ancient ordnance certainly improves our chances."

Daniel nodded.

"We've also got to keep people's spirits up," West went on. "Now isn't the time to let doubt and fear get the upper hand. That way lies chaos."

Daniel shuddered, his mind going back to the final days on Abydos. "You have my word that I'll keep my doubts private, General," he promised.

West briefly inclined his head. "Then, I'll have done my job."

When they'd left the general's office, Daniel shot Jack O'Neil a questioning glance. "Forgive my inquiring mind," he said, "but West seemed in a sort of crepe-hanging mood. I thought he'd be happier over getting new guns."

"He thinks he's living on borrowed time," O'Neil replied. "As long as repelling Hathor was either a hopeless task or a possible hoax, it was a perfect—punishment—for West's freewheeling approach to Abydos. But now the hardware is in place, and you've found an entire planetary defense system—"

Daniel's face tightened. "It's become a plum."

O'Neil nodded. "West is figuring he'll be kicked out of the way."

"And you?"

O'Neil's shoulders rose in a shrug. "I may yet get to see the wonders of Tierra del Fuego by winter. How about you? Unless you have any more bright ideas, your job here is just about over."

"I'd thought of heading back to Saudi Arabia, but Sha'uri has taken over as the liaison at Planetary Defense Control." Daniel sighed at the thought of the farther distance between himself and his estranged wife. "It's a good idea, I suppose. We'd need a real native speaker of the imperial tongue to interface properly with the computer."

He gave his military friend a wry smile. "So I'm thinking of going back to the beginning—to Creek Mountain and the StarGate. Your pal Travis and Barbara Shore are beginning a new investigation of the Star-Gate apparatus. The information we pulled from the good ship *Ra's Eye* discusses some maintenance aspects on StarGates. And since I've gone the most places through the damned things, they'd like me in on it."

"Sounds good," O'Neil said.

"You mean it's good that I'll be safely under wraps as we finish up this countdown to disaster," Daniel said with a cynical smile. "Who knows? Maybe we'll find another combination—the cosmic phone number for another world. It might be useful to have a bolt-hole to escape to, if things don't go well with Hathor."

His smile became even more cynical. "And, considering the way I've shaken up the last two planets I've been on, it might be good for me to have a third world to head for if Hathor *doesn't* show. People will be pretty pissed with me on Earth."

Barbara Shore stepped into Daniel's office to find him poring through a sheaf of photocopied hiero-glyphics. "Hey, master translator, find anything interesting?" she inquired.

"I'm going to kill Gary Meyers' tame Egyptologists," Daniel growled. "Only one person has looked at this since it came in from Abydos. And that person just gave it a quick read through. According to his notes, it refers to the music of the spheres."

Barbara rested one hip on his desk. "It doesn't?"

Daniel shook his head. "As near as I can make out, it deals with 'fine-tuning' a StarGate."

Barbara stood bolt upright. "Do tell." She peered at the symbols. "But if you're having trouble, and you're the best we've got—"

"Let's just say that this one is more cryptic than most. It refers to a couple of dinguses that must have been eternally available, because there are no diagrams on how to make them. And most of the commentary uses technological terms that later came to refer to music. A literal translation would be that they 'sing together.' "

"Clear as East Texas mud," Barbara agreed sourly. " 'Sing together.' Could that mean harmonize? Something to do with harmonics?"

Rereading the document, Daniel looked more closely. "No, it's the golden quartz that sings together—or should that be resonates?"

Barbara began to get more interested. "These dinguses—are they supposed to be nearby?"

"Thousands of schene away, apparently." Daniel read on. " 'Beyond the sky, before the stars.' The reference seems to be to sending it pretty high up in an udajeet. Then there are ways you set up the StarGate to make the things sing."

"It sounds as if they're somehow calibrating the

StarGate. Tuning in on distant resonators . . ." Her voice died away, then she tapped her finger urgently on the sheets of copy paper. "You damn well better make sense of those funny pictures, mister. This could tell us the basic coordinate systems for all these magic donuts!"

With Daniel and Barbara cracking the whip, the translating staff winnowed the mountains of copied hieroglyphics for any references to singing StarGates. Images and the usual frustratingly vague diagrams were located for Daniel's "dinguses." Then, after agonizing attempts to design the resonators, Barbara used her clout with Colonel Travis to get the damned things built.

They were small-scale, almost handmade mechanisms, but the prototype technicians who had turned out the original blast-rifles were able to construct reasonable facsimiles of what Barbara wanted.

Daniel reached out to Jack O'Neil for help in getting the resonators into space. "Can General West help?" he asked.

"The ax fell," O'Neil replied over the phone. "West still has a resounding title, but no command. They've got him in Cheyenne Mountain, reorganizing the U.S. Space Command into a war room."

O'Neil paused. "But the old man still has contacts. Let me see what we can do."

"What about you?" Daniel asked.

"Call it the military equivalent of limbo," O'Neil replied. "I'm still on the general's staff, holding the fort here in Washington—until circumstances dictate my transfer."

The resonator packages did find their way into space, delivered by the fledgling shuttle defense fleet. Although the seven orbiters had all been equipped with antigravity drives and energy cannon, they were a long way from becoming effective space fighters.

So pilots were off on constant maneuvers, which made it easier to place the dinguses in various orbits.

But after their success in getting the resonators out there, the research team couldn't get them to resonate.

The floor of the Creek Mountain missile silo looked more like a military fortress than a research lab. Earth's StarGate link was protected by the best antiterrorist security forces, both from outside attack—and from attack through the gateway.

Heavy machine guns commanded the focus of the carved golden torus. Any person—or thing—materializing there would have its structural integrity severely threatened by sharing space-time coordinates with a hail of lead.

The technicians and monitoring crew had been moved off the silo floor completely. They now occupied the conference room where Daniel Jackson had gotten his first glimpse of the golden enigma that was the StarGate.

Once again Daniel looked down at the StarGate through the heavy Plexiglas panel that looked down on the silo floor from several stories up. Barbara had managed to regather the scattered technicians from the original StarGate project. It somehow seemed right to see Mitch Storey in his beard and beret powering up the dimensional portal.

But this time they weren't shifting the carved representations of ancient constellations and other signs into the coordinates for Abydos. Following the instructions Daniel had translated, they were moving the StarGate characters almost infinitesimally, trying to focus the gate's energies on one of the small packages of golden quartz orbiting thousands of miles overhead.

And once again they were failing, in no uncertain terms.

When the StarGate was powered up, a low, almost subsonic, vibration pervaded the entire area. As each coordinate was locked on, the vibration grew in power, until, when the interstellar connection was finally made, the harmonics resolved themselves into a beautiful tone.

That experience was not being reduplicated here. As the technicians maneuvered the golden torus in infinitesimal arcs, Daniel felt as if he were manipulating a giant radio dial, trying to tune in an elusive FM station.

Failure, however, did not mean static instead of beautiful music. The subsonic emanations from the gate shifted into subtle disharmonies. Even at this distance from the gateway, with a window and wall between him and the source of the vibrations, Daniel felt as if every filling in his mouth were being redrilled.

Barbara clutched her forehead. "Hey, Jackson, did your hieroglyphics make any mention of this lovely effect?"

The technicians on the floor made another minute

adjustment. Daniel's breath hissed between his teeth as a new throb went through him. "If it had, do you think I'd be standing here?"

Barbara made a brief, throat-cutting gesture to Mitch Storey. "Stand down," he gratefully called into his headset. The vibrations faded away.

"Screwed again," Barbara said pithily. "I expect the only result of this experiment was to make half the coyotes in the state howl their throats raw."

Weeks passed without any trace of success to buoy the researchers' spirits. After yet another set of careful tuning with excruciating results, Daniel sat in Barbara's office for a late-night postmortem, going over the hieroglyphic manuals for what seemed like the hundred and fiftieth time.

"I got a complaint from the security commander this time around," Barbara reported. "Apparently, the vibrations wakened his night-shift guards out of a sound sleep."

"I can live with that," Daniel replied. "Remember the time the vibrations began resonating with everyone's bowel-muscle contractions?"

Barbara buried her face in her hands. "Please," she moaned. "Everybody in a hundred yards, simultaneously getting an urgent case of the trots."

"Thank goodness we didn't have any distinguished visitors around. Suck the shit out of some of those Washington types, and you'd have nothing left."

He caught his reflection in the glass of a framed diploma and was shocked to see the death's-head grin on his features. Daniel had lost weight on this project.

It showed most of all in his face, where pressure had honed away the last of his boyish softness.

"God, what time is it?" Barbara stood and stretched. Failure had also taken its toll on her, Daniel realized. Her pose did interesting things to the jumpsuit she wore, but the suit wasn't as snug as it had been once upon a time.

She seemed to realize his eyes were on her and lowered her arms, clenching her hands into fists and massaging her back. "Damn, feels like every muscle I own has gone into gridlock," she groaned. "When they're this tight, only one thing I know settles them down."

The words seemed to hang between them in the air.

For a second, just a second, Daniel considered the opportunity this very attractive woman was offering.

"I think that's frustration talking," he finally said carefully. "If you'd been talking this way back when I first came on board the StarGate project ..." He shrugged. "But now ..."

"Sha'uri." Barbara spoke the name gently.

"Sha'uri," Daniel said with a nod.

"It's been how many months since she hung you up to dry?" Barbara gently touched his elbow. "You know what they say about that—better to be hung as a sheep than a lamb."

"Hanged," Daniel corrected pedantically. "I know that when Hathor was spying on Abydos as an undercover, Sha'uri thinks she got under the covers with me. Lord knows Hathor tried, and it was pretty tempting." His lips twisted in a rough approximation of a smile. "But I guess I was lucky. The one time I might have fallen, Hathor found the amulet I was wearing—the key to the StarGate. So instead of getting the girl, I got the Vulcan nerve pinch."

"Did you explain all that to Sha'uri?"

"I'd say she wasn't really receptive," Daniel said, "and I'm not sure that I blame her. I failed her on Abydos. But since we came back here through the StarGate, everything I've done, I've done for Sha'uri." His voice got fierce. "I *won't* fail her again."

For a long moment Barbara looked at him in silence. Then she said, "I wish I had someone—anyone— who'd do the same for me."

The sensor package hung in space, out beyond the orbit of Neptune. Although it was the outermost, first line of defense, it had been the last element built and set into place. The underground relic in Saudi Arabia had offered diagrams—*proper* diagrams—for the circuits needed to detect Ra's space-warp drive.

That was lucky, because the originally planned detectors would have been too short-range to be of much use.

Detector components had to be fabricated out of the precious golden quartz, then hooked up to a small antigravity engine and boosted at top power to the outer solar system.

It braked in the void and then simply kept its position, with nothing between it and Alpha Centauri.

At least there *had* been nothing.

But, after some weeks, delicate circuits on board responded to a distant twisting in the fabric of the universe.

The sensor pack's engines burst into brief life one

more time, orienting the detectors directly at the oncoming space warp.

After the engines shut off, the unit would rely on passive sensors to observe the approach of the *Boat of a Million Years.* The huge vessel dropped out of warp and proceeded on antigravity drive. The sensor package computed speed, size, and course, encoded the data, and then pumped a tight-beam burst transmission to sensors farther in-system along the vessel's projected route. These would in turn orient themselves on the advancing behemoth and relay the data to Earth.

Then the sensor unit shut itself down. By the time the *Boat of a Million Years* passed, it was merely a small, inert lump of matter.

It had done its job.

Watching another abortive fine-tuning experiment on the StarGate, Daniel Jackson grit his teeth as another vibratory twinge went through his molars. "More static," he muttered in disgust.

Barbara Shore, also wincing, turned to him. "Static?" she said.

"This has always reminded me of trying to tune a radio to a faint, faraway station," Daniel explained, feeling a little lame. "Instead of music—"

"We get interference," she finished for him, frowning in concentration. "You know, in cosmic terms, those resonators we put into orbit aren't all that far away. It's a shame we had to depend on the shuttles to place the dinguses, because that meant they were somewhat closer than that hieroglyphic manual said they should be. The highest the shuttles can do is about six thousand miles out."

"I don't—" Daniel began.

"From a thousand kilometers to ten thousand kilometers—that's about six hundred to six thousand miles—lie the Van Allen radiation belts." She winced again at a particularly bad surge of vibrational static. "Maybe we are getting interference."

She turned to Mitch Storey. "What's the orbital period on our farthest resonator?"

Storey punched keys on a computer. "It's a little less than six hours—and it will be overhead in about twenty minutes."

"Cancel this test. We're going to concentrate on that outermost sucker. Use the settings we'd been trying on the *closest* resonators, then work your way out."

Under Storey's orders, technicians scurried and the great outer wheel of the golden torus began to revolve to a different set of coordinates. All that remained was to enter the final hieroglyph—the one for Earth.

Storey watched a readout on his computer, counting down the seconds. "Okay—it's in position," he reported.

"Then hit it!" Barbara commanded.

A high, thin whine came from the StarGate, combining all the worse aspects of nails on a blackboard with a dentist's drill.

"Well, this is different," Daniel said over the noise.

"Tune that bastard," Barbara cried. "Tune it!"

Operating his keyboard with the most delicate of touches, Mitch Storey sent almost infinitesimal surges of power to the rollers controlling the movement of the outer torus. Back and forth the great wheel moved, as he minutely changed each coordinate. Sometimes the interference got worse. But as he kept fiddling, the earsplitting quality of the sound diminished.

And then the sound wasn't just noise, it was the clear harmonic of the StarGate in operation.

"Lock that into the computer!" Barbara shouted, pounding on Daniel's shoulder. "I'd do this to Mitch, but I don't want to joggle his elbow right now."

"It's entered," Storey said.

"We did it! We did it!" Barbara shrieked, spinning Daniel in an impromptu dance.

"I'm glad you've had some success," a familiar voice said, cutting over the sounds of celebration.

Barbara, Daniel, and the technicians turned to find Colonel Jack O'Neil in the doorway, backed by a squad of marines. "I'm afraid we have to close you down."

"What are you talking about?" Barbara said pugnaciously. "We're finally getting a handle on this coordinate business—"

"The outer detection line reported a blip—a *large* blip—heading our way."

Daniel swallowed. "So. It's started."

"Things have suddenly become much more real to the Joint Chiefs—like the possibility of an incursion through the StarGate. They want me to insert a metal plug into the focus of the gate to block anything from coming through." O'Neil paused. "We're also setting up canisters to flood the whole silo area with nerve gas. If the Horus guards manage to come through—"

"They get a sarin cocktail," Daniel finished.

"Couldn't happen to a nicer bunch of guys," Barbara said cold-bloodedly.

"But it means you'll have to vacate—at once." O'Neil's square-jawed face was set like concrete—a soldier doing his job.

Daniel looked at Barbara. They'd already been through a scene like this when they'd proven the Star-Gate worked only to be thrown out on security grounds. "Déjà vu all over again."

CHAPTER 16
GUNS

The news of the enemy's arrival came to space station *Mir* during the dinner break. An urgent voice rattled from the control console at the far end of the main module, "This is Case Red, I say again, Case Red!"

Oleg Kuzma, one of the caretaker cosmonauts, glanced over at the two military men who'd come aboard. "This sounds like bad news," he said in Russian.

"The worst," Colonel Grigori Vorodin agreed. "It means the enemy has been detected."

"Or that we're undergoing a most annoying drill," growled Vorodin's co-commander, an American colonel named Allen Balent. The search for military personnel to serve on the space platforms had been rigorous. Each platform had two weapons officers, of high rank, one each from the U.S. and the Russian Federation. Balent had won the junior's position on *Mir* thanks to a pair of refugee parents. His Russian was as good as that spoken by the cosmonauts.

Both colonels went for the recently installed weapons consoles.

"No countermanding order has been sent," Vorodin

said, punching buttons. "I am activating the Orbital Weapons Platforms."

"Our own weapons systems are operational," Balent reported from his board.

Vorodin turned to the cosmonauts. "Don your space suits. Then I will put on mine, then Balent."

"Begging the colonel's pardon, but I think you should don yours first of all," Balent said. "In the absence of information about the enemy's arrival, one fire-control officer should be in a position to operate our weapons, even if the structural integrity of the station is breached."

He met Vorodin's eyes. "This is a case of commanders first, sir."

The Russian colonel made a face as if he were swallowing very bitter medicine. "Very well. Kuzma, monitor the detection systems. Galitsky and I will suit up."

"Not that I know why we're bothering," Nikolai Galitsky muttered to himself. "If they get a hit that breaches the bulkheads, that should be enough to vaporize us all."

The two stations continued in their orbits, *Mir* sinking below the horizon to cover the Western Hemisphere, *Freedom* swinging around to extend its protection over the eastern half of the Earth.

Astronaut Deke Farnham sat at the detection boards. "We've got the enemy on the display," his voice crackled in the crew's helmet speakers. "And it's a big mother!"

"Calculate how long it will take to reach extreme

missile range," Colonel Craig Hastings ordered. He turned to his number two, Colonel Valeri Rodenko. "We have no idea of the countermeasures the enemy may have available. I want to try a general launch, one missile each from all our OWPs."

"These are dumb missiles, sir," Rodenko responded in only slightly accented English. "They'll have exhausted their fuel. All the enemy has to do is avoid their flight vectors—"

"Then, at least we'll know something about the enemy's evasive capabilities. If they don't duck, we may be able to overwhelm them. It's worth a shot."

"Yes, sir." Rodenko got to work on his console. "Entering target for all available OWPs. Programming firing orders for distance of four thousand miles."

After a moment he said, "Input and transmitted."

"Prepare for execution on my command," Hastings said.

"Course projection holding steady, Colonel," Farnham reported.

His backup, Ron Dessarian, confirmed from his board. "They're almost on your mark, sir."

A moment of tense silence followed as the intruding spacecraft continued closer to Earth. Then both men cried almost in unison. "Target within range!"

Hastings took a deep breath. "On my command— fire!"

Seventy-two weapons platforms swung slightly in their orbits, focusing on an area of what was now empty space. Soon enough, the trespassing space-dreadnought would occupy that spot. Launch structures shuddered slightly as the engines of former intercontinental ballistic missiles suddenly flared, boosting their cargoes to accelerations just slightly below one mile per second.

Behind his helmet visor, Craig Hastings' face was an impassive mask. It would be at least an hour before that flight of missiles arrived, each loosing eight warheads into the enemy's course. Such a cloud of destruction must turn the invading ship into radioactive vapor, or at least render it a lifeless hulk.

His fists clenched in their protective gauntlets. If not . . .

"Continue to monitor the enemy's course," he ordered. "If there's any sign of deviation, I want another flight of missiles ready."

Seated behind his targeting board in the fire-control section of the *Boat of a Million Years*, Nekhti stared in astonishment at the holographic display. The closer they came to Earth, the more orbiting hardware was detected and entered into the image glowing at eye level.

Nekhti felt his hackles raise, and an incipient snarl wrinkled his muzzle. He could scarcely credit what he was seeing. According to his father and the Elders of the Setim, their homeworld Tuat had once been ringed by minor satellites in this way. They had conveyed communications, monitored weather patterns, even conducted detailed surveys of the ground below—before the ecological disaster that had slowly worked to render Tuat uninhabitable.

But those forays into space had required a substantial technological base and years of effort. What was all this ironmongery doing in orbit around an undeveloped world like Earth?

Had Ra finally listened to Ushabti's pleas and allowed some of his technology to filter down to the lesser humans? But the transfer must have been massive, and the humans incredibly apt pupils to put so many objects in orbit in so short a time. A technological society must have spread all across the globe from Ra's initial landing point by the great river.

Yet technology would also mean a better living standard. So why had the mass of humans revolted?

Nekhti reviewed his memories of the holo-records that Lady Hathor had shown of the rising. The Ramses guards had carried only wooden batons, their traditional weapons. The fellahin rioters had used the usual improvised weapons of a mob—farm equipment, clubs, stones, even fists. There had been no sign of enhanced technology evident on either side.

What could that mean? Were the rebellious fellahin manual workers left behind by the march of progress, trying to tear down something that appeared to be their livelihoods? Had the keys of technology been passed to the masked human godlings who clustered around Ra? In such hands there would surely be inequities enough to rouse even the most sheep-like farmworker to rebellion.

But the question that had troubled Nekhti from the moment he saw the holos remained. How had the rebels succeeded? If they were ignorant of the mechanisms that allowed Ra such power, how could they overthrow them?

Furious crowds might overwhelm and slaughter the baton-wielding Ramses guards. But they would have to suffer serious losses to tackle a Horus guard with his blast-lance. And how could they hope to deal with a strafing udajeet?

Perhaps it would be possible to coordinate a rising while all the udajeets were grounded in a single locality, like Egypt. But all that orbital ironmongery argued a more widespread base than Ra's original toe-hold. Success in one location would be met with vengeful udajeet squadrons from other locales. A worldwide attack argued either considerable sophistication on the part of the rebels—or Setim involvement.

Teeth showed under Nekhti's muzzle. Hathor's whole story had smelled somehow wrong. Were they being brought to put down a rebellion of their own people?

Yet, again, the artificial satellites would seem to show a sharing of technology. That was one of the things Ushabti and the older Setim had argued for— that, and a world of their own. If *that* promise had been repudiated . . .

But the bargain that had bound the Setim had been a long way from fulfillment when Nekhti and his mates had boarded the *Boat of a Million Years*. Ra's rule had been established in Egypt, but not over the whole planet.

Attaining that goal would have taken long years. Long enough to fill Earth's orbit with machines?

Nekhti had to face a single, supremely unsettling question. How long had he and the rest of the crew actually been in stasis?

According to Hathor and the readily available ship's records, little more than half a score of years had elapsed. But Nekhti's surreptitious forays into the computer had turned up . . . anomalies.

He'd been infuriated at how much of the computer systems had been declared off-limits for the crew. Did Hathor expect sabotage from within? Did she not realize that there was a difference between concern for the miserable situation of the fellahin and support for rebels who would kill Setim?

Some of the interdicted data seemed of little help to anyone trying to hinder the progress of the *Boat of a Million Years*. Whole directories of maintenance records, for instance, were prohibited from Nekhti's access. He could not read them, but he had insinuated a utility program which showed that enormous files worth of data lay behind the interdict.

Nekhti had no idea what size those files had been when he had begun his service to Ra. But if they recorded the minimum operation of the ship's systems while crews remained in stasis, the history of the *Boat of a Million Years* must be long indeed.

Circuitous checking of files more directly used in the ship's housekeeping provided clues that again disputed with Hathor's tale. A systems calibration check accomplished only four times a century was listed as just recently accomplished. Yet a similar check had occurred when Nekhti and his crewmates had just boarded this vessel.

Something was definitely wrong with the timescale of their period in stasis. The amount of material floating in space before them only made the incongruities in the records more palpable.

Nekhti pulled his attention back and realized that a change had taken place on the display before him.

Before, the images of the orbiting mechanisms had been colored a pale green, roughly translating as "enemy artifact, potentially hostile."

Now an entire constellation of satellites glared out in the blazing green that categorized them as definitely hostile. Stretching from each of the newly identified enemies was a flight path, bright orange denoting the space already traversed, a paler shade showing the predicted vector. All vectors coincided on the projected location for the *Boat of a Million Years.*

Orders lashed through the Detection and Imaging crews, demands for information. Hieroglyphs began to crawl through the air beneath Nekhti's holographic representation. Size, speed, estimated propulsion—

Chemical rockets? Why would anyone use such expensive and slow engines?

Radiation emissions detected from on board the advancing motes. Nekhti whined in disbelief at Fire Control's analysis. Multiple-warhead thermonuclear weapons?

During the all-too-short breaks between gunnery practice, Nekhti and his crewmates had speculated about the coming battle with the terrestrial rebels. Most had envisaged it as a long-range affair. The *Boat of a Million Years* would serve as an untouchable safe harbor, receiving udajeets ferrying refugees from the more vulnerable havens . . . and, of course, acting as a stratospheric firebase directing its armament on the larger rebel formations.

It seemed a reasonable enough theory, based as it was on the example of the empire's earliest wars with certain intransigent tribes. Udajeets would harry would-be invaders, herding them against a fixed position of Horus guards with their blast-lances. If the enemy force was large enough, Ra's flying palace came overhead to add its firepower. A few survivors were allowed to escape and spread the word. This not only stopped present invasions, but pacified neighbors, making assimilation much easier.

The tactical traditionalists had been quite amused at gunnery simulations against computer adversaries with varying degrees of technical advancement. Now Nekhti saw why. Instead of mattocks, sickles, clubs, and a few liberated blast-lances, the rebels of Earth had much greater resources. Why hadn't Hathor explained this?

How *could* anyone explain the hodgepodge of technologies the rebels seemed to be deploying? The weapons platforms carried both chemical rockets and a blast-cannon similar to the ones in the battery Nekhti controlled. Why supplement one weapons system with another so much cruder?

The display now showed a flock of antigravity craft, larger and considerably slower than udajeets.

Nekhti guessed they were hybrid craft, udajeet engines grafted on to other bodies. But the weapons platforms were obviously designed specially for their roles. How had the fellahin been able to develop and emplace so many so soon after their rebellion?

It had to be reckoned a remarkable achievement— yet, somehow, a pointless one. If all the orbiting metal were of some military use, it still wouldn't be enough to stop the *Boat of a Million Years*.

The motes on the tracking display continued to crawl closer. Hieroglyphics sped by, announcing that most had consumed all their fuel and were continuing on ballistically.

Then came the orders. Secondary batteries were to serve as point defense. Nekhti received his targeting instructions. No. These would never stop the *Boat of a Million Years*.

Shuttle *Endeavor* achieved station five hundred miles above the Earth, its nose pointed at the oncoming invader. Commander Neil Antonelli brought the vessel to rest, awaiting the rest of the tiny shuttle flotilla. To avoid a Pearl Harbor scenario, the orbiters had been scattered around the globe for safety.

Antonelli watched the display on his computer and radar consoles as the other vessels scrambled into position. They moved with incredible speed and precision. He'd never expected to see flying refrigerators move more like fighter planes.

The question was, would they be nimble enough to survive the coming fight?

Every officer at the helm of these babies was military trained, most of them ex-fighter jocks. During the maneuvers to familiarize them with the capabilities of their reconstructed craft, Antonelli had come to know his fellow commanders and their copilots, as tactical mates . . . and as friends.

No one was playing hot pilot, trying flashy maneuvers. The orbiters were all business as they rose and adopted a line-abreast formation.

Antonelli activated his mike. "Gunnery."

Christy Manville responded. "Yes, sir."

The payload specialist had developed into an excellent fire-control officer. Antonelli was glad he'd been able to keep her as a member of his crew. "Open payload-bay doors."

Even with her advanced propulsion system, the shuttle needed those doors open for heat-exchange purposes.

They also had to be open to deploy the orbiter's weaponry systems. Sliding up from the shuttle's former cargo area was a latticework construction that held the best armaments Earth's mind had been able to assemble. A half-dozen missiles powered with tiny antigravity engines rode on launch rails clustered around the crane-like body of a heavy blast cannon.

It still felt strange to be carrying weapons in an area that had been supposedly demilitarized for more than thirty years. And even stranger to maneuver in sync with pilots who had been enemies not so long ago.

An order from Space Command crackled in Antonelli's ear.

"Everybody ready?" he asked into his mike.

One by one the responses came. *Discovery, Atlantis,*

Buran-1, *Ptichka*, the second Buran-style shuttle, incongruously named *"Little Bird." Enterprise* and *Columbia* All reported themselves ready for combat.

"Assume Formation Bravo," Antonelli commanded.

The line of shuttles turned into an arrowhead with *Endeavour* at the point.

Steadily accelerating, they took up a position midway between *Freedom*'s orbit and the outer ring of OWPs. Antonelli still kept his craft's nose aimed straight at the enemy. "Backfield in motion," he muttered. "Get ready to rumble."

On the bridge of the *Boat of a Million Years*, Hathor sat enthroned in the captain's chair, a seat built for a creature somewhat taller than her height. Her head was craned back, staring at the air above her head. The vessel's grand tactical display put to shame any other holograms she'd ever seen before—and she had seen the best that Ra's empire had to offer.

The huge vessel's computers had allowed her to play god on Abydos, bestriding a virtual-reality battlefield where the foot soldiers had been like ants and their vehicles like water bugs. Extending a pointed finger had triggered heavy batteries of blast-cannon. It had been a heady experience, but merely an improvisation, a useful interface while she was controlling the ship only with automated systems.

With the crew out of stasis, however, the grand tactical display offered a more abstract representation of the near space around the planet Earth—though it was considerably more detailed than any other she'd used.

Hathor stared in quiet amazement at the number of artifacts in orbit. Two good-size installations floated in the lower orbital areas, their icons shifting from potential threats to active ones as weapons were detected. Numerous weapons platforms held higher orbits, while an intermediate group of flickering sparks represented a mobile force, operating on antigravity drives.

They couldn't have salvaged that many udajeets, she thought, considering the battlefield. Most of those must have been fabricated from nothing but samples and manuals.

Almost unwillingly, she felt a certain admiration for these rogue fellahin. The profusion of objects in orbit showed that they couldn't all have been put in place with antigravity. These people had been reaching into space without the aid of Ra's technology.

They could learn, she thought, which is a good thing. But their defenses were still crude enough to be easily handled, which was better. She had learned the mechanics of conquest bringing new tribes under Ra's dominion. While those had been cases of blast-lances against arrows, the principles were still the same. Destroy the enemy's strongest defenders. Humiliate and then eliminate the leaders. Balance ruthlessness with economy in turning the surviving population into slaves.

First, however, she'd have to survive the initial onslaught of simple nuclear bombs. According to the intelligence she herself had gathered, one of these devices had destroyed Ra aboard his flying palace.

But it had been materialized inside the vessel through the short-range matter-transmission system. These weapons were crawling their way through space, unable even to maneuver.

As they passed into effective range for her energy weapons, Hathor gave the order. Searing lances of incandescent energy stabbed out from the facets of the *Boat of a Million Years'* pyramidal hull. Where one of those bolts intersected the oncoming missiles, a halo of energy marked the vaporized remains.

Not every thrust connected with a missile. But the crude weapons still had minutes before reaching their envelope of danger, and there were ever more secondary batteries available for point defense as the number of targets decreased.

One missile, however, reached its terminal phase, scattering ten warheads across the area the monster ship's pyramidal apex would occupy.

Her gunners would hear of this—after the action. "Erect energy barrier now!" Hathor ordered crisply.

The North American Air Defense command had been allowed to wither on the vine from its heyday of the Fifties and Sixties. As ICBMs edged out manned bombers, the headquarters facilities in Cheyenne Mountain, Colorado, had seemed increasingly irrelevant to America's defense. They'd gained a new lease on life as the headquarters of the U.S. Space Command. General West had concentrated every communications system available for the coordination of Earth's defenses, including a direct holographic line to the ancient planetary defense net.

He'd also concentrated the experts he considered necessary for a defense. Daniel Jackson was in the room as translator in case the invaders communicated, and as the expert on Ra's empire. Across the room stood Sha'uri as the liaison with the planetary defense control center in Saudi Arabia. And serving as West's aide was the ranking military man to battle the Ra's empire and live—Jack O'Neil.

Like everyone else in the room, their eyes were glued to the holographic tactical display hovering in the air of the command bunker, showing the death agonies of Earth's first launched nuclear strike.

Colonel Jack O'Neil stood in a neat, clean uniform at the edge of a knot of generals following the battle. This was like no war he'd ever participated in. He was a hands-on kind of guy, a blood under the fingernails warrior.

What was happening here was more like a video game. The generals groaned as their team was steadily whittled down. Then came an excited shout. "One got through!"

The screen switched to a telescopic view, greatly enhanced by the planetary defense computers. Men sucked in quick breaths as the warheads exploded—only to have their energy absorbed or deflected by some sort of impalpable barrier protecting the *Boat of a Million Years*.

"Force-fields?" one of the younger generals blurted in dismay. "Why didn't we hear about force-fields?"

Because Ra always kept an ace slipped up his pectoral necklace, O'Neil thought grimly.

"Well, we know about force-fields now," General

West said quietly. "What we need to learn is how to overload them. Otherwise our entire nuclear arsenal will be nothing more than the biggest light show in the galaxy."

CHAPTER 17
SUNDAY PUNCH

The war room in Cheyenne Mountain became quieter as the generals tried to devise some way to pierce Hathor's protective shield.

Sha'uri turned from the console that maintained her link with the ancient planetary defense computer. Her lustrous dark hair was pulled back to accommodate the ear set and microphone she wore. "Sir," she reported to West, "The Setim relic has no information on any technology for an energy defense system. It was apparently kept secret from its builders."

"Well, we know about it now. Damned thing's got to be strong, to shrug off the effects of a nuclear blast," an air force general muttered.

"It shook off ten of them," an army representative pointed out.

"So we need twenty—fifty—a hundred!" another officer cried.

Jack O'Neil shook his head at this brute-force approach. It smacked of desperation.

But in moments the OWPs were launching missiles as quickly as they could possibly fire. Motes of red swept across the tactical display, arriving in waves against the advancing poison-green tetrahedron that represented the *Boat of a Million Years.*

The number of motes drastically diminished as they came closer to the invader, like bugs flying around a candle. A few missiles managed to survive, however, to release their warheads. But the enemy's icon on the display continued to advance, apparently untouched.

"Ask for another look at the ship," West said to Sha'uri. She translated the request to the central control computer—the relic—in Saudi Arabia, and an enhanced image pulled together from all the detectors, visual, electromagnetic, and holographic, appeared below the tactical display. As the *Boat of a Million Years* came closer to Earth, more information was gathered. The flashes from exploding warheads showed more clearly. The initial impact with the field of force was a pinpoint of searing light, quickly expanding into a prismatic display—a huge circle of shimmering, lambent energy. Firefly flashes appeared as the field moved through the residual blast, creating smaller ripples of color. As the energy was absorbed, the disklike shimmers shrank, then disappeared.

O'Neil looked hard at the light show. Those impact zones looked familiar—though without those regular color changes . . .

"The StarGate!" Daniel Jackson burst out. "Those blotches look like the interface on the StarGate. Except there the color pattern isn't as defined. It's more like a film of oil on rippling water than a series of concentric halos."

"You think this has some sort of connection to the matter-transmission technology?" West asked.

"Damned if I know," Jackson replied. "Except I don't think you'll get much in the way of results with that scatter-shot approach. You see how new halos form as the field swallows up hot spots within the warhead's explosion? If you focused enough shots at one part of the field, maybe you could attain a local overload."

New orders flew out, but the OWPs couldn't succeed in concentrating their missile fire. Several lucky hits stressed the energy shield, but nowhere were the defenders able to rend Hathor's protection.

One of the technicians monitoring the battle spoke up. "Sir, the enemy is entering extreme energy-weapon range."

"This may be our chance," O'Neil whispered to Jackson. "The OWPs are organized into sub-constellations, to coordinate into battery fire. Maybe they can weaken the force-field enough to let a warhead through."

"God, I hope so," the scholar whispered, watching as various groups of OWPs lit up, indicating their fire attacks. "So far, we haven't been too damned successful at stopping Hathor's Flying Circus."

"Damned Urt-men," Hathor snarled, picking up the Abydan's derogatory terms. They were annoyingly persistent, and certainly prodigal with their limited stock of nuclear weapons.

As she monitored the progress of the Urt-man attack, she decided that heads would not necessarily have to roll in Fire Control. Even as the volume of enemy fire increased, the kill ratio for her secondary batteries improved dramatically. Except for the attack missile that apparently malfunctioned, failing to release its war-heads separately but delivering them in one package, Ra's energy barrier had not even been remotely threat-ened with failure.

On her grand tactical display, the small orbiting fortresses suddenly gleamed into a new level of threat assessment. The barrier was suddenly pockmarked with energy bursts.

Ra's teeth and toenails! she swore silently. They've switched from missiles to energy weapons!

A quickly voiced demand for information from her vessel's computers brought surprising answers. The weapons now pounding on her shields were not merely weapons scavenged from the wreck of *Ra's Eye*. There were too many of them, and each blast-cannon was slightly more powerful than the arma-ment of her lost cruiser.

They built these themselves, she realized in won-der. From her contact with the scientists, technicians, and translators—primarily Barbara Shore and Gary Meyers—Hathor hadn't expected so much from Earth's research establishment. Crafty little Urt-men, she thought. Using my own weapons against me. I can't blast energy-beams with my secondaries.

Her beautiful lips twisted in a mirthless smile. But I can blast those beam projectors.

"Fire Control," she spoke into the air, confident that the ship's computers would route her commands to the correct officers. "Independent fire on all the enemy's operating blast-cannons."

* * *

Aboard space station *Freedom*, the cramped displays told the grim story.

"They're picking off the OWPs," Dessarian reported. "There's nothing we can do to stop them."

Craig Hastings was already busy on his computer console. "Order all surviving platforms to fire the last of their missiles," he ordered. "We'll give them something else to shoot at."

He ran several simulations on his console, taking into consideration the information that was coming up from Space Command. The intruder would be in range of *Freedom*'s energy-cannon soon. If they could concentrate sufficient fire on one spot . . ."

"*Freedom* to Space Command," he spoke into his microphone, changing command frequencies. "Permission to release shuttle fleet. Gambit Tango."

"Permission granted" came the word from Cheyenne Mountain.

"We're going in!" Neil Antonelli spread the word to his command as soon as it came over his earphones. "Gambit Tango. I repeat, Gambit Tango."

For the shuttle flotilla, this meant a fairly simple maneuver, a strafing flyby. The mobile units had practiced trying to focus their firepower, in hopes of creating what the attack planners had called "the big hole"—sufficient damage to impair or destroy the *Boat of a Million Years.*

Too bad they didn't know the enemy had the "big shield," Antonelli thought. He proceeded forward, flying on instruments, the other shuttles maintaining their standard echelon behind him.

A sudden, novalike flash appeared in the cockpit window, far off to port.

There went an OWP with a full stock of warheads, Antonelli thought. Must have just come over the horizon.

He started to jink his craft, taking evasive maneuvers the OWPs couldn't even try. Ahead, ghostly lights beckoned like a thunderstorm in space, or an interplanetary aurora borealis. It had to be the *Boat of a Million Years,* its force-field still bearing the brunt of the OWPs' attack.

Craig Hastings' voice suddenly blared in his ears. "*Endeavour,* we're about to launch G. Answer. Do you copy?"

"We copy. G Answer."

So Hastings was going to light off some of his special Roman candles—antigravity drive versions. Antonelli saw the plan. His flight would launch a manned strike at a particular spot in the impalpable wall protecting the boss bitch and her ship, hopefully weakening it enough to let *Freedom*'s heavy missiles through.

They were definitely in range of the *Boat of a Million Years* now. As he gave his orders to the rest of the flotilla, a lash of blinding energy swept below and past *Endeavour*'s starboard wing.

MIssed that time, honey, Antonelli thought.

"*Endeavour*?" Hastings' voice came back. "We're engaging."

"I stay," Antonelli replied. The flotilla would continue its mission.

The glow ahead became less auroral and more satanic. *Freedom*'s blasters, pumped with a heavier reactor, were more powerful than those on the OWPs or the mobile units. They splashed into the force-wall.

Giving us something to aim at, Antonelli thought. He contacted Christy Manville. "I think you've spotted our target. Fire energy-cannon at will."

"Yessir!"

"Engage missile," Antonelli ordered his copilot.

"Engaged."

"Fox One!"

Their first missile leapt from its latticework launching cradle, accelerating at a speed that would have jellied a human passenger. As soon as it was free of *Endeavour*, it began a wild flight pattern, generated by a tiny electronic brain. In practice the shuttle pilots had called the damned things "jiggle birds," from a long-standing term for evasive maneuvers.

With its speed and jinking course, it was hoped that the jiggle birds might evade defensive counterfire from energy weapons. They'd done well against human defenses.

"Fox Two!"

That was a third of his available magazine. Time to get out of Dodge.

As he peeled away, a godawful flare of energy ignited behind him.

"*Endeavour!*" That was the shaken voice of Dick Conway, commander of *Atlantis*. "*Ptichka*. It's gone!"

So the little bird had been slapped out of the sky, Antonelli thought. That leaves us fourteen percent less firepower to bring up against that big bastard. "Evasive Four!" he snapped into his microphone. That called for the most strenuous maneuvers as the flotilla banked away from the invader and moved off to regroup.

It wouldn't be the neatest-looking return from a sortie, but with luck it might keep his people alive to fight another hour.

"We've lost a shuttle," Dessarian said from his boards on space station *Freedom*. "I think it's one of the Russians."

"First blood to the enemy," Colonel Hastings said grimly. "I hope it was worth it. Where are our birds?"

"About to impact . . ." Dessarian drew out the last word. They were just far enough away that the speed of light began to become a slight limiting factor in getting information back. "I think we did something! That big mother jolted for a moment!"

"Ammit take them!" Hathor ground out the curse as she clung to the arms of her seat. The Urt-men had actually managed to overload Ra's barrier of force—not decisively, but enough to allow some residue of their blasts to sieve through. The outer shell of the *Boat of a Million Years* had taken collateral damage.

An image of her vessel rode before her on the air. A smear ruined the line of the craft's apex. Repairs would have to be initiated before the ship's pinnace would be able to dock there.

The ship's pinnace—Hathor's lips twisted. That had been the vessel she'd always thought of as Ra's flying palace.

Her eyes went back to the tactical display. The Urt-men had managed another technological hybrid she hadn't expected, crossing their missiles with the empire's antigravity drive. The ones from the small vessels were annoying enough, skittering madly around the secondary batteries' point-defense fire. But the ones that had followed had completely deceived her. They'd come on much as the weapons had from the orbital platforms, following a straightforward ballistic course. Then, as they came in energy-weapon range, they'd begun a crazy dance, too.

Moving her hand over her command console, Hathor placed a Fire-Control signal over the larger platform that had launched these more dangerous weapons.

"Main batteries," she ordered. "Fire and destroy."

Freedom never knew what hit it. Colonel Hastings was just getting new orders from Space Command when hellish bolts of energy sheared through the spindly construction. The latticework back of the station was broken, and the separated pieces began to spin on their own axes. The boom separating the nuclear pile from the rest of the station separated, and the main power source undertook a new orbit. Astonishingly, the tiny crew quarters was unhit—by the energy beams.

But one of the energy-cannon, slashed loose from its mounting, swung around to collide with it . . .

Hastings recovered consciousness to find himself floating in the midst of the living quarters. He managed to snag a handhold, and turned . . . to find a breathtaking view of space where the forward part of the cabin had been.

The whole living space had been unzipped. Dessarian and his consoles were gone. Rodenko lay across his action station, chunks of visor and reddish ice dancing around his head.

The colonel shook his head, trying to clear his ears. But those bubbling sounds weren't coming from him. They were being transmitted over his radio.

Farnham!

A dislodged microcomputer had landed against the caretaker astronaut's chest, weightless, but deadly in its mass. Farnham had been driven up against the wall, the microcomputer had rebounded to float over him . . .

But the upper half of Farnham's suit had been stove in. This was the hard portion of the EMU, and while it hadn't been broken, the dent in the fiberglass extended too far into the astronaut's chest cavity. That indicated broken ribs, perhaps a punctured lung . . .

Then Hastings realized what he was hearing. It was the sound of a man drowning in his own blood. And there was nothing he could do about it. They were surrounded by hard vacuum. He couldn't even remove Farnham's suit.

Trying to push the noise out of his ears, Hastings turned to the battered consoles. Astonishingly, some battery backup was still connected, enough to give the grim readouts. Their energy weapons were wrecked, and there was no power for them without the reactor. But six antigrav missiles survived in their cradles.

Hastings worked painstakingly over a keyboard,

punching in the target coordinates with his gauntleted fingers. Immersed in the work, he didn't notice when Farnham's noises stopped.

"They kicked our ass bad, Farnham," the colonel said as he initiated the sequence. "But we'll give them one kick back."

Aboard the *Boat of a Million Years*, Nekhti quietly engaged a program he'd worked out on the library computers. To Fire Control, it would seem that his console had developed some sort of critical malfunction. In moments he was getting queries from one of the gunnery officers.

"Sir, I don't know what the problem is," he responded. "I'm running diagnostics programs, but as yet they fail to find the fault."

Instead, his console computer had been subverted from its Fire-Control functions and was now attempting to interface with the empty communications sector of the bridge. Nekhti's sharp nose for deceit had twitched when Hathor had turned the entire Comm crew to gunnery. The head of Communications, a fourth-rank officer, had wondered out loud why Lady Hathor wouldn't give Ra advance warning that rescue was on the way.

Hathor had responded that the appearance of the *Boat of a Million Years* would be message enough. Soon after, the officer in question had suffered a gorily fatal accident using the matter-transmitter to get to the bridge. Nekhti suspected Khonsu. But he had no theory as to why the crew was being held incommunicado.

When he saw the missile strike launched on antigravity drive, Nekhti knew the time had come to implement his diversionary program. The weaponry being used against the *Boat of a Million Years* seemed incredibly crude, but more and more, he believed it had to be Setim work. Which raised the suspicion that he might be fighting on the wrong side.

His trapdoor program allowed him to take control of a Communications console. Quickly, Nekhti checked for incoming messages. None.

Nekhti's throat felt the cold breath of phantom jaws about to tear vulnerable flesh. But he prepared a brief burst transmission on a special frequency . . . a specially coded message for Ushabti. He touched the *transmit* icon.

And suddenly, the *Boat of a Million Years* heeled madly.

A major icon on the Cheyenne Mountain tactical display disappeared. "Gentlemen, it seems we'll have to scratch *Freedom* from our defense," General West said after getting a report from Sha'uri. "After that second launch of antigravity missiles, the remaining components of the station were vaporized."

Jack O'Neil felt his face harden as he stared at the backs of the generals entrusted with Earth's defense. They were fighting this battle as if it were truly a Nintendo war—with the endgame coming rapidly upon them. The *Boat of a Million Years* had chewed large holes in the OWP constellation, had shrugged off an attack by the shuttles, and now reduced Earth's close-in defenses by fifty percent. Human casualties would hardly constitute a corporal's guard, but the eight dead also represented more than a fifth of their forces in space. The losses in material were already in the tens of billions of dollars.

What the hell were they waiting for?

"Message from Saudi Arabia, General," Sha'uri spoke up.

"The Central Control computers have activated the planetary defense system. The enemy is in range of three Northern Hemisphere installations—designated Bermuda, Gibraltar, and Hindu Kush."

General West gestured toward the tactical display. "Tell the computers to synchronize its fire with the arrival of the antigrav missiles."

Silence fell over the room as everyone watched the missiles crawl nearer. One fell to counterfire, two more . . .

Sha'uri got another message from the ancient computer. "The *Boat of a Million Years* is using its main batteries in a point-defense role," she announced.

"We're keeping them busy, at least," a general muttered.

At ten widely spaced points on the globe, core taps went fully operational, powering up enormous accumulators. In three locations, two underwater and one set in a remote mountain valley, sensor nets aligned huge discharge tubes of golden quartz.

Thousands of miles above, a fourth missile vanished in a ravening flood of energy. But two reached the forcefield. They detonated.

Ocean water vaporized into storm clouds as the ancient planetary defense installations fired. In the mountains, villagers stared upward in fear at the enormous, dazzling-bright spear of lightning that lashed upward, straight and true—and at the thunder that rocked the heavens after its passage.

In a Colorado bunker dug into the bowels of a mountain, a group of military men examined a holographic display of the course of battle. The oncoming bilious-green pyramid slewed slightly in its course.

But it came on.

"Gentlemen," General West said in a hollow voice, "that was our Sunday punch. We may have staggered Hathor and the *Boat of a Million Years* . . . but we haven't stopped her."

CHAPTER 18
SACRIFICIAL VICTIMS

Aboard the *Boat of a Million Years*, the sculpted lines of Hathor's face were twisted in an expression of incredulous rage. Her defenses had failed *again*?

Serious damage reports flooded her secondary displays. A holographic image showed an ugly gouge down one facet of the *Boat of a Million Years*. The scar went decks deep. Atmosphere was leaking. Heavy blast doors slammed shut. Several batteries had been put off-line.

"Fire Control!" she shouted. "Dispatch all idled gunners to Engineering for damage control."

She continued to peruse the floating readouts. Engineering had been all but untouched. Engines had not been damaged. They regained their course and continued.

What in the name of Ra had struck them?

The ship's computers played back the jarring blow. Multiple nuclear explosions had weakened the force-field. Then unimaginably heavy energy-beams had pierced the energy-barrier.

Hathor's eyes narrowed. Beams—*from the surface of the Earth?*

Conjectures ran through her head almost as quickly as the hieroglyphs scrolling before her eyes.

If the Urt-men had such weapons in hand, why had they wasted time and materials the paltry spaceborne defenses that faced her? With more of those damnable antigravity missiles and such heavy energy weapons, they could threaten sufficient damage to the *Boat of a Million Years* to keep her at bay.

Why divert effort to produce the toys she'd almost casually been wrecking? The incongruity nagged at her.

She'd been surprised that the Urt-men had even managed to reproduce cruiser-level energy-cannon. How could they develop ground-based energy ordnance that rivaled the *Boat of a Million Years'* main batteries?

Hathor looked across the echoing emptiness of the bridge, at the scattered red-furred backs hunched over control consoles.

No, the jumped-up fellahin of Earth had not created those weapons . . .

Those blasts had to be the work of Setim! Nekhti thought desperately, following the damage reports on his console. Should he venture another attempt at contact?

"Second Officer Nekhti," the voice of the Fire-Control officer interrupted his musings, "your battery is still off-line. You are reassigned to Damage-Control Party Fifty-one, now located in the prime power traverse, level Seventy-four."

Nekhti did not wish to lose the use of his console. But he dared not disobey a direct order and call attention to himself. Nor could he disengage his diversion program to effect a miraculous repair.

Reluctantly, he acknowledged the command and rose from his place. He'd have to travel down to his assigned location by foot. A power fluctuation while using the matter transmitter could have fatal consequences.

Perhaps somewhere in the course of his new Damage-Control duties, Nekhti would have access to another computer—a chance to send another message.

General West aimed bulging eyes at Sha'uri. "What do you mean the damned computer refuses to fire? That was the best shot we managed to get off against the enemy."

Sha'uri shook her head, listening to the report coming through her ear set. "Central Control detected a message coming from the *Boat of a Million Years*. The frequency and code indicate the message is for Ushabti."

"This Ushabti has been dead and dust for thousands of years!" West burst out. "Why—"

"The planetary defense network is prohibited from attacking Setim, General," Sha'uri explained. "The computer is suffering from a conflict in its programming directives. Until it resolves them—"

"It won't fire?" West turned from anger to calculation. "This order. Could it be some sort of ECM?"

He caught Sha'uri's incomprehension of the acronym. "A false signal—a countermeasure to keep the planetary defense network from firing?"

Daniel Jackson suddenly spoke up. "That bitch!" he

growled, his voice hoarse. "What if Hathor never told the crew how much time has passed? Maybe there are genuine sympathizers with Ushabti's cause up there, trying to get an idea of conditions down here." His face twisted. "They don't know that the empire doesn't hold Earth—that their people were exterminated . . . or that Hathor was the exterminator."

"If these people are for real, we've got to get in touch with them." West turned to Sha'uri. "Can the computer talk to whoever sent that message?"

Sha'uri listened to her link. "The computer has been attempting contact—no one is answering."

"Then, it could be a trick," the general said. "Remind the computer of that—and that it's vulnerable until it resolves this personality disorder."

The village was no different from many scattered through the mountains, a small collection of stone and plaster houses in the center of some hardscrabble farms. Nothing notable ever happened there. The march of history, changes of government, even the withdrawal of the British, pretty much failed to affect the general tenor of life.

Young Ali shepherded his goats off to pasture, one eye on the sky, the other scanning the valley for the scorched spot from the great lightning bolt. The brush was dry, and wildfires were a distinct possibility.

Paradoxically, the valley seemed no different than on other days. The sere vegetation was untouched. There was no fire, not even a blackened scar. Perhaps the bolt had landed in stony wasteland.

Ali laughed to himself, looking down at one of his goats. "Not a sign from Allah, not a wonder," he said whimsically.

He never saw the counterblast of energy lashing down from the sky—or rather, from far beyond it.

In an instant, the valley hiding the ancient defense installation and the valley that housed Ali's village became one, large, lifeless, *molten* hole.

In her command chair Hathor nodded in satisfaction. She had elected to target the land-based blaster installation because it was the most accessible of the targets her computers had identified. Still better, computer projections indicated that blasts from the other two locations would not be sufficient to penetrate the energy-barrier.

"Resume operations against the weapons platforms, and target the other large orbiting installation when it moves past the horizon."

Beneath Cheyenne Mountain, the points of holographic light in the tactical display were just as bright, but the picture they presented was a dark one. *Mir* scarcely got into the fight before it was silenced. The Russian station had privately been considered the more vulnerable of the two. It had a larger pressurized area, and bulkheads that could have been used to seal off areas had to remain open to accommodate cables snaking the length of the station to various pieces of equipment.

Jack O'Neil was astonished the Russians had managed to light off any missiles at all. They must have known they were hanging out there as sacrificial victims, and determined to do what they could while they could do it.

There was some good news from the main battery attack on Pakistan. Direct hostile action had brought the planetary defense network back on-line. The bad news was that it didn't seem able to get through that damned force-field. Firing through the windows of opportunity provided as the Russian antigravity missiles detonated against the field allowed the good guys to do some more minor damage to the *Boat of a Million Years*. But Hathor was still coming on.

The slower ballistic missiles from the OWPs were being consistently zapped hundreds of miles from the force-field. And, indeed, the weapons platforms themselves were being sniped out of existence, sometimes as soon as they appeared from behind the bulk of the Earth.

O'Neil glanced at his watch, amazed to see that barely forty minutes had passed. In that short time the outer defenses were shredded, the inner defenses destroyed, Earth's most powerful weapons diminished by ten percent. If Hathor really wanted to pour on the antigravity and come hell-for-leather at the Northern Hemisphere, there were only six shuttles and four planetary defense installations between her and most of the developed countries.

But, for the present, Hathor seemed content with her slow progress, knocking out all of their space-borne defenses before taking further action.

There was nothing they could do to preserve the

OWPs except put them in the line of fire as surely as targets in a shooting gallery.

The problem was, Earth would be the sharp-shooter's prize.

Daniel Jackson turned up at O'Neil's elbow. Apparently, the Egyptologist had worked out the math, too.

"In less than an hour, we're going to run out of weapons platforms. We've got to do something before then."

"If you've got an idea, now is the time to share it," the colonel replied.

Jackson licked his lips. "All right." He pointed to the lividly green tetrahedron that represented the *Boat of a Million Years*. "Suppose we could sneak something onto that damned thing?"

"*What?*" O'Neil ignored the three- and four-star heads turning at his outburst.

"When you threw us out of Creek Mountain, Barbara Shore and I were experimenting with fine-tuning the StarGate. We might have roughed out the coordinates for a spot directly above Creek Mountain—about six thousand miles up."

"Might have?" O'Neil repeated dubiously.

"We'd have known for sure if we hadn't been evicted." Daniel shrugged. "Anyway, I didn't think there was any practical use for that information—until I realized that there's a StarGate aboard the *Boat of a Million Years*. If we lured it to the right spot, we might have a chance at getting past that energy-shield."

* * *

Daniel Jackson nearly felt his arm come out of its socket as O'Neil grabbed him and hustled him over to General West. "Sir!"

A dubious expression replaced the general's usual poker face as O'Neil explained the desperate gambit. "What are you suggesting, Colonel? That we try to slip a warhead through the StarGate—?"

"No, sir. We don't know if the onboard StarGate is monitored or guarded. I'd recommend a boarding party."

O'Neil's face was tight and grim, the mask of the warrior, a killer with a cause. "The party that accompanied me to Saudi Arabia has been transferred here as part of the security team. I'm sure Lieutenant Kawalsky and his men will volunteer. I, of course, will command."

"I'll go, too," Daniel said.

He concentrated on the general's face in front of him, trying to ignore the startled female exclamation from behind him. "I'm the only Earth-human who's been on board that big clunker. I speak the enemy's language."

West nodded grudgingly.

"But we've got to make this happen, General. Somehow, we've got to decoy Hathor to the one point we have rough coordinates for. She's been coming straight in. What do you think would make her turn left and head for Colorado?"

West looked mildly ill. "The shuttle group."

Daniel nodded. "We'll also need some time to get ready."

"Chopper transport to Creek Mountain," O'Neil said. "Transport of a backpack nuke. MOPP-4 gear."

"Wha-who gear?" Daniel asked.

"Mission-oriented protective posture," West translated the acronym.

"The silo has been mined with chemical weapons," O'Neil pointed out. "I want full protection for anyone going in—or coming out. That means rubber gloves and boots, charcoal-lined pants and jackets, and a gas mask."

"Yeah," Daniel said. "We'd hate to get killed by our own side."

"Daniel!" In her agitation, Sha'uri slipped back into her slightly slurred Abydan pronunciation of his name. "Dan-yer!"

Jackson turned, slightly surprised at the emotion in his estranged wife's voice. Sha'uri wasn't giving him her usual woman-of-stone impersonation this time. Shock made her face vulnerable, revealing her feelings.

If I were John Wayne, I'd just tell her, "A man's gotta do what a man's gotta do," kiss her soundly, and amble on out of here, he thought. Then Daniel remembered one of Feretti's combat aphorisms: "There are two ways to do everything—the right way, and the John Wayne way."

He made his voice gentle as he pointed to the ear set she wore. "You have a place here—an important job. That computer you're talking with controls our last-ditch defenses if O'Neil and I fail." He shrugged. "I was just part of the audience here. Now I have a chance to make myself useful."

She suddenly switched to Abydan. "You don't do this because of me, do you?"

Daniel actually smiled. "Surely, not to impress you," he replied in the same private language. More seriously, he went on. "O'Neil will need my knowledge on the *Boat of a Million Years*. I offer it to stop Hathor and to save everyone on my world." He looked at her. "Though, to tell the truth, those I know and love best are my strongest reasons for fighting."

Sha'uri stepped from her console and flung her arms around him. Daniel enfolded her in return, conscious of a lot of generals' eyes studiously observing the tactical display overhead.

"Come back," Sha'uri murmured.

She released him and went back to her place.

Daniel stepped over to Jack O'Neil, eager to get out of there. He was trembling like a damned virgin.

"Here we are, together again," Feretti muttered to Lieutenant Kawalsky. "Right down to our favorite no-hope pope."

It could have been worse, Kawalsky thought. There had been a time when the brief helicopter journey from Space Command Headquarters to Creek Mountain would have left Daniel Jackson a teary-eyed, sneezing, runny-nosed wreck. It seemed that the academic's barnstorming across the country to support Earth's defense had finally defeated his psychosomatic travel allergy.

Now, if they could only do something about his innate ham-handedness . . .

The lieutenant sighed as he watched Jackson don

the suit that would defend him against the deadly chemicals now stockpiled in the Creek Mountain missile silo. Kawalsky's marines were trained to get into the NBC (nuclear, biological, chemical) protective gear in under eight minutes. Jackson was considerably slower as he slipped into the green, rubbery garb.

"Feels like I'm dressing up for a kinky evening in," he said, wrinkling his nose.

He tried to flap the rubberized, chemically treated jacket to start a breeze inside his clothes. The bulky material didn't cooperate well. "Sort of warm in here."

"Well, it will give you a warm feeling if you've got to walk through a cloud of poison gas," Feretti said. He held out a web belt and a holstered Beretta 9mm pistol. "I'm sorry we don't have any blast-rifles to spare. But I thought you should be carrying some sort of equalizer."

The attack force would be lean and mean, squad-size, ten men in all: two fire teams, one led by Feretti, the other by Kawalsky, the colonel, and their idiot savant. Each team consisted of three men with blast-rifles and one with an M-16 rifle set for launching grenades.

Kawalsky would be carrying the backpack nuke, so he'd go with a grenade launcher. The battery packs for the blast-rifles made it impossible to add more burdens. Feretti had shuddered at the idea of Jackson traipsing around with an M-16. He'd used the Beretta before and survived.

The Egyptologist seemed oddly reluctant to take the pistol. Belatedly, Feretti remembered the trouble a similar weapon had meant for Jackson, getting him accused of shooting his father-in-law.

With a sudden, decisive movement, Daniel removed the pistol from its holster, released the magazine, and checked the action. "Thanks for thinking of me, Feretti."

Holstering the weapon, Daniel slipped the web belt around his middle.

"I thought I'd have to depend on my monster routine," Daniel went on. Slipping the hooded gas mask over his head, he raised his arms, turning into a snouted, goggle-eyed apparition. "Whoooooooooo!" he moaned through the filtering apparatus.

Feretti rolled his eyes. Just when you began to think he'd gotten some sense . . .

Peering through the plastic goggles of his gas mask, Daniel considered the canisters of nerve gas lying on the floor of the converted missile silo, then turned his gaze to his companions. Everyone around the Star-Gate was dressed in the essentially anonymous protective gear.

Daniel recognized Lieutenant Kawalsky because of his deadly burden, not a backpack, but a large cylinder of high-impact plastic. Jack O'Neil had gotten himself a submachine gun for this sortie, the distinctive weapon making him stand out. Otherwise, he'd just have been another grunt in rubber suit, mask, and Kevlar helmet. Daniel hid a grin behind his mask. It would have been pretty ridiculous for Jack to wear his trademark black beret on top of the protective hood.

The grin faded as Daniel remembered the last

words he'd had with the colonel. "I just got off the phone with my wife," O'Neil had said. "Told her I had a mission, though not what it was." Jack's warrior mask was off. He looked less like Joe Uniform and more like a human being. "After seeing you and Sha'uri, I thought it was the least I could do, to tell her once more that I love her."

The ends of O'Neil's lips twisted upward in an ironic smile aimed at himself. "You know, when I first met you, I'd have leapt at a mission like this. High-risk, no net. Well, here we are again, and I discover I want to survive, I want to come back to Sarah. Funny, huh?"

Daniel hadn't felt like laughing.

Now he stood in the staging area, watching an anonymous crew set the StarGate to the coordinates he and Barbara Shore had stumbled upon. The room was already humming with the power being sucked into the glassy-gold torus.

Nothing now remained except to see if the *Boat of a Million Years* could be diverted to the magic spot indicated by the coordinates.

Daniel wondered if he should worry about whether the giant starship would make that rendezvous . . . or should he worry about the consequences if it didn't?

CHAPTER 19
INTO THE WOLF'S MOUTH

Space Command had ordered *Endeavour* and her fellow shuttles beyond the horizon in an attempt at least to salvage what was left of the manned space forces.

With the planet for a bulwark, Christy Manville felt safer from those ravening beams of destruction the *Boat of a Million Years* was using to scourge Lower Earth Orbit. At least they'd be safe for a while.

But it was harder for the crews to follow the course of the battle. Reports were coming from Space Command, although the ships were maintaining position over the United States. Nonetheless, Manville could see that the tide hadn't turned. Orbital Weapons Platforms continued on their appointed rounds, swinging past the shoulder of the Earth. But damn few were returning from the battle beyond the horizon. What happened when all that had been on this side of the planet rotated through?

Manville had caught the hellish flare representing the extinction of space station *Freedom*. But the shuttles had already retreated—what was the military euphemism? engaged in retrograde movement—before *Mir* got it.

The shuttle crews had caught that report, and the news that one of the vaunted planetary defense installations had also been scragged.

Manville's short brunette hair was damp with sweat under her "Snoopy hat," the cloth communications carrier assembly astronauts wore like a skullcap beneath their helmets. She knew it wasn't a case of her suit's environmental controls going on the fritz. This was cold sweat from pressure, and yes, fear.

All too soon, Space Command would have to call the shuttles out of hiding and send them against the huge invader.

No, Christy Manville interrupted herself, editing her thoughts with scientific precision. Soon they'll have to throw us against the *Boat of a Million Years*, because they'll have nothing else left.

Neil Antonelli sat tight-lipped as he got the word from Space Command. Then he looked surprised. He'd expected orders to engage the enemy head-on, or perhaps to take a desperate parabolic course, attempting to catch that monster pyramid from behind. Instead, he was not ordered to commit suicide—at least, not immediately.

Cheyenne Mountain wanted his flotilla to try a hit-and-run attack, with the idea of drawing the *Boat of a Million Years* off its present course and into a pursuit. Antonelli couldn't see what that would do, except maybe allow new planetary defense installations to have a crack at the enemy. Well, those weapons had put the most hurt on Hathor's behemoth spaceship. Maybe they could hurt the bad guys again.

As General West went over the timing, he promised that all possible cover would be provided for this sortie. "We're launching every remaining bird we've got. You'll come up while the enemy is busy dealing with them. With luck, a surviving warhead might even open a hole in the force-field. We need you to hit with everything you've got—sting them. Then redline it out of there."

Exit stage right, pursued by a bear, Antonelli thought. If we can get the bear to notice the wasps trying to sting it. Or, dealing with an enemy of that scale, would we even appear as wasps. Maybe houseflies—or gnats.

Neither Antonelli nor West mentioned cover for escaping away from Hathor's pursuit. West had admitted that just getting them in would exhaust Space Command's remaining resources.

If they stung the bear, the shuttles would be strictly on their own.

Antonelli asked where the planetary defense blast had landed. "Did it catch the ship straight-on, or is one of the pyramid faces more damaged than the others?"

A moment of silence went by as West checked for the information.

"The eastern face of the pyramid has taken the most damage," West replied. "Good thinking, Commander."

"We'll aim for that aspect," Antonelli said. Because we'll need every scrap of tactical advantage, he added silently.

"Good luck, Neil," the general said.

Antonelli began barking orders into his mike. His flotilla reorganized into two three-ship echelons, moving across the dawn line massing at the eastern horizon.

"Launching missiles!" came the report from Cheyenne Mountain.

Antonelli crunched numbers on his computer, calculating the fastest course to the enemy ship. Then he ran the fastest course with the greatest evasive deviations. He transmitted his second set of figures to the whole squadron.

"We'll proceed with maximum evasive maneuvers, boosting in six minutes. Echelon Two will go in first, under Commander Conway. *Endeavour* will bring up the rear of the second attack."

From her place in the command chair of the *Boat of a Million Years*, Hathor examined the grand tactical display, an incredulous expression on her perfect features. The Urt-men's shattered defenses seemed to be attempting a dying effort, pumping ballistic missiles in her direction. It was simply pitiful. The weapons platforms still in the battle had only a few missiles left or had already exhausted their store. The newly arriving platforms survived only long enough to boot a missile or two before being vaporized.

Hathor's gunners had learned the orbital planes and speeds of the platforms. They were already targeted in, and another platform-icon vanished on the display.

If their full complement of defenses could barely penetrate the barrier of force, why would the Urt-men try this new attack? Were they already flailing desperately? Were they merely determined at least to use their weapons before they were all destroyed?

Then Hathor saw the icons for the mobile forces swing out from behind the green globe representing Earth.

Excellent, she thought. After these little motes are extinguished, nothing stands in my way.

"Fire Control," she spoke up. "Target the ballistic devices first. When they are destroyed, eliminate the antigravity craft."

The tiny shuttle flotilla came screaming around the shoulder of the Earth, drives at maximum.

Antonelli sucked a dismayed breath between his teeth. There were hardly any OWPs left, and the ballistic missiles from that forlorn hope were being slashed out of existence even as other blast-bolts obliterated the launching platforms.

"We'll have to give them something else to shoot at—besides ourselves," Antonelli said in to his mike. "Each unit, fire one on my command . . . fire!"

Behind him, Christy Manville and her second aimed and launched a jiggle bird. The lighter missiles pulled ahead of the shuttles, dancing just as furiously through space, doubling the enemy's targets.

Bolts of pure destruction lanced out at them like giant, poking fingers. Even though the gunners commanded light-speed weapons, their targeting had to choose among several possible positions for the madly flitting attackers.

Antonelli grinned. Maybe his gnat analogy held truer than he thought. Hathor was striking out at a cloud of no-see-ums, but she wasn't connecting.

Right then one of the advancing missiles vanished in a soundless glare.

Lucky shot, Antonelli told himself, gripping the control stick tighter. "Engage with energy weapons," he ordered.

The folks on Earth did their bit, too, lashing out with the pair of surviving planetary defense beams. Empty space before them lit up like a pyrotechnic display. The ballistic missiles from the OWPs had been wiped out before they could even discharge their warheads. Three antigravity-driven missiles reached the force-field and detonated.

Antonelli saw a flash from *Atlantis*. Dick Conway was trying to squeak a second missile right on the ass of the detonating one. It struck the dissipating circle of light bare seconds too late, failing to pierce through.

The other two ships in Conway's flight aimed missiles at the baleful scar cut by one of the planetary defense beams. They added to the garish light display, but also failed to penetrate.

There went the last of the second echelon's missiles.

"Dick, get out of there," Antonelli ordered.

The orbiters pulled a parabolic turn that would have been impossible in an atmosphere ship and hauled ass back toward Earth. Each still had its energy-cannon trained on the enemy's force-field.

An immensely thicker gout of energy blasted from

the *Boat of a Million Years* like a brief lick of flame from a furnace. It touched shuttle *Atlantis*, and the craft and its crew became nothing more than a brief afterimage.

"Scumfucks," Antonelli snarled. He keyed in his mike. "Echelon One! Go in!"

Shuttle *Enterprise* fired its three remaining missiles, following Conway's example of aiming for the marks left by planetary defense bolts.

The gunner on *Buran* followed suit, and one of his warheads partially broached the shield, sending a whiff of hell onto the already smeared apex of the *Boat of a Million Years.*

Antonelli allowed himself a wolflike grin. The pyramid was somewhat truncated now.

Again, however, *Hathor*'s gunners lashed out.

Buran bounced into a fresh evasion as several beams converged. None hit, but they were all horribly close. Thermal tile blackened, then ran.

Antonelli had trained with *Buran*'s pilot, Vitya Chorni, for months. But with all his knowledge of the guy, he wouldn't have predicted what happened next.

Perhaps Vitya had been flash-roasted in the near miss. Perhaps he'd been blinded. Antonelli wouldn't have put the pilot down as a kamikaze.

But *Buran* struck the impalpable wall of force that separated them from the *Boat of a Million Years*, and the result was hellacious.

Buran crumpled in on itself as if it were crashing, igniting like a candle as its velocity burned out against the force-field. The greater mass of the shuttle created a huge, burning star. Then the ship's reactor hit the white-hot impact zone, creating a new blast in the very center of the already stressed shield. The usual coruscating disk became a torus, the irregular "donut hole" representing a huge failure in the force-wall, tattered streamers of energy still trying to hold . . .

It's a weird way to aim a weapon, Christy Manville told herself as she manned the improvised weapons console at the aft of the flight deck. She acquired targets by television, facing the opposite direction from the cockpit windows.

Buran's impact, therefore, was a glaring nova effect over her left shoulder. But her screens showed what the shuttle had done to the force-field. Christy's face was merciless as she launched the three missiles she'd carefully hoarded right into the suddenly opened maw in front of *Endeavour*.

"Hold tight, everybody!" Neil Antonelli warned as he swept the shuttle into a parabolic turn.

Manville's number two somehow managed to keep the vessel's blast-cannon more or less centered on the hole in the shield, which was healing before her eyes on the targeting screen. The blast-bolts finally fizzled out, merely making pretty sparks in the shimmering disk of roiling energy.

But Christy's were through!

The *Boat of a Million Years* ponderously tried to shift on its axis, attempting to bring a new facet—fully armed—to bear on the oncoming missiles. Every beam-weapon that could fire was concentrating on the three tiny intruders.

One was caught in the blast from a secondary battery. Even as it was incinerated, the warhead went off.

The titanic vessel staggered as if it had been struck.

Two main-battery blasts vaporized the final missile of the trio. Manville couldn't be sure of its effect on the slewing behemoth.

The middle missile survived until it was even closer. Its blast was literally lost in the blinding convergence of half-a-dozen energy blasts.

But the results could be seen. The already gashed pyramid wall writhed and ran as the blast-wave turned golden quartz into incandescently glowing wreckage. The truncated nose of the vessel slewed around, as if the *Boat of a Million Years* were a human being, folding under the impact of a kick in the gut.

It wasn't enough to break the ship's back, Manville knew. But it was an impressive sight to see—as was the continuing damage being done to the vessel's flank. The *Boat of a Million Years* had been in the midst of its roll when the warhead ignited. Destruction continued to vomit down onto previously untouched parts of the pyramid face. The edge between the two facets shriveled out of true, and the scar continued across the new plane, gouting atmosphere and debris.

"Now, that's *got* to hurt," Christy Manville said with savage exultation.

Hathor's hands were claws as she clung to her command seat, nearly gouging into the golden quartz on the chair arms . . . just as those damnable Urt-men were flaying whole decks on the outer sides of the *Boat of a Million Years*.

She ignored the screech of alarms and the computer-intelligence's reports on the damage. Curtly, she'd told the computers to dispatch Damage-Control parties to the most critical locations and oversee the necessary work.

Instead, she continued to examine the grand tactical display, watching the little motes retreat back around their world—only four of them now. She could not have conceived of mere fellahin selling their lives to breach her armor. And that final vessel—whoever commanded there was a clever warrior, conserving his strength for when it would do the most good—or, rather, evil.

Hathor could feel the anger pulsing through her veins. These stiff-necked fools with their pitiful weapons had visited serious damage on her ship, the tool she most needed to achieve her ultimate aspirations.

A conquered Earth would provide limitless man power, useful manufactories for weapons, and the base for using both to capture imperial worlds. But if she wished to conquer the throne-world, Tuat-the-Moon, and deal with her too clever husband, Ptah, she needed a spaceship. Ra had isolated the center of his rule from the StarGate webwork, making Tuat impossible to seize with mere troops. The space defenses were also impressive, requiring a powerful weapon to cleave them.

Hathor had intended to use the *Boat of a Million Years* as her sword to cut her way to the throne. But now the blade was cracked, because the Urt-men didn't know when they were beaten!

Well, she would teach them.

"Computer," she called. "Change course to pursue hostile craft."

Then she contacted Fire Control. "We will be overhauling the spacecraft who attacked us. I wish them all destroyed . . ."

She reached down to a console to indicate the final fleeing craft. The one that had caused the most damage. "But you will destroy this one last."

Harsh laughter forced its way past Neil Antonelli's lips as his reduced flotilla fled through space. His screens told the story. The *Boat of a Million Years* was diverging from its course and coming after them!

The bulk of the enormous spaceship was damned hard to turn. But once it had taken its new heading, the ship was damned fast to come after them.

"Sir!" Christy Manville's voice crackled in his ear set. "The enemy is in beam range. Permission to engage?"

"Granted." It might be as useful as throwing lit matches back at a pursuing bear. On the other hand, their lucky shots might have damaged some of the gear that projected that force-field. If so, they should test and report.

An eye-searing glare seemed to lash past them on all sides. For an instant it was like flying through a radiant tunnel. But the blast-bolts converged up ahead.

"The *Enterprise!*" a shocked voice came from Stan Lundeen on board *Discovery*. "It's—gone!"

A shockingly inappropriate TV voice echoed in Antonelli's brain. "They're dead, Jim."

"Abandon formation!" Antonelli cried into his mike. "Scatter!"

Even as he shouted, he was again surrounded in that coruscating cathedral of light. This time it was *Discovery*'s turn.

Antonelli suddenly realized what the enemy was doing. It was a high-tech variant of the poor man's air defense. The Iraqis had used it in the Gulf War. Without the radar and sophisticated target-acquisition hardware to focus fire on a single plane, air-defense planners broke up the sky into a vast imaginary checkerboard, with gunners assigned responsibility for a singe square. The hope was that sooner or later a plane would pass through a square already inhabited by a blind-fired shell.

In this case, Hathor's gunners were targeting the space around a single fleeing shuttle. Sooner or later, the craft would jink into a beam.

Antonelli passed his analysis to *Columbia* as they flashed over the last of the Atlantic Ocean. The United States spread below them, and they still had to lead the big bogey on their tails to their final destination.

"Fly 'er by hand," Antonelli suggested. "The less we jump around, the less chance they have to hit us."

The wall of light surrounded them again, but this time, the target survived.

But *Columbia* wasn't as lucky the next time.

"Just down to us," Antonelli muttered.

The Rockies were below them now as the pilot pushed *Endeavour* into a dive. Maybe he could hoax the *Boat of a Million Years* into thinking he was trying for a landing, although this glide path would put him well past Vandenberg and end him up somewhere in the Pacific.

The blare of blaster-fire surrounded him now, but Antonelli held his course, crossing the target area Space Command had given him.

The *Boat of a Million Years* was right behind him.

Antonelli threw the antigravity drive into full reverse, essentially braking in midair. "Why don't you stick that big nose of yours right up my ass?" he gritted.

He wasn't able to broach the force-field.

Every weapon on the *Boat of a Million Years* blasted the *Endeavour* before it was able to do any more damage.

Standing in the Creek Mountain silo, Daniel Jackson felt as if the subsonic energy rippling from the StarGate were strong enough to push him to the far wall. Every tracking system in the United States was feeding information about the epic chase far, far overhead.

"They did it! They're coming!"

Was that muffled voice Barbara Shore's? Daniel couldn't tell in the all-swaddling protective gear. Technicians advanced the final symbol on the Star-Gate—the inverted-V pyramid that stood for Earth.

The deep rumbling of power turned now to the golden harmonic of a completed StarGate connection. The rippling disk of light suddenly filled the center of the StarGate's torus.

"Let's go!" Jack O'Neil yelled.

The man's got a point, Daniel thought. We don't know how long the connection will last.

Sprinting after the marine attack party, he dove into the undulating pool of light.

CHAPTER 20
ALIEN INVASION

Harkhuf was panting from the heat before the glowing tip of his multitool finally triggered the desired biomorphic switch in the golden quartz circuitry. It was bad enough that the Earth-rebels had somehow managed to bite a few chunks off the *Boat of a Million Years*. Whole sections of the outer corridors were now open to space on the scarab face of the ship. Blast panels had to drop in the apex of the ship before the bridge lost its air.

And enough Ra-be-damned power cascades had surged through the ship to turn the usually smart circuits into cybernetic morons.

A sigh whistled between Harkhuf's fangs, and he checked the golden-quartz slate that hung on his red-furred chest. He'd been glad to get the lone job of tracing and repairing circuit glitches. Things had gotten just a little too tense in his work party.

Harkhuf was part of the regular Damage-Control detail aboard the *Boat of a Million Years*. He and his teammates had been trained for the job when Ra had taken them aboard as caretaker crew.

When events outran the pack, they were always glad for extra claws. But when Second Officer Nekhti turned up on Level Seventy-four, ordered out to work as a common laborer, Harkhuf smelled trouble.

Nekhti had seemed angry—but not at being effectively downgraded twelve levels. Something else was gnawing at him. He'd asked if there were any communications or computer repairs to be done, as those were areas he knew.

Instead, Fourth Officer Rekhmere had put Nekhti to work hauling debris, just to show who was in charge. Harkhuf half expected the superior officer to go for Rekhmere's throat in all earnest, but Nekhti had simply gone to work.

He had not, however, offered his throat in salute.

Harkhuf queried the ship's computers as to the next nearby circuit jam. There were quite a few in the now-empty Astrogation command deck.

With his multitool in one hand and the slate in the other, Harkhuf set off for his next job.

He'd used the key setting on his multitool to cycle a control panel through all its modes when an odd, low rumble caught Harkhuf's attention. What the—?

He turned just in time to see the StarGate set in the center of the deck's workstations suddenly flash into life.

The multitool in Harkhuf's hand instantaneously switched to the vibrating blade option. He couldn't believe that the rebelling fellahin of Earth could have learned to operate the portal between worlds. But who else could it be? The Lady Hathor had said that

Earth's Setim had been attacked and besieged. Perhaps some of them had seized control of the StarGate and were trying to communicate.

Thus, Harkhuf was not at all prepared for the creature that emerged. It was vaguely Setimian, standing upright, two legs, two arms. But its skin was a curious glistening green. The head was a lighter green. Huge glassy eyes dominated the face, which was neither flat like the humans nor muzzled like the Setim. There was either a jutting jaw or a low, rounded snout that looked vaguely reptilian. It seemed to go with the turtle-like shell covering half the head. The mouth was round, its lips a darker green. And the creature smelled revolting!

As a Damage-Control tech, Harkhuf had worked on battle damage in dangerous positions. Before that, he'd fought for Ra. But this was something beyond his normal standards.

The multitool dropped from nerveless fingers as he turned and ran. It continued to chatter on the floor as more of the monsters arrived.

Jack O'Neil arrived on the *Boat of a Million Years* to find Feretti already establishing a perimeter in the enormous, empty room where they'd appeared. The men seemed steady—all volunteers for this foray were StarGate veterans. The last thing O'Neil wanted was someone having to upchuck in a gas mask.

"Report, Mr. Feretti."

"We spotted one of those alien guys. What did Jackson call them? Centimes?"

"Setim," the colonel corrected. "The alien escaped?"

"Garwood saw him, but he wasn't at his best, right after coming through the Puke Chute." Feretti jerked a thumb at the StarGate, where Daniel Jackson came tumbling through as the party's rear guard. Astonishingly, the Egyptologist didn't disgrace himself.

"Old red-hair took out of here as if his tail were on fire," Feretti went on. "But he left this."

He pointed toward an open control console. A golden-quartz tool with a vibrating blade buzzed viciously as it sliced its way through the deckplate.

O'Neil frowned. "The last thing I would expect in someone who works for Ra—even involuntarily—would be timidity," he said.

"It's our getups, I think, sir." Feretti ran a hand over his protective gear. "One look at Garwood, and he thought he was up against the Creature from the Black Lagoon. Anyway, that's why I've told people to keep the stuff on."

"Nowhere to stow it anyway," O'Neil muttered.

The colonel pushed that thought away and turned to locate Daniel Jackson. Kawalsky was already sending his people to check out the exits.

Jackson was on his feet but still a little wobbly when O'Neil got his attention. "All right, you know this bucket. Can you lead us someplace a few decks away from here, where we could leave our present undisturbed?"

The Egyptologist looked around the empty room. "What's wrong with here?" he asked.

"For one thing, we were observed arriving," O'Neil said. "For another, we're a little too close to *that*." He gestured to the StarGate. "Be embarrassing if they shoved our bomb right back on our doorstep."

Jackson, however, was still absorbing his first point. "Observed?" he echoed. "Who saw us?"

"A red-furred guy who looked vaguely like Wiley Coyote," O'Neil said. "He didn't break out his Acme welcome kit, though."

Jackson didn't respond to the sarcasm. O'Neil was willing to bet there was a thoughtful frown on the guy's hidden face.

"The library," Jackson finally said. "It's not too far away, I know a direct route . . ." He shrugged. "And I don't suppose anybody would go off in the middle of a battle to pick up a little light reading."

Nekhti was organizing his team to dig through a pile of gold-quartz ore that blocked the companion-way when one of the low-rating workers—Harkhuf—came running up, almost whining in terror.

"Aliens!" the tech shrieked, pointing back the way he'd come. "They must have invaded Earth—that's why all that tech stuff is opposing us. But they've found the gate—they're coming through in Astrogation!"

Nekhti knew only one gate in Astrogation. He snatched the tablet from around Harkhuf's neck and feverishly began inditing hieroglyphs.

Hathor sat at her leisure in the command seat, directing the mopping-up job of eliminating the weapons platforms on this side of the planet. This was the land-mass Daniel Jackson had identified as North Amer-ica—his home. Idly, Hathor tried to remember if he'd mentioned a town or city he'd come from. It might make a useful object lesson to obliterate it.

When the computer indicated a message from one of the Damage-Control teams, she was somewhat annoyed. "I told you to oversee the work—beyond your competence? Let me see."

Perfectly sculpted brows drew together as she read the message. "Boarders? How would anyone know our new coordinates? Computer!" she snapped. "Has there been any activity from the StarGate?"

"Ten-person transit, four minutes ago," the computer replied.

"Why was I not notified?" Hathor demanded.

"No information was requested from the StarGate log," the computer responded in the same even tenor.

Hathor paled. All the time she had been flying about, destroying the Urt-men on Abydos, they could have launched a counterattack, and she'd never had known!

"Lock the StarGate to all incoming traffic," she ordered.

"Only Ra may give that order," the computer said.

Hathor held out the golden amulet that fell between her breasts. "I carry Ra's key."

"Only Ra may give that order," the computer repeated.

Hathor sighed. She'd encountered several doors that even Ra's key could not unlock.

"Who submitted this report?" she asked.

"Second Officer Nekhti."

Hathor frowned. The astrogator. But perhaps a

useful officer to have on the spot to deal with a boarding party.

"Direct him to the nearest armory. Allow blast-lances for as many laborers as he may have. Then summon Khonsu to me immediately."

Daniel Jackson sucked air through the filters of his gas mask. What a time to discover a mild tendency toward claustrophobia!

The damned goggles were giving him tunnel vision. He squinted, not wanting to bang into the backpack in front of him. That was Kawalsky's nuke. They were traveling in the middle of the line of march—Kawalsky as the indispensable man, Daniel as the hopeless member of the team. Feretti was on point, scouting out the route from Daniel's sketch map. It might be rough, but Daniel knew it was accurate—the route was engraved in his memory.

What he'd forgotten was how bloody boring the endless corridors of the *Boat of a Million Years* could become.

They marched down another interminably anonymous hall when the ambush was sprung. Daniel was ambling along, trying not to yawn, when a maintenance aperture suddenly dilated in the golden-quartz wall. A lean, red-furred arm shot out to grab him, and then he was stumbling through. The guy behind him raised a blast-rifle, but another access hatch opened on the far wall. A blast-lance poked out and fried him.

Kawalsky spun, trying to grab for Daniel. But the blast-lance spoke again, and the lieutenant kept spinning, his hard-pack and his jacket smoking.

That was the last Daniel saw. The aperture biomorphically sealed itself, and he found himself struggling in the half dark. It didn't help that the grip on his throat had shifted the goggles away from his eyes.

Daniel grabbed onto the furred wrist of the hand that had twisted in his gas mask. The other was trying to get his pistol out of the holster.

Apparently, the Setim now realized that the fabric was a mask. It tore the hood loose nearly taking Daniel's head with it. "What"—the doglike muzzle creased in a snarl—"*who* are you?"

Daniel stumbled back in the confined space, finally freeing his automatic. "My name is Daniel Jackson. I'm a specialist in ancient cultures, which is why I can speak this tongue."

The red-furred alien paid no attention to Daniel's pistol. But with his fangs and those functional claws at the ends of his fingers, he had natural weapons enough. Eyes like black-brown marbles scanned Daniel's face, his pale skin, his blond hair.

"Take a good look at me, Son of Set," Daniel challenged. "You never saw my like in the First Days, when Ra appeared on Earth."

"No," the alien admitted. "Are you of some invading tribe—?"

Daniel shook his head. There was no way to make this gentle. "I am the result of eight thousand years of history since the slaves in Egypt rebelled against Ra."

"Eight thousand!" the Setim repeated.

"More than eight thousand, since the Setim walked the Earth," Daniel went on.

"You mock me!"

"Look harder!" Daniel replied, slapping the rubbery stuff of his protective jacket. "Is this gear I wear the work of Ra's fellahin slaves? Is it Setim work?"

Still holding the pistol clumsily in one hand, Daniel scooped up the gas mask and his helmet. He held out the Kevlar helmet. "Examine this, neither bone nor metal. Do you recognize it? It is—" he stumbled. What the hell would you call plastic in ancient Egyptian? "It is a made thing, from the components of petroleum."

The Setim returned the helmet, giving a low growl. "You cause me to wonder, Dan-yer, but not to believe."

"Would you believe Hathor instead?"

The growl turned uglier. "And what do you know of Lady Hathor?"

"I know she brought me here as a prisoner," Daniel replied boldly. "I managed to escape to Abydos, and when she used this vessel to destroy that planet, I escaped to Earth."

The alien face, and those fangs, came closer. "The tales you tell—" The Setim suddenly began sniffing the air around Daniel's face. "Your scent. It was in the library. I did not recognize it at first, from the abominable smells emanating from your garb."

"I was here. I did escape," Daniel said. "I saw you and the other crew members sleeping the sleep of ages. And I know that when Hathor awakened you, she told you lies."

"How do you know? What lies?" the alien demanded.

"Not long after battle was joined, a message was sent from this ship for Ushabti," Daniel began.

"And what of Ushabti?" Reddish fur raised in hackles.

"I know that Ushabti spoke for the Setim more than eight thousand years ago," Daniel said. "I know that Ushabti helped build the weapons which drew first blood on this vessel." He paused for a second. "I know that Ushabti is dead, probably murdered by Hathor. And I know that Hathor butchered the race of the Setim after they were sent in exile to Ombos."

Alien eyes examined Daniel's face for a long moment. "Tell me more, man of Earth," the Setim finally said.

Jack O'Neil was acting as rear guard for the strike team when Daniel Jackson was grabbed. "Get the sniper!" he shouted to the two men ahead of him as he turned to cover the rear.

Even as he moved, a stealthy rush of red-furred figures came charging from the cross-corridor they'd just passed. O'Neil hosed down the attackers with a stream of 9mm bullets from his submachine gun.

More combat noise came from the head of their little column, where the crash of blaster-fire was punctuated by the explosion of a grenade. S.O.P.—aggressive to ambushes. "Kawalsky!" O'Neil called.

"He's down but still breathing, sir," Feretti replied. "This is a complete rat-fuck. They're all around us, and can pop out of the walls to waste us!"

"We go on," O'Neil decided. He looked from the map in Feretti's hand to the featureless corridors ahead and beyond. It's the only destination we know, he thought. This is not a good place to get hopelessly lost.

"What about Jackson, sir?" Feretti asked.

O'Neil hesitated for a moment, then shrugged. "If we can find him on our way out of here, fine. But the mission comes first. Let's see if we can move Kawalsky and get out of here."

The lieutenant was on his feet, but his face was pale. He'd already removed his smoldering gas mask hood. "Hurts like hell, sir, but it sort of cauterized itself."

"Glad to see you're still around for the party, Lieutenant," O'Neil said, trying to keep the wounded man's spirits up. "I'll carry the nuke. Should I detail someone to help—"

His voice died as he saw the plastic pack Kawalsky had been carrying. There was a not-so-neat hole through the top section—right through the compartment that was supposed to hold the bomb's timer.

"Looks like we're always having trouble with these suckers," the lieutenant said. "Last one we used, the timer wouldn't stop." He pointed to the hole, wincing at the movement. "This one—I'm afraid it won't start."

CHAPTER 21
LIBRARY SCIENCE

Daniel Jackson slipped his hooded gas mask under his belt as his dubious ally Nekhti went to the wall to press several studs in sequence. The access hatch dilated to show a much-changed corridor.

Two dead marines lay on the floor, arms and legs straightened as if they were lying at attention. Daniel was glad to note that neither of them was Lieutenant Kawalsky. Seven Setim lay sprawled and contorted, three at either end of the corridor, like some sort of grotesque honor guard. Number seven was the sniper who'd appeared in the hatch across the hall. The quartzite wall was smelted and spalled, and he literally rested in pieces inside.

Four live Setim stood in the hallway. From their postures, Daniel couldn't tell if they were furious or appalled at their losses.

"Your companions fought well," Nekhti admitted in a low voice. "I had expected to find them wiped out."

One of the aliens, an older male with a graying muzzle, tentatively poked one of the dead marines with his blast-lance. The gas masks on both of the fallen had been removed, revealing human faces, and the older Setim seemed a bit embarrassed by this revelation.

Daniel registered something subliminally wrong with the picture. Then the Egyptologist in him took over. The weapon in the alien's hand must be a pre-imperial model. It was long and thin, tapering at one end to a small knob. The area around the trigger was slightly notched as if for six oversize fingers. Neither the Setim hand, nor, Daniel expected, a human one could hold it comfortably.

He'd holstered his Beretta, but as he stepped through the hatchway in the wall after Nekhti, he wondered if that were a good idea.

Four blast-lances snapped around to aim at Daniel even as Nekhti waved them away. One of the aliens brought his lance to parade rest, standing straight and raising his head in an oddly formal manner. The Setim salute? Daniel wondered.

"Second Office Nekhti!" the braced Son of Set cried. "We engaged the enemy, but they fought back with unexpected ferocity and unfamiliar weapons. We broke off contact, and the humans quit the scene. They did not, however, retreat toward the StarGate. I dispatched Niay to follow them at a distance."

"You did well, Tenth Officer Bak," Nekhti replied.

The gray-muzzled Setim seemed less into military formality. "They turned out to be humans. Sorry, sir. When I first saw and smelled them, they seemed so—" He broke off.

"Don't feel downcast, Harkhuf," Nekhti said. "I was just as surprised when the alien's face came off so easily."

Harkhuf looked up. "Why do they wear the masks, sir? Do they emulate the Horus guards?"

Daniel had to hide a smile at the idea of any marine imitating the group they referred to as "Whorehouse guards."

"We wear this gear for protection from—um—noxious mixtures we have placed around to defend our StarGate," Daniel replied.

"He speaks the tongue!" Bak, the petty officer, exclaimed. "The others jabbered among themselves in some sort of uncouth speech we did not understand."

"Much has changed since we walked the surface of Earth," Nekhti began. "For one thing, more time—"

His words were interrupted as another gang of Setim hastened into view. They carried an assortment of tools as improvised weapons and stopped short at the sight of the fallen Setim clutching blast-lances.

The leading alien dropped into an uncomfortable-looking hunched position to examine one of the fallen, and rose with the dead Setim's blast-lance in its hands. "What has befallen here?" the newcomer snapped. "We heard the firing of blast-lances in the distance and came to investigate."

The Setim spotted Daniel's alien face. "And what is *that*?"

"I was just about to explain, Rekhmere," Nekhti said calmly. "The great bitch Hathor has lied to us all. We have slept, not a couple of years as she told us, but *eight thousand years*. That is why we were banished from Astrogation and from so many records, so that we would not discover the lie. But there is worse. We

are the last of the Setim! Our race was exterminated—
by Hathor!"

"What nonsense is this?" Rekhmere interrupted.
"You talk rebellion—mutiny!"

"I do indeed. A free human society has developed
on Earth. That is what we're attacking, Rekhmere."

"Fourth Officer Rekhmere to you." Rekhmere swung
the blast-lance he'd just obtained so that it covered
Nekhti. "I know not why you seek to foment rebellion.
Perhaps it has something to do with the reason you
have been degraded so many ranks. But you will sur-
render yourself for justice at the hands of Lady
Hathor."

"Justice?" Daniel inquired ironically in the imperial
tongue. "Hathor is a bloody-handed monster trying to
conquer my world."

"Silence, human!" The Setim officer dismissed Daniel
as if he were a slave, keeping his lance aimed at Nekhti.
"You other men. Seize and bind Nekhti, unless you
wish to be considered mutineers as well."

"Enough of this shit," Daniel muttered. He drew the
Beretta from his holster, aimed, and fired.

Rekhmere spun around, the blast-lance in his hands
sending a bolt into the ceiling before he collapsed in
an untidy heap.

Half the weapons in the hall were immediately leveled at him. Daniel carefully dropped the pistol to the
floor. "Fourth Officer Rekhmere would not hear the
truth, and would have fired on Second Officer Nekhti,"
he said in the imperial tongue. "I merely acted so that
the truth could come out." He indicated the weapon at

his feet. "Could such a thing as this have been devised by lowly humans in a mere couple of years?"

The petty officer, Bak, stepped forward to reclaim the late Rekhmere's blast-lance. "There is much here we do not understand," he said. "But I begin to doubt the tales we were told."

"I wish you could present some proof to us," Nekhti told Daniel.

"I think I know where we might find some," Daniel replied. "The library—where we may also discover my friends."

The backpack nuke lay disassembled across the library floor, a collection of useless components now that the timer was a fused lump.

Might as well load it back into the case and bang the walls with it, for all the good it will do, Jack O'Neil thought bleakly. I should have remembered the trouble we had with the timer on the Abydos bomb, brought a backup . . .

It was too late for recriminations. No way could he send back to Earth for a replacement. Even if he got through the hostile alien crewmen and back through the StarGate, the *Boat of a Million Years* would have moved from the coordinates that would have allowed him to return.

No, he told himself, it's not just a case of trotting back to Radio Shack.

There is one answer, a cold voice whispered in the back of his head. *You could probably wire up a circuit to spark the detonator by hand.*

It would be simple enough. All it would require was

two wires and an electrical source. A literal dead man switch.

O'Neil began rooting through the bomb components, looking for wire he could cannibalize. Lieutenant Kawalsky watched him fashion his jury-rigged detonator switch. "Sir," he said through gray lips. "I wish to volunteer—"

"I didn't hear myself asking for volunteers, Lieutenant," O'Neil snapped.

It would be so simple to agree, he thought. So tempting. An easy out.

But Kawalsky was wounded. Walking wounded, certainly, but just as certainly impaired. If these missions had taught Jack O'Neil anything, he knew that this nuke needed a perfectly functioning timer.

The colonel began reassembling the bomb. "You'll have fifteen minutes to get the men back to the Star-Gate, Lieutenant. If you wish to spend part of that time looking for Daniel, that will be your decision. I'll fort up in here. If I'm discovered and attacked before fifteen minutes is up . . ."

O'Neil shrugged. "I think I've got this rigged so it will go off even if I fall."

"Permission to speak, sir."

"Lieutenant, there's nothing more to say." O'Neil tried to soften his tone. "We knew when we undertook this mission that all of us might not be returning. Two—maybe three of us—are gone already. I'm depending on you and Feretti to bring back some survivors."

He kept his eyes on the detonator circuit, ostensibly examining his handiwork. "You might also carry a message for me . . . to Sarah. Tell her—" The colonel paused for a moment. "Tell her I'm sorry. This time, I really hoped I'd be coming back."

"Sir!" This time, the interruption came from Feretti in the hall outside. "I'm hearing movement in the corridors. Coming this way."

"Get ready to boogie, Lieutenant," O'Neil said. "You don't want to get caught in here."

Kawalsky rose unhappily to his feet as a new voice came echoing down the hallways. "Hello, in the library."

O'Neil and Kawalsky stared at each other. "Jackson?" the colonel shouted back.

"Consider this a verbal flag of truce. I want to bring one observer in with me."

The two officers went to the library entrance. "Come on in," O'Neil shouted.

Daniel appeared at the end of the corridor, leading one of the red-furred aliens. O'Neil noticed that all the way in, the Egyptologist carefully covered the Setim with his own body.

Once I'd have considered that plain stupidity, O'Neil thought. But I think it may be sheer guts.

As they reached the library, Daniel handled the introductions. "Colonel O'Neil, this is Nekhti, son of Ushabti."

O'Neil did his best to minimize his reaction to that familiar name. Jackson kept talking. "If I can convince him of certain truths, we'll have gained an ally."

Nekhti began speaking in the ancient tongue of Ra's empire.

"He says that all access for crew people has been suppressed," Jackson translated. "That may be so, but

I was working here when we first arrived. And I'm willing to bet Hathor never bothered to lock me out after I escaped."

His confidence was justified. With Nekhti's technical help, Jackson soon was accessing the historical records kept in the computer.

A holographic image resolved itself over one of the consoles—a furious mob flinging itself over unmasked guards in uniform head cloths, armed only with batons.

"He says Hathor showed scenes like this to the crew to convince them that Earth was in rebellion." Daniel fiddled with the console, and now hieroglyphics were floating in the air. "That's the computer's record of when this image was stored, including the date—which is more than three hundred years after the crew went into cold storage here."

Nekhti almost came to point like a hunting hound.

Other images came up as Daniel called for records about a world called Ombos. Here were shots of hand-to-hand combat between Horus guards and Setim bearing a variety of weapons, including something that looked like a crossbow. Another record showed an aerial view of a family group—including Setim women and children—being exterminated by an uda-jeet. Daniel called up records showing Hathor in command of the genocidal campaign. He even found an image record of her being attacked by a Setim suicide squad.

"This is when she was brought back and put in Ra's sarcophagus." Daniel turned and provided his commentary in Nekhti's language.

Then the Egyptologist searched for references to

Ushabti. Hieroglyphics crawled through the air. "The official record," Daniel explained. "It says he was murdered, probably by thieves."

Then a new set of symbols appeared. "This is from Ra's personal archives." Daniel's eyebrows rose. "He knew all the time that Hathor had actually done the job."

Nekhti turned from the console, his fangs bared.

"Looks like you've convinced him," O'Neil dryly observed.

The alien stalked over to a set of golden-quartz slates—the equivalent of laptop computers in Ra's empire.

"He wants to make copies of these files and send them to various friends on board ship," Daniel said. "If we can guarantee refuge for his people, he'll help us sink the *Boat of a Million Years.*"

The library began to get crowded as more and more Setim showed up in response to Nekhti's messages. Some seemed furtive and worried. All were surprised to discover the Earth-human boarding party.

In between acting as translator, Daniel continued to hack into the computer's memories with the aid of some Setim technological types. Stumbling around in search of more theoretical information on the Star-Gate, Daniel came across a large file. When he came to display it, however, there was a list of place names in hieroglyphics, followed by a set of enigmatic little fig-ures—six of them.

Daniel blinked—then his eyes widened. "Holy shit!" he blurted. "I think we just got Ra's phone book.

This is a listing of StarGate coordinates—I recognize some of the constellation symbols!"

He fumbled around for a slate-computer. "We've got to copy this!"

As Daniel began the copying job, O'Neil and Nekhti called the milling crowd to order. There was a lot to discuss. The Setim crew people were shaken by the revelations they'd received. They were even more shaken at Nekhti's offer that they abandon the *Boat of a Million Years* and head through the StarGate to Earth.

"We are the last of the Setim," Nekhti said. "At least some remnant of our people must escape Hathor's schemes and live free."

Argument raged, however, on the question of destroying the *Boat of a Million Years.* "You would doom all of our people still serving," a female Setim accused. In the end, a compromise of sorts was achieved. A general warning would be announced throughout the ship once the StarGate was secured—and the destruction of the vessel put in motion.

That raised the next question. *How* were they going to destroy the vessel? One of Nekhti's top colleagues, the second officer in charge of Engineering, looked askance at the backpack bomb.

Daniel translated the engineer's comments. "Any improvised timing mechanism would be very vulnerable," he told O'Neil. "What this guy suggests is that they simply sabotage the engines."

The Setim went on for a moment or two, then gave a sharp yap of laughter.

Daniel glanced at his expectant human audience. "Boiled down, he says that these are interesting

engines, with lots of ways for things to go catastrophically wrong."

The final plan was a two-pronged attack. Nekhti
and the engineers would clear the engine room and
destabilize the engines. O'Neil would secure the Star-
Gate and help the would-be refugees escape.

"What about weapons?" one of the Setim asked.
"We have only those in the hands of the humans, and
the ten blast-lances that Nekhti drew from the mid-
deck armory. Should we not force our way in to one of
the other magazines?"

Nekhti emphatically rejected the idea. "Breaking
into an armory would undoubtedly raise alarms. Do
you wish to warn Hathor that we are attempting to
rise against her?"

His words left the Setim subdued but apparently
resolute.

"Tell Nekhti that we're ready if he is," O'Neil told
Daniel.

"You may be ready, but I'm not." The Egyptologist
pointed to the slate on the computer console, still
filling with characters. "This is a big mother of a file
I'm downloading."

O'Neil rolled his eyes, then looked thoughtful.
"Kawalsky," he called. "Dr. Jackson is staying here,
and you'll be staying with him."

When the lieutenant looked ready to argue, O'Neil
added, "Don't look at it as soft duty. I'm depending
on you to get him to the StarGate on time."

Khonsu stood at the foot of Hathor's command
chair, listening to the sounds of a large crowd leaving.

The Lady had already raised force-screens to keep the rest of the bridge crew from hearing.

"How fortuitous that they accessed special archive files," Hathor said, a ruthless smile on her perfect features. "Otherwise, the computer would never have alerted me."

"Now that you know their plans, Lady Captain, how will we counter them?"

"I think I shall dispatch you to the engine room. That would appear to be a task best left to your special talents."

The tall Horus guard merely nodded. Not for nothing was he known as Khonsu the Killer.

Hathor then glanced over at the bridge crew. "In the meantime, I shall take as many of these fine warriors as can be spared from destroying the last Urt-man space defenses. After a quick stop at the nearest armory, I'll deploy them to block access to Astrogation and the StarGate."

A small tinge of humor now entered her smile. "What better position for the cat than in front of the mouse hole, eh?"

The main engine room was empty except for Nekhti and four of the engineers who'd joined his plot. A brief showing of some of the more graphic images in Hathor's campaign of extermination had been more than enough to convince the crew that usually tended the huge engines.

Djedhor, the Engineering Second Officer, stood over the main control console. "It is accomplished," he said. "The system's safety interlocks have been rendered inert. Now I merely program a growing instability into the force-fields controlling the matter-antimatter reaction, until in the end it becomes a positronic bomb."

The engineer deftly traced symbols onto the console screen. "The human leader requested fifteen minutes. This will give us twenty."

Like any careful engineer, Djedhor made one last check of the hieroglyphs standing in the holographic display. "Satisfactory," he said, reaching for an icon on the console. "Now, to execute—"

An instant later the contents of his chest cavity sprayed through the hologram as a blast-bolt took him full in the back.

Whirling from the display, Nekhti desperately grabbed for the blast-lance he'd left leaning against the console.

Another bolt crashed, taking not him but his weapon down to destruction.

Nekhti glared at the Horus-masked intruder—Khonsu. "Your plot is known, mongrels," his amplified voice filled the room. "There remains nothing more except that you should die."

Three sets of fangs and claws against one blast-lance, Nekhti thought, his legs tensing for the spring. But one of us must execute Djedhor's program.

He glanced at the others, who snarled assent.

They leapt for the Horus guard while he whirled back to Djedhor's console.

The sound of two blast-bolts ripped the room as Nekhti returned to the control panel. His fur on his exposed back rose in hackles. Any instant, the third blast might come . . .

He stretched out a hand to the Execute icon, but hands like steel suddenly seized him.

Held by the scruff of the neck and the material of his kilt, Nekhti was whirled from Djedhor's console and smashed into another. They fell to the floor, Khonsu's knee landing in the small of Nekhti's back.

"Yap, hound," Khonsu mocked as he exerted more pressure, bending Nekhti's back like a bow. "For your jaws will never snap."

But Nekhti's back did.

CHAPTER 22
OF PENS AND SWORDS

Daniel stared at the still cycling symbols crawling across the golden quartz of the slate-computer. "Either Ra's empire is a hell of a lot bigger than we expected," he said, "or his original race must have been heavily into travel."

"What do you mean?" Kawalsky sat on one of the empty library consoles, like the Hunchback of Notre Dame from the pile of dressings on his scorch wound. He shifted slightly, trying to find a comfortable posture.

"Well, Ra was the last of his race, right?"

Kawalsky nodded, and instantly looked as if he were regretting the action.

"From all the records we were able to pick up, it looks as though he ruled about twenty planets." Daniel tapped his console. "But this file here, it's got to have *thousands* of StarGate coordinates."

"Well, maybe if you lined up all the planets between here and Abydos, a hundred million light-years away—" The lieutenant's voice faded. "Old Man West is going to have a coronary."

Daniel glanced sharply in his direction. "Why?"

"It was bad enough when we only had to worry

about Hathor coming through. Imagine how happy he'll be to discover that thousands of planets could dial our number and wind up on the front door."

"Maybe he should also remember that it works both ways," Daniel said. "*We* can dial up thousands of planets."

Kawalsky looked pensive. "Colonization?"

"It's a possibility." Daniel's voice was tentative. "When I saw all those coordinates, I thought maybe this could be an answer for the Abydans. Skaara's been very concerned about his people being swallowed up and losing their identity. Sha'uri, too, although I didn't hear that from her."

The lieutenant looked at him with compassion in his eyes. "If Sha'uri went off to another world to keep her people together, what would you do?"

"I don't know," Daniel admitted. "I really don't—"

His words were interrupted by a voice that seemed literally to come out of thin air. Both men looked around the library, but there were no speakers visible.

"Shipmates! Attention, shipmates! All heed to the Lady Captain Hathor," the voice cried in the imperial tongue.

A second later a seductive contralto voice began speaking.

Faizah's voice, Daniel thought, then sternly corrected himself. Hathor's voice. There was a cold quality, a remoteness, as if she were speaking through her golden cat-mask.

Daniel remembered the bright, lively, and yes, flirtatious young woman he'd known as Faizah, comparing her laughing face to the masklike, ruthlessly controlled features of Hathor. Had she enjoyed putting aside her godhood for a little while to be just a human being? he wondered. Or was it all the cold-blooded action of a master spy and assassin?

He pushed those thoughts away as he listened to what Hathor was saying. "Loyal Setim! Be warned that our vessel faces a double threat! Human rebels have boarded us by way of the StarGate, and traitorous elements have used this crisis as an excuse for mutiny. All Setim who hold to the vows given to our great lord Ra are ordered to the main bridge immediately! We will cleanse this ship of enemies, then turn our attention to the world below."

When Kawalsky heard Daniel's translation, he yanked the slate-computer way from the console. "That's as much as we're going to get," he said. "I want to catch up with the colonel before something more than words hit the fan."

The disembodied announcement caught Jack O'Neil still scouting the ways back to the Astrogation deck and the StarGate. He understood about one word in eight, but he could tell there was trouble from the reactions of the Setim accompanying him.

I wish Jackson would get the hell finished in the library, the colonel thought. We could use a decent translator.

Instead, he turned to second best. "Feretti, you learned a bit of Abydan. What were they saying?"

The little recon man shrugged. "It was pretty fancy, but it sounds like Hathor knows we're here—and knows that some of these folks are helping us."

"Won-der-ful." O'Neil spaced out each syllable of the word. Hathor had just demonstrated that she could talk in every compartment aboard the *Boat of a Million Years*. What if she could listen in as well? She might know all their plans.

"The boss lady wants all the loyal Setim to head up to the main bridge."

"Out of the way," O'Neil mused.

"Or available as hostages," Feretti suggested.

"Somehow, I don't think she'll be down here to face us alone," the colonel said. "We're going to end up in a fight, and that means we need more weapons for our allies."

Feretti immediately turned to a gray-muzzled Setim carrying a blast-rifle. Poking a forefinger at the weapon, the marine asked, "Where?" in Abydan.

That prompted a longer response completely unintelligible to the officer. But Feretti turned with a grin. "He can lead us there."

"The three of us will go. Garwood!"

"Yessir!" the young marine leapt to attention.

"Hold the unarmed refugees here, and post the armed people as pickets. You know how to set the StarGate to get yourself back?" He'd had Jackson drum the necessary sequence into every member of the team.

"Yessir!"

"We're raiding an armory to get additional weapons. If we're not back in five minutes, or hostiles come down these corridors, head for the StarGate. Understood?"

"U-understood, sir," Garwood gulped.

* * *

Pain. Deep, grinding pain flared with every breath when Nekhti opened his eyes. He blinked in confusion. Where was he? All he could see were the bases of control consoles. But where?

Then memory returned—Khonsu killing Djedhor and the other as efficiently as a machine, their unequal wrestling match. . . . The program! He had to execute the program!

Nekhti tried to push himself up. His head swam, his arms trembled.

His legs and lower body lay like a deadweight.

The final moments of their struggle came back, and a howl burst from Nekhti's lips. Khonsu hadn't failed to kill him. He'd merely broken Nekhti's back!

Peering up from the deck, Nekhti scouted around for the live terminal, the one with a holographic display still flickering.

There it was. And there was Djedhor, lying sprawled in front of it.

Nekhti let his head back down and extended his left arm. Inch by inch, he pulled himself forward.

To Jack O'Neil, the door to the armory looked no different from the entrances to any of the other compartments along the corridor. But the older Setim warrior—Harkhuf, Feretti had called him—went to this entryway like a hunting hound on the scent.

Harkhuf slapped his hand against a raised, panel-like section of golden quartz. Nothing happened.

Feretti translated the brief spate of speech. "Guess it's authorized personnel only, sir. He says something about a key from above."

Curtly, O'Neil reached over to pat the muzzle of Feretti's blast-rifle. "Tell him *that's* your key."

Harkhuf caught on pretty quickly when Feretti opened up on the door, enthusiastically adding the bolts of his blast-lance.

When the door suddenly jerked open, the colonel thought that perhaps they'd fused some control circuit.

Then the blast-bolt came from within, scorching Harkhuf's fur and flinging him back. A big, muscular figure in a kilt and Horus-mask burst through the doorway, swinging his blast-lance like a quarterstaff. The butt of the lance caught Feretti in the temple, dropping him like a poleaxed steer. Then the golden baton went into a complex figure-eight movement. One end slashed through the power cable connecting Feretti's blast-rifle even as the recon marine went down. The other end landed with stunning force on Jack O'Neil's wrist, making his submachine gun clatter from his hand.

Despite his aching wrist, O'Neil tried to grab the attacker's blast-lance and pivot past. Instead, he was rammed hard and sent staggering down the corridor. He leapt back at the guy before he could bring the weapon into firing position, throwing a high kick that connected with both the staff and the enemy's chest.

O'Neil rebounded. God, it was like kicking a wall!

A sound that might be described as a laugh came from the hawk-mask, and the Horus guard tossed his weapon away. The big man was on him with frightening speed, lashing out with a series of blows that used his heavy bracelets as a sort of wristy edition of brass knuckles. O'Neil tasted blood in his mouth, but was still on his feet.

He threw a punch to his adversary's stomach, feeling his knuckles skid against washboard muscle. The damned golden Horus-mask protected the guy's face. O'Neil spun aside from a body blow, threw another kick—and didn't just get blocked, he got thrown.

The colonel went cartwheeling through the air to impact heavily against the corridor wall. Then he went bouncing to the deck. He was still scrambling to his feet when a big hand caught him by the arm and sent him flying again.

"Gotta stop meeting like this," he muttered as he crashed into the wall again.

Somehow, he kept his feet, but the world was blurrily out of focus as he tried to backpedal, clawing for the Beretta in his holster. The big Horus was on him all too quickly, knocking the pistol from his hand, pounding him with body blows.

"You die, little man," the deep, hollow, accented voice came from the mask. "You die like Nekhti and his friends."

O'Neil froze in dismay. If Nekhti were dead, then his sabotage plan was dead as well!

The Horus made his move. He lashed out, half spinning O'Neil around. Then he seized the marine by the right shoulder of his rubber suit, lifting him up while he got a hold on the colonel's right leg.

O'Neil suddenly remembered one of the dead Abydan guards they'd found after the infiltration attack that had brought Hathor to the planet. The guard had had his spine broken, and then his neck.

The colonel clawed around, catching hold of the killer's hawk-mask. The big guy staggered, caught off balance, and O'Neil swung his left leg, as hard as he could, into the Horus' family jewels.

The big man pitched forward, and O'Neil landed jarringly on the deck. He didn't know what Horuses wore under their linen kilts, but apparently it wasn't a box.

Amazingly, the masked warrior forced himself upright and came at O'Neil yet again.

What the hell did they do? Give him a Novocain injection down there? Staggering to his feet, the colonel prepared to meet the inexorable advance.

The breath shuddered in Nekhti's chest as he clawed his way up to the top of the console. He'd never have made it, except that he used Djedhor's corpse as a sort of grisly ladder. Clinging with one hand, Nekhti scrabbled along the smooth surface of the console with the other. Even propped up against the cooling form of his friend, he couldn't pull himself up to eye level. He'd have to guess where the Execute icon was.

Praying to the gods of his homeworld that he wouldn't land on Delete, Nekhti pressed down.

Then he lost his hold and slithered to the deck.

Even though he'd come back into the fight after O'Neil's below-the-kilt shot, the big Horus was moving slower. He tried to pound down on the colonel, but O'Neil slipped by, ripping off a couple of pounding punches to the big man's stomach. The Horus gave ground, and O'Neil risked a high kick, not for the chest, but for the joint between helmet and flesh at the guy's throat.

The big warrior was flung back right to the juncture of the next corridor . . . right as Daniel Jackson and Lieutenant Kawalsky came around the bend.

Daniel had no idea what to expect. He heard a scuffling sound, and suddenly a fully masked Horus guard was flying into him and Kawalsky.

The Horus' flailing arm crashed down on the lieutenant's wounded shoulder, and Kawalsky was sinking to his knees.

That left Daniel alone to face what seemed like a clockwork monster.

"You!" a voice rumbled from the mask.

A tag of half-forgotten Theban poetry ran through Daniel's mind as he recognized the man in the mask. *Khonsu the Killer is . . .*

Daniel had been carrying the precious slate-computer cradled against his chest. Now he flung it in Khonsu's face as he clawed out his pistol.

All he saw was the poison-green glare in the mask's eyes as he fired.

Jack O'Neil came staggering up as the big Horus crashed to the deck. The killer lay like a discarded rag doll, the baleful light gone from his eyes. Then O'Neil looked more closely. No, the glow was gone because each eye had been penetrated by a 9mm bullet.

The colonel sent wondering glances from the dead man to the pale Egyptologist.

"I didn't break the computer, did I?" Daniel asked nervously.

"Jackson," O'Neil said, "you are either the greatest snapshot or the luckiest bastard in the solar system."

They managed to revive Feretti and help Kawalsky get back on his feet, then, carrying as many blast-lances as they could handle, they set off to join the remainder of their strike force and the would-be refugees.

"We'll have to get them started through the Star-Gate," O'Neil said. "Feretti, you send a patrol to pick up more blast-lances. I'll make contact with Nekhti."

Strictly speaking, it's the truth, he thought. *After I go to the library and connect the dead man switch on the nuke, Nekhti and I will both be dead.*

Up ahead, they heard the snarling roar of blast-bolts being traded. Pushing into a jog trot, O'Neil led his men to see what new disaster awaited them.

The refugee column was hunkered down just one corridor short of the huge compartment that held the StarGate. But it might as well be down on Earth or off on Abydos.

Hathor and an armed party of Setim held the entrances.

"Sir, we waited as you ordered," Garwood reported as O'Neil and the others handed out their blast-lances. "But when we arrived here, the Lady and the others were already forting up. They used the matter-transmitter to slip down from the bridge."

The colonel ran a quick count of his available

STARGATE: RETRIBUTION   293

troops, including the armed Setim. Then he risked a quick look around the corner at the enemy's position.

O'Neil leapt back hurriedly after blast-bolts carved a new set of scars in the wall of the corridor.

It was bad. They'd have to make a frontal assault down the empty corridor into the teeth of an enemy firing from a prepared position.

"Any hope of using the same trick Nekhti did? Could he get behind them through the maintenance accesses? Or at least open a couple in that hallway to provide some cover for a rush?"

Daniel conferred with some of the Setim officers. "They can't get any of the hatches open," he reported. "Hathor must be using the ship's computers to shut everything down."

They didn't have time to waste. While they played besiegers out here, Hathor might be ordering the ship's computers to start bombarding the Earth.

The colonel gripped his blast-lance, about to order the suicide charge, when the air filled with the sound of alarms.

Yet another alien voice resounded from thin air, its inhumanly calm measured cadences ringing through the decks.

Daniel turned to O'Neil. "That's the computer, telling everyone to abandon ship. It seems the engines are about to blow."

Daniel watched the Setim crew members working themselves up into a pretty fair panic when Hathor's voice suddenly cut across the crowd noise. "Attention

mutineers and invaders," her clear contralto reverber-
ated through the ship. "You will not escape the effects
of your perfidy. We, the loyal followers of Ra, hold the
StarGate. None shall pass."

Daniel had just about had enough. Handing his
blast-lance to the one of the Setim, he began inditing
hieroglyphs on the slate-computer he carried. If Hathor
still hadn't canceled his access . . .

She hadn't. Daniel arranged a data shunt from the
library to Astrogration, hit the Execute icon, and
handed off the computer.

Then, empty hands raised high, he stepped into the
disputed corridor. "Look at me!" he shouted in his
best version of Ra's ancient tongue. "I do not look like
the human fellahin you remember, nor am I garbed as
one. The reason why—and the truth about the Lady
Hathor and your people—can be seen on any of the
Astrogation consoles."

A brighter glow came from the barricaded command deck as every console in the stadium-sized
chamber began to play the bits of history that Daniel
had culled from the files.

A wordless scream overcame the exclamations of
the Setim inside.

Hathor leapt over the barricade, stalking toward
Daniel with a leveled blast-lance. He couldn't see the
expression on her face. It was covered in her golden
cat-mask. But her voice couldn't have been colder if it
had been dipped in liquid helium. "Fool from a world
of fools, you will regret this final interference in my
plans."

She raised her blast-lance. A bolt ripped through the air.

And Hathor crumpled to the deck, struck from behind by one of her own Setim guards.

"Come!" a voice cried from behind the barricade. "There is little time to escape!"

Jack O'Neil and his marines led a flood of Setim into the command deck. Daniel could hear the subtle harmonics building, indicating a connection with the Earth StarGate had been made.

He didn't really pay much attention, kneeling over the stricken figure as the marching columns of escapees split around them.

Gently, he pressed the switch that turned Hathor's cat-mask back to a necklace. She was icily beautiful as ever, though a bright-red line of blood oozed from her lips.

"Fool," she muttered, making the blood bubble. Whether the remark was directed at him or at the poor aim of whoever had laid her low, Daniel couldn't say.

"I've got to get some help," he said. "We'll take you through the StarGate, get you treatment down on Earth—"

"No!" The will was strong as ever, but the voice grew weaker. "I have lived long enough, Daniel Jackson. I saw the First Times of Ra's empire. I do not need to see the end."

She raised a hand, to indicate the *Boat of a Million Years* around them. "Who could ask for a better, if ephemeral, tomb?"

The hand dropped, those magnificent eyes glazed.

Jack O'Neil stood beside him in a suddenly empty corridor.

"Come on!" the colonel said roughly. "This damned thing is supposed to go up any second!"

Daniel didn't even feel the extradimensional jolts of the fun house ride through the StarGate. He landed in the Creek Mountain missile silo still dazed and confused from the death he'd just seen.

The bemused defense force was still trying to bring order to the milling crowd of refugees.

"A new set of aliens for the government to deal with," O'Neil muttered. "We may be glad you got those new sets of coordinates."

He looked hard at Daniel. "I think you need a little air."

Daniel breathed deep as they stepped out of the elevator and onto the brief concrete ledge on the mountainside. It was evening, and the stars were brilliant in the Rocky Mountain sky.

As Daniel looked up, he saw a sudden flash—a new star. "It's the end," he whispered, looking up at the funeral pyre of a woman who would be a goddess, who died in the same fashion as her own god.

But Jack O'Neil was looking into the sky with an entirely different expression, gently tapping the thin, golden-quartz computer he held. "I think maybe it's the beginning."